MAR − 2006

THE BLOOD KNOT

THE BLOOD KNOT

A Fly Fishing Mystery

John Galligan

BLEAK HOUSE BOOKS

MADISON | WISCONSIN

Published by Bleak House Books Inc.
953 E. Johnson St.
Madison, WI 53703
www.bleakhousebooks.com

Published 2005
07 06 05 04 03   1 2 3 4 5

This is a work of fiction. Any similarities to people or places, living or dead, is purely
coincidental.

ISBN 1-932557-12-1
Library of Congress Control Number: 2005924205

Jacket design and cover photograph: Peter Streicher
Book design: Peter Streicher
Author photo: Ya-Ling Tsai
Text set in Adobe Garamond

Printed in the United States of America by McNaughton & Gunn.

Every time, for Jinko

Acknowledgements

A place makes a story, and people make a place, just as the place makes them. For any beauty, inspiration, grittiness, and sheer kinkiness my readers may find in this story, I wish to thank the Kickapoo Valley of southwestern Wisconsin and the people brave or lucky enough to live there. If not for their decency, things might really happen as they do in this book. I also want to thank the dean of rural Wisconsin writing, Jerry Apps, both for his work on the excellent *Barns of Wisconsin* and for his generous reading of *The Blood Knot* in manuscript form. Any remaining irregularities in Wisconsin barn architecture are the work of my hammer alone. Thanks also to my ready core of readers in Japan: Iain, Tom, Troy, and my wife, Jinko, who provided me with invaluable challenge and support when I was far from home. Finally, as always, thanks to Ben LeRoy, Blake Stewart, Julie Kuczynski, and Alison Janssen of Bleak House Books. I couldn't ask for better.

The Rhabdo Virus

There are two types of rabies: mad rabies and dumb rabies. The labels are perfectly descriptive. You snap, unprovoked, at everything, or you drool at nothing, or you do them in sequence, like entrée and dessert. It all depends on the mechanism chosen by the Rhabdo virus to effect what will become, either way, your total cerebral derangement and horrible death.

Hence, this introduction to the quality of my thinking on that chilly September morning, in the moments before I found the Barn Lady's soggy, bullet-riddled body in the West Fork of the Kickapoo River.

My brain was doing this: *If one is prone to* both *snapping and drooling—at everything and nothing, simultaneously—and these symptoms have persisted since long before the beaver bite—say, since a certain unforgivable disaster in one's past—then one is in the clear.*

One cannot have rabies.

Right?

One can't.

Digman and Magritte, that pair of fools

Bang!

A rifle shot. I sat up in my bunk. It was just after dawn at the cold tail-end of September. I was beginning my sixth day in Avalanche, Wisconsin, camped within a stream's murmur of the sleek and purling West Fork. The windows of my Cruise Master RV were frosted over with three or four hours of restless exhalations. But amazingly, given the shock of my injury, I had experienced some sleep-like moments, my brain toiling all the while on the rabies question.

As I sat shivering, the small-bore rifle discharged a second time. *Bang!*

Just for good measure, I mumbled as I swung my legs off the bunk—first the healthy leg, getting solid purchase on the Cruise Master's gritty floor, and then the injured one. Pain erupted across my right calf. But I assured myself the wound was not infected. Beavers were rarely rabid. My problem was nothing more than the fact that 8X fly fishing tippet, used as suture, wasn't as flexible as the stuff real doctors used. I was fine.

Bang!

A third shot. Anyway—for insurance—now the bastard was dead. Now I could fish his contentious ass out of the creek, drag him in to the state health office, test him, confirm what I already knew, then burn his sorry remains.

So, get up, Dog.

I shoved the good leg into my second-string waders. The injured leg, tight-skinned and throbbing, didn't want to go down, but I gritted my teeth. *Come on, Dog.* Beneath the galley sink I found a box of garbage bags—I would just roll-float-scoot the bloody carcass into a bag—and from there I stumbled to the Cruise Master door, where one of the vehicle's previous owners had hung a grimy little mirror. I scrutinized the Dog. My eyes were no more bloodshot than usual. A small amount of ice flecked the corners of my five-day beard—but that was breath, not drool. I was fine.

But I thought I might as well probe a little deeper—test the whole "snap, unprovoked" idea—and the silly postcard I had tacked beside the mirror presented the perfect opportunity. Three years back, on the heels of the aforementioned tragedy, I had left Boston behind, had left everything behind except a few thousand dollars in the care of a trusted friend. Fishing had then ensued—three solid years of it—infused by small rations of wired cash. Of course things had kinked, and twisted, and dwindled, and then finally, on the way to Avalanche ten days back, I had phoned my pal—my tax guy, Harvey Digman—and asked for my last few dollars. Harvey's little package had reached Avalanche by two-day express. I had opened it to find five crisp one-hundred-dollar bills, paper clipped to the back of the—

Bang!

Another gunshot.

—back of the silly card. The card was one of those fine-arts jobs that young lovers like to send each other when their feelings grow especially incoherent. But this card was weird. The painter, some Belgian guy named René Magritte, had painted a dull-brown picture of an ordinary tobacco pipe. And beneath that pipe, in French, our Monsieur Magritte writes: *This is not a pipe.*

The Dog kids you not.

The artiste writes: *This is not a pipe.* Beneath a pipe.

And when I unclip the five hundred bucks, I see that my tax guy, Harvey Digman, has written on the back of the postcard: *Dog, this is not a fishing trip.*

I said it aloud: "Hah!"

That cold September morning in Avalanche—as I was about to limp forth across frozen grass and find the Barn Lady's ruined little body—I coughed out "Hah!," proving my sanity, my perfect state of health, and then I shook my head and cursed Digman and Magritte, that pair of fools.

Mad.

Dumb.

My breath steamed the tiny, frozen mirror. I wiped it clear. Hell—the Dog was fine. I shoved my hat on. I was on a fishing trip. So what if the trip was three years long? Those other guys—Digman, Magritte—what the hell bit *them*?

They were—*Bang!*, a fifth shot—Digman, Magritte, they were the sick ones.

Dog, this is not a fishing trip

Ned Oglivie was the name on all the mortgages, licenses, lawsuits, bankruptcy papers, and assorted ravaged savings accounts I had left behind in the care of my old Boston friend Harvey. But look closely. Look where the Ned meets the rest of me. Find the self-inflicted nickname, the d-O-g that morphed from the brimstone moments of an upright, humdrum, middle-class existence. The Dog in the middle was the heart of the matter.

The Dog had been good once. The Dog had been obedient. The Dog had been loyal. I had served. But then—long story, not germane to how Barn Lady ended up dead in the creek—the chain of my good life had broken, the muzzle had come off, and by the time that beaver rose out of the West Fork to bite me, I had gone beyond trout bum to trout hound. I had gone feral. I had spent three years on the road, in the sun, in my tattered chest waders, subsisting on peanut butter, vodka, and Tang, dialing dear Harvey from truck stops for small shipments of precious cash. A thousand times I had pushed up one stream or another, my fly flicking, my eyes tight to the current, my intellect as empty as I could make it, my raw thoughts as rooted and twined to the art of catching trout with a fly as I could keep them.

At least that's my excuse for not seeing the beaver. It was just be-yond dusk on the night when the woman died, and I was fighting to land a big brown trout in the boggy stretch below the campground. I had the trout on the reel, but he was taking line. He was digging through a black reef of weeds toward the downstream corner. The Dog was pursuing blindly, mashing through a hip-deep mass of flotsam, when out of the churning ink in front of me a slick, seal-like head rose up.

I sloshed to a stop. I clicked on my headlamp and we looked at each other. The beaver had bad, busted teeth, orange with beaver-plaque. He woofed at me, then added two more low yips, and the Dog in me snarled back, "Then just get out of my way, Bucky."

He cocked his head as if to ponder my guff…the fat, glassy-eyed bastard, looking as healthy as the stream he defended.

"Go on," I said. "Move it."

In the slight pause that followed—eyeball to black eyeball—my big trout had gained the upper hand, and I sensed he was about to rip the gears out of my reel and escape. And in those days, let me tell you, the Dog could not afford to lose a big fish. In those days, losing a big fish shot an emptiness through the Dog that could take miles and miles…and miles…of stream to wash away.

So I charged ahead. And the beaver, unrushed, sank slowly, its dark eye upon me. Inexplicably—my intellect as empty as I could make it—I considered the bastard vanquished. I considered the stream bed mine. So I plowed ahead through the space where the creature had been, and on my third step, my right leg bent like a black willow sapling. Paws—front paws, heavy and sure—braced against my shin to leverage the muscles of the jaw. Down in the murk, those big orange teeth sheared my waders, my trousers, my long johns, and carved a downward curd of flesh from the meaty outside of my calf.

You bet your bead-heads I howled my pain. But on top of that, I howled my fury, I howled my surprise, and I howled my insult—and then somehow, from the hills of Avalanche, I heard tumbling back, crashing down on me, that echo I couldn't shake: *Dog, this is not a fishing trip.*

What the hell did Harvey mean? The old fart was a tax accountant. What the hell did he know? And as for Magritte, the artiste, how could a pipe not be a pipe?

I threw my rod at the bank. I hurled limestone grenades at the black water where the beaver had disappeared. I hopped backwards on one leg and toppled over a wedge of muddy coontail weed... *splash!*...and then I was alone in the dark, in the blank spot after echoes, wet and bleeding.

The trout was gone.

The beaver was gone.

My rod was somewhere among the wet nettles on the bank. Downstream I heard a heavy tail whack the water.

Maybe the beaver was sick, I thought suddenly.

Him...*and* Digman...*and* Magritte.

Was she Amish, not-Amish?

Bang!—once more, a rifle shot spanked the wet morning air.

That was six shots by my count. Six shells seemed like a lot of ordnance to bring down upon one beaver, no matter how big and deranged. But I appreciated the sentiment. I appreciated that some Kickapooian was up early taking care of business. Up to that point, the folks in Avalanche—by whom I mean the long-term survivors of that wild and gorgeous little wrinkle of Wisconsin—had taken wary but decent care of me.

"But no," I had told Harvey from a pay phone the morning before. "No Amish bent-hickory rockers ready for sale. Six months on backorder, and no delivery."

Harvey wasn't giving up. "Nice place, Avalanche?"

"Sure—nice enough—but Harvey, don't start—"

"Nice...whachacallums...trout?"

"Of course."

"Lots of Amish? You went down every driveway?"

"Harvey, look. I took the detour over here. I did my best. I know your collection needs a chair with the special...Amish...whatever—"

"Spindles, Dog. Amish steam-bent hickory spindles."

"Right. But I'm staying here six days, not six months. I gotta get up north before the season ends. The woman at the store said—"

"This woman...she's Amish?"

"Yes, she's Amish. I mean, no—not really. I'm not sure what she is. Look, Harvey. Cut it out. The woman at the store said Amish furniture is only made to order around here. It's all spoken for long before it's made. You want a rocking chair, you place an order. In person. You pay cash up front. In person. And then you come out here to Wisconsin, in person, and you pick up your chair."

"I don't know, Dog. Which subway stop is Wisconsin?"

"Harvey—"

"I'm asking a favor, Dog. If this Avalanche is a nice place, why not hang around? Get to know people."

"I'm on a fishing trip. I don't—"

"Fishing trip," he scoffed, interrupting me once more. "Fishing trip my spotted old ass. Dog, come home then. The coast is clear. The ground did not collapse beneath Boston."

"I'll tell you what." My brain was suddenly stimulated by the way the phone gulped at my next-to-last calling card, about to take it whole. "There's an older woman in the campground here who paints pictures of barns. The barns are famous around here, really special. Historical, I guess. And you collect...um...just about ev-erything...right, Harv?"

"Except old lady amateur painters."

"She's good, Harv. She's very good. She gets good money. She even pisses off the local barn-owners because they haven't figured out their own way to cash in. And she owes me. I taught her to tie fly fishing knots for her husband. He's got hands like you, old buddy. Lotta turbulence. And this Barn Lady is supposed to stop by tonight with her sketchbook because she wants to make me a special painting of this big Amish gambrel that sort of just looms up behind the creek..."

"Dog, please—"

"Harv, listen—"

And there my phone card expired.

Six shots, I mused again as I shoved out of the Cruise Master and stepped gingerly onto frozen grass. Too much for a beaver. Unless the shots were misses—and it was hard to imagine anyone I had met in Avalanche missing a beaver with a rifle. A Bud can on a fence post at two hundred yards, in a gale wind, maybe. Maybe one miss. But six times?

I tried to guess where the shots came from. It was a cold-soup morning, sounds battened in fog, and I hunched against the chill, listening. Shoot once more, I requested, so the Dog can locate.

But of course it was quiet then. Somewhere, my beaver was shredded. I looked around. The campground was long and narrow, hugging the creek. Its tattered grass was half-mowed by the boy I called the Avalanche Kid. The boy was ten, maybe. He lived at the store, with the woman who might or might not be Amish, and he was trouble. He shot grackles in the campground and teal in the sinkholes. He chucked wild apples into the stream while I tried to fish. I had caught him inside the Cruise Master, twice, his dirty fist in my Tang jar—and I had gotten my ass kicked, twice, in the ensuing clash of words. The Avalanche Kid was ten, I had found myself thinking...going on twenty-one.

But there was no one in the campground that morning besides the Dog, plus the Barn Lady and her husband, still at slumber, I gathered, in their teepee at the far north corner of the camp. A good hundred yards to the south, the Cruise Master moldered beneath a tall, yellow cottonwood. Behind that to the east about twenty paces was the bathroom (with a hot shower that took quarters I couldn't spare), and from my low creek-side vantage, those three points—teepee, RV, and WC—were about all the Wisconsin geology allowed me to see. This was the Driftless Area. The last glacier had failed to grind it down. The bluffs were tall and ragged, level with the surrounding plains. The valleys were deep and kinked, carved by spring water. The corn and weeds were high. As I hobbled in a circle, a fresh sweat broke on my face and met the cold air. I couldn't see jack shit.

Then a softer crack—not a gun shot—led my gaze uphill and east beyond the bathroom, into the tatter of damaged trees that lined the road. I looked for human shoulders, a hunting hat, the glint of a rifle barrel. I listened again for the snap of a stick. But only the Avalanche Oak stood out, a towering but frail and twisted specimen in dull fall brown, leaning over the top end of the narrow campground drive. Crack went the old tree again...a soft crack like a sigh...and then the Avalanche Oak settled back into its slow and silent death.

I limped to the higher ground beside the tree, where I could see better. Now, looking back, the whole campground snaked out its tattered green pattern before me, and I could see the red barn and the blue store across the creek and soybean field to the west. I stood warily, ears tuned. Nothing. I touched the old tree and looked down. A carved stone in front of the tree's wormy trunk said, *This Oak Survived the Avalanche of 1913*. I turned east. Behind the Avalanche Oak, across the road, the coulee walls climbed sharply, but with a kind of doddering ruggedness, their ancient catastrophe long ago scarred-over and now flocked in autumnal sumac, birch, and hickory.

I turned back and listened again. Above me, a woodpecker thumped a rotten elbow of the Avalanche Oak. Hoof beats—an Amish horse and buggy—echoed *clip-clip, clip-clop* to the west, and as I watched, the black buggy rounded County Y and descended beyond the red barn, the horse stepping high, its shoes ringing through the coulee. The buggy disappeared for a moment behind the barn. Waiting, I gazed idly at the faded orange-and-blue billboard mural on the barn's east wall, knowing the Amish conveyance would reappear just below the R in King Midas Flour. Then the buggy did as I expected, rolling out under the R and alongside the blue-sided Avalanche Mercantile before the horse pulled north up Avalanche Coulee Road and the buggy showed me the orange caution triangle on its back.

Then: *Bang!*

A seventh shot. That direction. Creek-wise. Buggy-wise. West of me. North of the store. Beyond the snarl of box elder and black willow that blocked my view of the County Y bridge.

But my eye lingered on the Avalanche Mercantile—a tall and sun-bleached blue building, country-school shaped, capped with a red tin roof, ringed by woodpiles and junked pickups—and again I felt the attack of the beaver, and the bite of Harvey Digman's words: *Dog, this is not a fishing trip.*

"Help me," I had begged the maybe-Amish woman, inside the Avalanche Mercantile the night before, minutes after the beaver bite.

I was bleeding on her floor. My bloody right hand gripped the top of her popsicle-and-cube-ice freezer and left a pinkish, gelatinous mess.

"I...a beaver bit me...help me...please."

She was bent down behind the Mercantile's counter. I remembered that Eve Kussmaul was the name she had reluctantly traded me for "the Dog," when we had dealt some days ago. She was letting me camp for free in exchange for some chainsaw work on a dead elm that had fallen on a camp shelter.

"Eve...right? I'm Dog. The guy in the RV." I had to wait for more air. "And I remember you mentioned that your brother-in-law...the guy that brings the firewood...and normally would cut up anything that fell...but he's busy these days...in school for medical stuff..."

She raised up sharply. As always, she wore a white Amish kapp, an indigo dress, and a white apron, but that prim and quaint picture would be complicated—as I had indicated to Harvey—by the arrival of her hands on the counter. She had painted her nails a deep grape, then chewed them ragged, and seeing the mess of the Dog failed to modify the bitter blankness on her young face. Plus, she smelled like stale tobacco.

I wobbled, grabbed at a shelf, and panted at her. "I need stitches…" I gasped. "Maybe your brother-in-law…"

She regarded me with close-set eyes that were dilated wide, their jittery black centers rimmed by a strangely luminous acorn-brown. I wondered again: was she Amish, not-Amish? Weren't her dark eyebrows plucked? Wasn't that a tattoo around her stiff, sinewy neck? Was I seeing correctly into the pocket of her apron? Wasn't that a pack of Drum tobacco?

When she finally spoke, she did so with no breath, no lip movement, and I had to limp in closer.

"I'm sorry…I didn't catch that."

"Tell you what," Eve was mouthing. Her eyes darted to a dark doorway behind the counter and back to the bloody wader shreds below my right knee. "I need a little help too. Maybe we can make another deal…"

Startled, I blinked at her.

"I know what you're thinking," she whispered. "A good person would just help you. But it's too late for me to be good. I have to do what I can, when I see a chance."

"I just need you to call someone. You mentioned that your husband's little brother had some training…"

She turned toward the doorway. Two white kapp strings swung across her neck. Through the fog of my panic I finally recognized the voices from the other room. Al Michaels. Dan Dierdorf. Monday Night Football.

"What I need…is just somebody with a little background in first aid…some peroxide or something…just some gauze and tape…to hold the thing together…I'll be fine…"

I was peeling down my waders. I pried the boot off. I sucked my foot out of the neoprene sock and looked for a place to set the bloody thing down. Her head snapped back around. The hot brown glow of an idea pushed out around her pupils.

"That beaver might be rabid," she told me.

"Yeah…well…"

"It must be rabid," she decided.

"Small chance," I argued weakly.

She stepped farther out around the counter. I didn't expect the raw whiff of sweat that came with her. I didn't expect the red Chuck Taylor basketball shoes, high-top canvas, beneath the Amish dress. They startled me. I hadn't seen a pair since high school, and those weren't red. She kicked a bucket toward me.

"You need rabies treatment. Put your leg up here. I can fix this."

I backed away. "You don't look like a doctor."

She glanced again toward the doorway. "I've helped out with a midwife," she whispered hotly. "My mother is an Amish apothecary. I own a madstone. And that's what you need right now. A madstone. And I need help with my son. So we can trade."

"No," I managed, picturing the menace who threw apples at my fishing. "No deal. I'm sorry."

"Oh, everybody's sorry," she shot back. "Especially me. But that never changes anything."

I blinked back at her jittery eyes. She was stealing my lines. In the Dog's world, Sorry was a board game. I flopped my bloody wader foot over the bucket and challenged her. "I never heard of a madstone. What is it?"

"A hairball," she said. "From a white-tailed deer. It's hard like a stone. You boil it in sweet milk and then put it on the wound. It sucks the poison out. When you boil it in milk again, the milk turns green. That means you're okay."

"Sounds great," I grunted, twisting the foot to fit it over the bucket. "And then you sew me up with a nice Amish cross-stitch?"

She put a grape-tipped finger to her lips. Small gray teeth appeared. As she gnawed the nail, she took on a vaguely rodentine look, furtive and determined.

"For your information," she said around the tortured fingernail, "I'm not Amish. I got kicked out."

This must have just happened, I noted inwardly. No time to change out of the Amish wardrobe. But then she added, "Ten years ago," just as the Avalanche Kid wandered out through the doorway behind the counter. A brown lab puppy writhed uncomfortably in the boy's arms.

"Put Wally down," his mother commanded. The puppy wrenched around hopefully. "Wally wants down," she repeated tightly. "You're hurting him. Put him down."

The Avalanche Kid jammed the puppy's front legs onto the floor. He walked the puppy like a wheelbarrow until the fat little creature collapsed, whining, onto its face. Then he picked the puppy up again and goosed its privates. Wally was a boy dog, I saw, nuts and all. Eve Kussmaul turned away and set her eyes on my foot in the bucket.

"Here's what I want," she said quietly through her teeth. "I fix you up with the madstone, and you teach my son fly fishing."

"Ha!" The shock of surprise set fresh blood flowing. "No."

"He's a good boy. He just doesn't have anything good to do."

"Hasn't he got a father to teach him stuff?"

She didn't answer that. The puppy yelped. The Avalanche Kid had the chest freezer open. He was trying to put Wally inside.

"Deuce!"

"Ma, I wasn't *doing* anything," the kid lied. "He just wanted to lick the blood."

"Take Wally outside," Eve Kussmaul commanded. "Put him in his house and leave him alone."

"But I wasn't doing anything…"

"Go."

No response…no response…like the kid had no ears…like his mother didn't exist…and then she raised her mop handle like she would crack bones with it…and the kid finally picked up his Chipmunk .22 rifle and slouched out.

"He just doesn't have anything good to do," Eve repeated as the door swung shut. She gnawed a different finger. "Now his father thinks it's okay for him to have a rifle, start hunting, but I think fishing would be so much better—"

Bang-whang!—the kid gut-shot a mailbox, or maybe a junked car.

"Look," I told her, thinking maybe some background would help. "I used to pay taxes. A lot of taxes. I ran a private security firm. The old guy that did my taxes, back when I paid them, he saved my ass a thousand times. He's the one who wanted the Amish rocking chair. I told him no deal this morning. So as soon as I get this leg sewed up, as soon as I get that beaver into the state health office, I'm going to commission my friend one of the Barn Lady's paintings…get the two of them hooked up…and then I'm out of here."

She blinked at me.

"You could just make an order for an Amish chair," she said. "Then you could get started fishing with Deuce…get him started this fall…and then come back—"

Bang-whang!

"—in six months."

The shock was getting to me. I was drifting. "I'm sorry…just call someone for me…please."

Eve Kussmaul ground her small, hidden teeth. She stared at me hard, and somehow I knew we weren't done dealing. But I faded again, dropped my head, and a dark moment slipped past. Dog— this is not a fishing trip.

I looked up.

With all my might I said: "No."

"Okay," she sighed. Then she was wheeling away, skirts swelling, kapp strings whipping. Into the flickering TV-darkness of the house behind, she called out, "Hey, King!…King Midas!…Git your butt off the sofa!"

So this was King Midas Kussmaul

Bang!

Eight shots now. I took my eyes off the Avalanche Mercantile and hobbled over frozen grass toward the snarl of trees around the County Y bridge. Fat, broken-toothed *Castor Canadensis* was meeting his maker, Avalanche-style. But I was worried. Eight shots was a lot. Eight shots was a statement. I wondered to whom I was indebted. The Avalanche Kid and his little Chipmunk .22, I was guessing. I knew his name now. Deuce. And I knew that when Deuce Kussmaul hit a bird in the campground, he whooped with glee, then laid back down and kept firing, taking potshots at the dead body.

As I stumped forward, the previous night still clung to me. I heard the kid's mama again, yelling, "Hey, King Midas!" into the room behind the Avalanche Mercantile. "Git your butt off the sofa!"

There came a snarl, a pop of TV static, and amidst the thumping and growling from the back room I woozily recalled what the Barn Lady had told me at one of our morning coffee-and-blood-knotting sessions: the Kussmaul men were known by their barns.

So…I was catching on now…Eve Kussmaul's husband…the father of the Avalanche Kid…must own the barn behind the store, the red bank barn with the snug-dutch roof and the King Midas Flour billboard from the 40's. So this was "King Midas" Kussmaul, stumbling out in a Monday Night Football daze, beer in hand.

"He needs help," Eve said stiffly. "A beaver bit him. But he's got no money. He wants Half-Tim."

"What the hell for?"

"Medical stuff. I told him Half-Tim was at the tech college."

"Oh," said King Midas, scratching his belly. "Yeah. I guess I heard that."

"So call Half-Tim."

Then Eve retreated among the shelves. I could just see the white arc of her kapp, moving behind a summit of Off! spray cans.

Her husband stared at me. He waved the beer can at me. "Fifty bucks the fucker's rabid."

"Yeah…well…not likely…"

I couldn't stand up any more. I knocked over the bucket, slumped down against the butt end of the chest freezer, and stuck my legs out across the store floor.

"Hell. I'll take a hunnert on it. Fucker's rabid. Betcha."

"Beaver's don't normally…" I couldn't finish a sentence. "It's rare…"

King Midas suppressed some beer–gas into his flannelled shoulder and stepped out toward me. He was a sizeable guy, if you measured lengthwise where the flannel split above the belt buckle that anchored a pair of filthy discount blue jeans. He was barefoot and hammer-toed, and his extreme blondeness cast an eerie sleet-white across the pinkness of his unshaven skin. I experienced what I thought was a brief bolt of clarity, vis-à-vis Eve Kussmaul being ex-Amish: if my sister married a guy like King Midas, we'd kick her out of the family too.

If I had a sister…or a family.

"We'll see one way or t'other," King Midas was telling me.

"Morning, I'll have the kid go out and shoot every beaver in the crick. Kid's a helluva shot."

"Yeah..." I said again. "Well..."

"I shit you not. You oughta see him. He's all Kussmaul."

"Yeah...well...actually..."

"Have a beer, man. It kills germs."

Some time later...maybe just seconds later...or hours...I was suddenly awake again, gripping a Bud Lite can so tightly I was squeezing the beer out of it. Rudimentary medical supplies had been positioned between my legs, and a second Kussmaul brother leaned over me. This one was soft-bodied and long-haired, sweating and puffing, his lungs blasting me with gusts of ketchup and fried chicken—in other words, this was the younger brother, the one who brought me more free firewood than I could burn, the one I had asked Eve for...Half-Tim.

"Sure," Half-Tim Kussmaul was saying. His voice trembled. "Sure. I can handle this. We covered this last term."

"Fucker's rabid," put in his big brother, King Midas—and right there I remembered another tidbit from Barn Lady, describing additional Kussmauls that morning over blood knots and coffee. Half-Tim was Half-Timber...a quaint little half-timber barn, Bohemian-style, with rare stovewood nogging, up at the tip-top of the coulee.

Half-Timber leaned over me. His wide-set eyes, Kussmaul blue, hung aglow upon my wound. His small, pink hands gathered up shoulder-length hair that looked like wet, matted corn silk.

"We covered this in Rapid Med I," he assured no one in particular. "And beavers...um...beavers...are almost never rabid...I think." He gloved himself. He tucked his wet wad of hair beneath a hair net. He belched nervous chicken breath. Eve shot me a look from under her kapp. I should have gone with the madstone, she was telling me.

But Half-Tim was scissoring off my waders and pants. He put the bucket back under my leg and drenched my wound with warm, soapy water. He unspooled my 8X tippet and fit it through the eye of a sewing needle.

"That's why I can do this," he informed Eve and me. "Rapid Med I. That's the only reason."

King Midas had gone somewhere. He came back loudly. "I called Salt Box and Lightning Rod and them," he said. "They gotta see this. They gotta see Half-Tim in action."

The younger Kussmaul kept his head down. "You didn't have to do that."

King Midas sneered. "Say what?"

The younger Kussmaul responded quietly and shakily, though clenched teeth. "I don't want an audience."

"Better get used to it," King said. "You gotten used to worse."

"Asshole," Half-Tim muttered at my leg. King Midas grunted something I couldn't catch, tipped his head and glugged beer. Families, I remember telling myself. I was lucky to be so free. I'd take a beaver bite any day.

Half-Tim resumed his tentative pose over the bloody gash, breathing greasy dark meat on me, adjusting the angle of his knees, his wrists, his hands, the needle, then adjusting everything back again. To distract myself from the pain ahead, I sat down with Barn Lady again—I mean, within the reeling space of my mind—I eased down again with a tin cup of hot coffee across the picnic table from my new friend, and I watched the old girl mis-tie blood knots as she told me all about the Kussmaul barns: the King Midas barn and the Half-Timber barn…the Salt Box Barn…the Lightning Rod Barn…the Potato Barn…the Round Barn…the Tobacco Barn…all Kussmaul barns, all famous in the barn-lover community, all on preservation lists, all fetching good money for Barn Lady as paintings on calendars, greeting cards, and canvas.

Then the actual pain of Half-Tim's stitchwork came and I faded altogether…and while I was out, the Kussmaul barns became Kussmaul brothers and uncles and cousins…leaning over me, the venality of each Kussmaul as startlingly clear as if Barn Lady's handy tags hung about their necks: oldest brother Salt Box, the one she told me was a tax cheat…cousin Lightning Rod, who cooked methamphet-amine in his barn…Uncle Tater and Uncle Roundy, who ran cock fights and poached…Uncle Beechnut, he of the tobacco barn, who had no lower jaw…all of them above me, breathing down in gusts of booze and Skoal and gingivitis, all the florid, blondine, manure-scented Kussmaul barn boys, the ones who kept coming after Barn Lady for money, not a single one of them ever asking nicely.

"Hey," one of them whooped, "look at little Half-Timmy go!"

"I didn't ask for an audience," the youngest Kussmaul com-plained again. "EMT work is not a show."

King Midas had gone somewhere again. Again he came back loudly. "Yep. Half-Timmy's all changed-up this year. He's in tech school now to be one of those guys who comes to accidents and pries you out of the truck. So you all drunk-ass sidewinders best be nice to him. But anyway, friend, if I was you—"

King Midas was speaking to me now. He took my beer can away. He handed me a half-done fifth of Jack Daniels.

"—I'd go ahead and graduate before he does."

The Kussmaul barn boys liked that. They snorted. They hoot-ed. They guffawed. A woman whinnied *tee-hee-hee* through her nose. My head jerked up. No—the pony-laugher wasn't Eve. The sound had come from a fried-out girlfriend on the arm of Lightning Rod. Eve…she was right beside me…on her knees, my hand trapped in her rough, grape-tipped fingers.

Tee-hee-hee, whinnied the girlfriend again. "I never seen rabies before." She nudged me with the toe of a cheap black cowboy boot. "Is that why he looks so scruffy and mean?"

Then the Avalanche Mercantile's outer door creaked open and slammed back shut—and all the Kussmaul fun stopped dead.

Too much lead for a beaver

Bang!

That was nine shots now. Nine rifle shots in the span of about two minutes, while the sun still clawed its way through cold morning fog.

I hobbled toward the bridge. My leg pounded from the 8X surgery. My head pounded from the Jack Daniels. I didn't remember leaving the store and getting back to the Cruise Master the night before. Someone had helped me, obviously, but...

Bang!

Ten. Damn it. That was too much lead for a beaver.

As I pushed through the high weeds that rimmed the campground, I stumbled on the rubber tube from a tractor's back tire, five feet round, blown open and deflated. I snatched it up. I figured I could use the tube to snag out the carcass, kind of wrap the beaver up, then ease him into the garbage bags for the trip to the state health office. And all the while I was hearing that door slam, feeling Eve's hands vanish, hearing the laughter stop dead, and thinking: *She was lucky, after all—the Barn Lady—that those Kussmauls hadn't killed her...*

As I lay there taking stitches and bad jokes, the Avalanche Mercantile's outer door creaked open and slammed back—*Bang!*—and everything had stopped. The snickering, the surgery, everything.

"Hey," said King Midas, "it's the goddamn poacher."

"Sticks and stones," sang Barn Lady, as she traipsed in. She was a plump little woman, an ex school teacher, gray-haired, apple-cheeked and cheery, tough as a goddamn nut. An "alternative learner," she called herself.

"I never gave you permission," King Midas growled, "to paint my barn."

"Oh, honey…" She laid a motherly hand on his beer arm. On her right wrist she wore hippie-style bracelets—braided leather thongs, slightly smelly but kind of cute—lots of them. "I didn't paint your barn. I painted a *picture* of your barn."

"I never said you could."

"But I don't need your permission."

"That's my property."

"Oh, but sight lines," she sang, "are *public* property. If I can see it, it's mine, artistically speaking." She waited for agreement on this obvious point but got none from the Kussmaul crowd. "Same for you, dear," she told King Midas. "What you look at is yours to keep inside your mind. Or else your big brother Salt Box could charge you for the sunrise."

"I ain't into the goddamn sunrise. The sunrise can go screw itself."

"But my point—"

Barn Lady stopped abruptly. I sat up a bit, saw Salt Box Kussmual spit a toothpick aside and step into her path. "But you're making real money offa us. We oughta get a piece of that."

Barn Lady sighed. Then she raised to her tiptoes, coming up to the red knob in Salt Box's throat. She shook her bracelets back and poked Salt Box in his round, tight gut. "Like you Kussmauls don't use *my* sunshine to make *your* money!" she exclaimed. "And no thank you, by the way, for all the methane gas your cattle send up into *my* air." She paused. She turned to all of them. "Not to mention, my dear friends, that our history, barns included, is the landscape of our minds and therefore belongs to all of us."

Then—as if we were engaged in high school forensics, as if logic were decisive, or even recognizable—the Barn Lady made a polite little curtsy and turned her attention to me.

"Oh, dear. Poor Dog. I was afraid you'd been hurt. I heard you yell…"

I told her why.

"I'm so sorry. But beavers are rarely rabid, you know. I do have those sketches of the Amish barn with me, the ones you wanted to see, so that we can get started on that special painting for your special friend. But of course this isn't a good time for you…"

I gasped something. No. Not so good, as times went. The Barn Lady glanced at my surgeon, he of the half-timber barn, and she bugged her eyes a bit, as if to wish me luck. Then I watched her return a small, hard-backed sketchbook to the baggy breast pocket of her paint-specked overalls, squaring it in beside a small yellow paint brush that stuck up and tickled her plump neck. "You'll feel better in the morning," she assured me, "and I'll show you then." She smiled at me. "I'll bring some of Howard's coffee." Then she turned her back to do her business. Her windbreaker said BARN AGAIN! "Eve, Sweetie," she said, "I'll have two candles, please, the tall white ones, and that new jumbo Snickers bar."

I felt a hard prick in the leg and looked down. Half-Timber had gone back to stitching. I know that in the renewal of my pain, I missed a line or two of conversation, because suddenly Salt Box was in full throat, woofing at the fearless little woman.

"Hey! Lady! You didn't hear him? You deaf? My Uncle Roundy says how about you give us some of that money?"

"Because," said Barn Lady with polished calm, not turning, "it's my living. I've got a husband who is retired and a son heading for college. Painting pictures of *your* barns is *my* work."

Salt Box—a beefier, older, cleaner-shaven King Midas—grabbed his pants and gave them a tug. "Well you ain't asked to come up on my property."

"I have riparian rights," she replied. "Just like the view, navigable water bodies are public. I have researched the state laws. I can wade up the West Fork anywhere I want."

The Kussmauls were silent for a long moment. Then the girlfriend made her eyes big and gave Cousin Lightning Rod a shove. On the Kussmaul spectrum, Lightning Rod was the runt. He was about a year or two older than Half-Tim—twenty-four, maybe. He had a gold hoop in his left ear and a permed mane of hair in streetlight-white. "We built them barns," he rasped.

Barn Lady turned and smiled sadly at Lightning Rod. His barn, I recalled her telling me, had exquisite wrought-iron weather vanes, complete with glass balls and tall copper lightning spires.

"No, dear. That's not correct."

The girlfriend, tall and skinny and a good decade older, made a kabuki face at the Barn Lady and re-shoved the young Kussmaul, but Lightning Rod was speechless.

"You telling me," Uncle Roundy spluttered finally, "my great granddad didn't build that round barn of mine?"

Barn Lady had received from Eve her tall white candles and her jumbo Snickers bar. As Eve tried to bag her purchases in a clear plastic, she said noisily, "Oh, no, Sweetie, I don't need that—no bags, please—just more trash—but…or then again, yes, I will take it. I can always use a bag."

I caught Kussmaul eyes rolling as the old woman wadded the plastic into her hip pocket. She tucked the candles and the Snickers bar carefully into the bib pouch of her overalls, between the sketchbook and the small yellow brush that stuck up perkily toward her dumpling chin.

"As a matter of fact, my dear man, your lovely round barn was built by a black fellow—a freed slave—who made it round so the white devil couldn't hide in the corners."

She smiled nicely at Uncle Roundy. This Kussmaul was pushing an age where he didn't care if his cap was on straight or if his fly was up—and neither could be said for Uncle Roundy at the moment. He was the shortest Kussmaul, with dirty hands dangling like hacked-off tree roots at his sides. He had grown into his nickname—his high, hybrid belly-chest, his red cheeks, the sagging aperture of his tobacco-stained lips—everything about him...round.

"Your great granddad Bertram Kussmaul got the barn when the poor black fellow went to jail for whistling at a white woman in Westby...or for whistling at a spotted dray horse in Coon Valley...it depends on whom you ask...and on how much you want to have another man's barn—"

Uncle Roundy glowered, flexing his dirty fingers.

"Hell you needem candles fer?" burst a tortured, high-pitched voice. I looked at the jawless Uncle Beechnut. But it wasn't him. It was Uncle Tater—lean and breathless, consumptive-looking.

"None of your business, dear."

"You stay oudem my barnem candles! I got hayender!"

Then the door swung again and the Avalanche Kid returned, his Chipmunk .22 slung over one shoulder, the puppy squirming and gagging under the opposite arm. Silently and seamlessly, he took his place in the Kussmaul gallery, ducking his father's beer elbow as it swung down.

"I'm missing stuff from my barn," grunted Uncle Roundy, turning back to the Barn Lady. "Tools. Gas."

"Now we're talking," growled Salt Box. "I had a gas can walk away about a week ago. And I lost a lamb the other night." He looked accusingly at the lady artist. "I ain't found that lamb. And I ain't found out how that lamb undid a head-high latch neither."

The girlfriend said, "Hey, lady. Us too. A twelve-pack of Mountain Dew and a whole side of bacon."

"Boy calf!" squealed Uncle Tater. "Gonis morning outem calf pen!"

The accusations went on, but Half-Timber shocked me back, tugging crudely to make a knot. "Sorry," my surgeon mumbled. I slugged down Jack Daniels and waited for the world to come back to me.

"You stay outa my barn!"

"You put one foot out of the crick and you're trespassing!"

"Where you gonem candles?"

The Kussmaul voices ricocheted around me. The puppy licked my face. The Barn Lady laughed gaily. "Let's just settle this," Salt Box was saying when I could hear the finer points again. "Nothing to settle," she replied. Half-Tim was wrapping up now. He was drenched in sweat. The chicken smell was coming out his pores. Salt Box had followed Barn Lady menacingly toward the door.

"Messing with livestock is a felony. Even if you just get all sweet and PETA and let a lamb out, the coyotes get it and then you killed that lamb—which is just as good as stealing it. But even though you been trespassing and killing and stealing, we don't go to the law. We forget about it. And you give us Kussmauls some of that barn painting money."

"You give us half," said Uncle Roundy.

"And then you stay the hell out of this coulee," said King Midas.

I came up on my elbows. Barn Lady wasn't frightened yet. Not a bit. Not even with the Avalanche Kid squared up on her, his little .22 rifle aimed just inches south of the angle where someone might claim he was pointing it at her. Barn Lady looked like she was having fun. "Should I dance, Deucey?" she asked the kid, and then she danced—a careless, loopy, bracelet-shifting, flower-child twirl into the rifle's purview and back out, her wobbly old arms pulling her hair up and letting it fall.

"I'll tell you what I'll do for you gentlemen," she said grandly. "Since you're such a fine bunch. I'll tell you what I'm going to give you."

She paused with the door open.

"Nothing!" sang the Barn Lady, and let the door slam.

And *Bang!* cracked the eleventh gunshot across the West Fork the next morning.

I staggered through the tangle of tree scrub and saw it was the Avalanche Kid, in the cold light of dawn, firing his little Chipmunk .22 rifle from the County Y bridge. He aimed down, into the un-

seen region below the bridge. The concussion spanked the heavy
air: *Bang!* An even dozen.

"Hey!" I yelled at the kid. "It's just a beaver. There has to be
something left of him. Enough!"

I fumbled the tire tube and the box of garbage bags as I smashed
through streamside asters.

"Stop!"

Bang!

Thirteen.

The kid stared down, ruinously defiant, purely Kussmaulian,
his dirty little chin stuck out at me. Then he swung the rifle butt
down to his hip and hauled open the bolt. He was going to re-load
and shoot again.

"Christ, kid!" I squawked. "Stop! Don't pulp the thing!"

But as I stumbled up I could see that the kid's target was still
plenty intact.

I could see the Barn Lady. Her plump little body rolled and
tossed at the tail of the bridge pool. Her thin gray hair trailed away
in the current, and the push of the creek ballooned her overalls. Her
left arm bent grotesquely above her head, wobbling like a trout. A
final shot slammed past me—*Bang!*—and jolted the body.

"There," said the Avalanche Kid.

He coughed words down at me.

"I shot her."

I stared up, disbelieving. The kid's puppy was nowhere in sight.
Beside him on the bridge was Barn Lady's easel, her paint box,
her little red wagon. The canvas on the easel was the whitewashed
Amish barn she and I had spoken of, the one with the blue monitor
roof—the actual barn itself just becoming visible at the edge of the
fog, about two hundred yards north of the bridge.

"Hey..." I stammered up. "What the..."

But now the Avalanche Kid was trembling, tears streaking
down his dirty cheeks. He tried a deep breath. I heard a cry of
shock behind me: the dead woman's husband had finally struggled

from the teepee, thrashed his way up through the high weeds and slag beyond the bridge. He was seeing it.

"Go ahead," managed the Avalanche Kid.

I gaped at him.

"I killed her," he said. "You saw me do it."

I sat back in cold mud beside the body. I was going to be sick.

"I let go them animals they was talking about last night, too," the Avalanche Kid said. "Then I killed her."

I tried to move my eyes bankside, to neutral ground. There, cased in the clear plastic bag from the Mercantile, and stuck in dewy purple asters, was the sketchbook—the one I was supposed to look at.

"I killed her," repeated the kid. "You saw me."

He shivered. He croaked, "Right? You saw me hit her. Now go ahead and tell somebody."

It's just a sticker…it came with the vehicle

Eve Kussmaul was in the store, mopping up mud tracks to the beer cooler. She waited for me to speak, but I couldn't find my tongue right away. I was shivering too hard.

"I heard shots," she said wearily, dropping the mop back into a bucket. "So I guess they got your beaver."

I managed to say no.

No.

That wasn't the case.

"Is my husband out there?"

I leaned on the counter and got the weight off my leg. A whiff of death seemed to rise from my sleeve, and I gagged back an upsurge of last night's Jack D. and Tylenol. I had knelt in the water beside Barn Lady to see if there was something I could do. But the woman was beyond dead. She lay half in the water and half ashore among the coon and heron prints on a little mud spit that formed in the wake of a bridge piling. Her right arm was mangled from the fall over the guard rail, and the leather bracelets were gone. Her skull, on the left side, was dented and her scalp was bloodily torn. She had taken one of the fourteen shots square in the jumbo Snickers bar as it peeked from the bib pocket of her coveralls. The result was a grotesque little mass of blood and chocolate, congealed in cold water and slipping infinitesimally south as the stream shoved dumbly on its way. The long, white candles were gone.

No, I told Eve Kussmaul. Not her husband.

No one was out there but her son.

She made a sharp little frown and brought a purple thumbnail to her mouth. "Deuce is still in bed."

"No. I'm afraid he's not."

She turned her head toward the door to the living quarters and hollered, "Deuce!"

"He's down on the Y bridge," I told her. "With his rifle."

She looked at me a moment, suspiciously, like I had already gone rabid. Then, thinly concealing a bolt of panic, she hauled the mop back out of the bucket. She stood on a stool, mop strings dripping everywhere. She reached to the tiptoes of her red Chuckies and banged on the pressed tin ceiling. "Deucey! Git your butt up! Git down here!"

"He's not—" I began.

"If you think I'm a bad person for yelling and cussing like that," she interrupted, suddenly red-cheeked as she stepped back down to the floor, "you're right. You won't be the first person to tell me that, so go ahead."

"I'm not going to tell you anything."

She slopped the mop back in the bucket.

"I used to get high a lot," she said. "With King and them. On meth. Do you know meth?"

I nodded. The Dog knew meth. Stimulant. Powerfully addictive. Crank, in Boston, in the nineties. People stole for it, whored for it, even killed for it—or because of it. It was a vicious-circle drug. But Eve Kussmaul seemed relieved that the Dog knew meth. She said, "My father writes me a letter once a week to tell me that I'm going to Hell." Again, she waited for a response. I gave her none this time. "He's a bishop. He moved them all away to an Old Order settlement in Kentucky," she said, "after King and I, you know…"

We heard a distant *Bang!* Her kapp strings whipped as she glanced sharply toward the streamside window. But the wall was blocked head high, corner to corner, with twelve-packs of beer. The morning sun cut over the beer boxes and filled the top half of the store with mote-struck, pale-yellow light.

"I'm just sure they got that beaver," she blurted. "The Kussmaul boys are all real good hunters. That middle farm, the one those new Amish are on now, my father bought it from King's Uncle Beechnut after he couldn't farm anymore, and you should see the side of that barn. The Kussmaul boys used to nail their beaver tails up there. There must be dozens of them."

I put my hand up. My voice was rough. "No—forget the beaver. Your son shot the Barn Lady."

Eve Kussmaul stopped. She shut right down. She kept her eyes on me for a long, expressionless moment. Then she lowered her head and stared at the streaky floor.

"King got me into drinking first," she went on, as if in a separate conversation. "My sister Rachel and me. Rachel went with Salt Box, and it was just a lot of fun. I never laughed so much...and I...I...maybe I...well, I'm sure you don't care..."

"I need a phone. Just get me a phone."

She moved tightly, silently. She gave me a cordless phone and I faced away from her. I hit 911. I said my piece. When I turned back, Eve Kussmaul was pale and shaking, tugging at her wet apron.

"There's some mistake," she said.

I told her I didn't think so.

"Yes," she said desperately. "There's some mistake. Deucey wouldn't shoot...a person. He...he...gets into a lot of trouble...but he's a good boy. He just doesn't know how to please his dad. He loves animals...and he and Annie were friends...and he..."

And there she lost the threads of hope. She began to shake.

"M-maybe," she stammered, "maybe you could help us."

"Help who?"

"Me and Deucey."

I looked away. I looked at canned peaches. There were nine cans of peaches, in heavy syrup. I was going to shoot that goddamned beaver and hit the road.

"I don't see how I could help."

"Maybe you could tell the sheriff you didn't see who shot her."

"That would be a lie."

Her brown eyes bugged. Her thin neck gulped. "Well...I could pay you. I sell eggs and pumpkins, and I do mending. I have three hundred in my own money that King doesn't even know about. I could pay you..."

"Pay me to lie? About a murder?"

"I told you. I'm going to Hell anyway."

"And you think I'd go too, for three hundred bucks?"

We looked at each other. For a split second, I wondered if she knew how close she had come to the Dog's price.

"Please," she begged finally. "Things around here...I mean, I don't know what happened...I can't explain it...but someone made Deucey say that...someone is taking advantage of him...and...these Kussmaul barns that Annie was painting, everybody's got something going on in there. King parties with the Amish kids in ours. He sells meth. He messes with girls. When an Amish kid wants to run away, King lets him stay in the barn. The sheriff is on his case about it. And King's Uncle Roundy has cock fights in his barn. And he butchers poached deer in there. Uncle Tater too. Maybe Annie was going to tell on them. And then Salt Box put an apartment in his loft and rents it to his milker and doesn't tell the government..."

I looked away from her. *Creamed corn. Three cans.*

"...and Lightning Rod," she said, "...his barn...that's where we...I mean, where King gets his meth...Lighting Rod cooks methamphetamine in his barn..." Her eyes pleaded. "And Ma Kussmaul...she lives with Half-Tim, up on the tri-county farm...she wants to tear that old half-timber barn down completely...And Annie was against that, because it's the only half-timber ever built around here...so she riled up all her barn friends..."

French cut green beans. One can. Tell her again, Dog.

"I saw your son shoot the Barn Lady. More than a dozen times. I saw the bullets hit her body. Nobody made him do it."

"You didn't see. You couldn't have. Please."

I looked toward the beer-blocked window. *Bang!* He was still shooting her.

"Sorry. I can't help."

"You have to."

"No, I don't."

"But…but…I saw the sticker on your camper car…"

Now I looked at Eve Kussmaul squarely. What the hell? Her throat had reddened. Her dark eyebrows seemed to bristle. Her armpits were suddenly black with sweat.

She told me, "The Good Sam Club sticker. On your camper. You can help. You're supposed to help. That's the way it is in the Bible. You're supposed to do the right thing for people in need. You're a member of the Good Samaritan Club…"

I raised my sunglasses from the twine lanyard around my neck. She was grasping. I reminded myself that *she* was the one who had broken the Good Sam code, the night before, trying to profit from my injury.

Go, Dog, go.

I settled the sunglasses on my nose and the store went dark.

"It's just a sticker," I told her.

Eve Kussmaul's face became stone. Blotchy red stone. Already, I could tell, she was looking for another way out.

"It came with the vehicle," I told her.

And I gave back the phone.

To Annie, everything mattered

It was dark again before the detectives were done with me and the crime scene tape was rolled back from the bridge and the stream bank.

I put my last, carefully nurtured nine-volt battery into my big Oglivie Secure flashlight. I loaded my Glock and packed an extra clip. I taped a garbage bag tightly around my wounded leg. On the way out of the Cruise Master, I checked my face again in the mirror. Blood shot eyes. Cracked lips. A peeling windburn around the white shadow of my sunglasses, a slight orange vodka-Tang stain at the mouth corners. In other words, vintage Dog. Status quo. No rabies. But still—no Good Sam either—the beaver had to die.

The postcard beside the mirror told me: *This is not a pipe.*

"Bullshit," I muttered.

"I saw what I saw," I grumbled.

And I reached out to pop the door. But the door opened without me. The husband of Barn Lady, the brand new widower, pulled it back and let me limp out.

His shoulders sagged. His mouth hung open. What little hair he had was badly askew. He had a big, square oil painting propped between his knees. His eyes rose to me behind thick glasses, great sad orbs, large as fried eggs.

Go, Dog, go, I thought again. But I managed, "I'm sorry."

"Thank you," he whispered. "Thank you, my friend."

I moved the Glock to my jacket pocket. I scowled at the bat-ripped sky. *My friend.* But it was fair enough, at this juncture in the man's life, to call me friend. We had met. That was enough. I had bonded—to the extent that my style allowed—with his wife. I had taught her how to tie blood-knotted leaders for him, advised her on which fly she should tie on for her husband before she went off to paint barns. A handful of times, in my six days in Avalanche, I had come across the old man trying to fly fish, finding him snagged in a tree, or snagged about himself, or posted up on a big hole, passionately addressing a rising fish…without any fly on at all.

I had fixed him up. I had retied his leader, sometimes from the nail knot on down. I tied fresh tippet and aimed him toward an ambush-feeding fish that would tolerate a bad cast.

His old eyes would swim up at me.

"There? How could a trout fit in there?"

"Put your fly in there. You'll see."

"I can't hit that kind of spot. Hell, I can barely wipe my own ass. I need Annie to button my shirts."

Annie. That was it. The dead lady was Annie. He was Howard. Annie and Howard Adams.

Now Howard Adams trembled as I closed the Cruise Master door and faced him. He sagged, almost sitting on the framed canvas between his legs.

"I'm sorry," I said again. "I've been where you are. I've had a loss like this."

"Yeah, sure," he said blankly. "Sure. Yup."

"You want a drink?"

"Jesus Christ," he said. "I thought you'd never ask."

I went inside the Cruise Master and fixed him a strong vodka-Tang. I doubt he'd ever had Dog Juice before, but he didn't flinch. I could have handed him diesel fuel. He gave back an empty cup.

"See," he said, "here's what gets me. Annie liked that kid. When Annie's own boy didn't come back to Avalanche this summer, that kid was heartbroken. He followed Annie around, tossing apples at her, but she knew why. She pretended not to notice. God damn it, she liked him. Then he guns her down."

"Another drink?"

"You got one?"

"I got several."

"It's getting cold out here."

"Then come on in."

I caught my breath after I said it. I had gone too far. I hung anxiously on his reply, picturing Howard Adams in the warm light of the Cruise Master, weeping onto my galley table, messing up my maps. Then I pictured him in the passenger seat, rambling morosely into the dark windshield, on our way up north to the Big Two-Hearted River.

"Naw," he said finally, to my great relief. "Thanks. I just came to ask you something. I need your good eyes again."

A feeble yard light had fizzled on between the Cruise Master and the bathroom, and Howard Adams carried the painting into the cone of pale yellow. It was a half-finished painting of the Amish barn, the painting set up on the bridge that Annie Adams had died beneath. But she and I had talked about something special for my tax guy, Harvey: a view from down inside the creek bed. "What do you make of it?" her husband asked me.

"It's very good."

"Yeah," he said forlornly, "yeah, Annie was very good. But that's not what I mean."

His brain was moving slowly. I waited. Moths and bats intersected above us. Barn owls called across the creek.

"No," he sighed. "Look here."

I looked. Leggy orange crane flies and tiny, speck-like midges crawled all over the completed structure of the barn itself, but the background was still a streaky sketch—a vague outline of fields and hills around the handsomely tall, whitewashed, blue-roofed barn.

"You see this here?" Howard Adams put a shaky finger on a dim grid of brown specs, a couple dozen of them, indistinct blobs of paint, about head high on the barn and to the right side of a big, double-railed door. I put my big flashlight on them. They were oblong, brown, faintly cross-hatched.

"Beaver tails," the old man told me, and I remembered what Eve had said. "From when Kussmauls owned this barn," he said. "But the beaver tails are nailed on the *north* side of the barn. Annie was set up on the bridge, which is *south*."

"She was just doing background," I said. "Fields and sky and hills. Maybe it didn't matter."

He worked his dry, purple lips for a long moment. "You didn't know Annie," he said finally. "To Annie, everything mattered."

I said I guessed I did know that. He drained his second drink and handed me the cup. "Hell, she would get into a barn just to touch the wood, measure the plank width, find out how many coats of paint it had. She had to get it right. Then she would sketch everything around it. A tree wasn't just a tree to Annie. A silver maple and a cottonwood are both tall and green, and their leaves are both white on the back, but the cottonwood forks higher," he said. "And silver maples bust up real easy, so there's always dead wood inside, hanging upside down." He shook his head again. He let the painting rest on the ground. "God, she would talk about that stuff forever. She would talk me to sleep with that stuff."

I put a paw on his shoulder. "I'm really sorry."

"I got so sick of it," he sighed. "She couldn't leave anything alone. Everything had to be just right. Other people too. Or Annie would step in and hassle them. But shit—okay—fair enough, I drink too much."

I raised my tin cup. "Join the club."

He made a sad little smile. He said, "Oh, well. Nothing's stopping me now."

"Get a hobby," I suggested, though I knew it was way too early in the course of his grief. "Get obsessed with something. I can't drink when I'm walking a stream. I don't even think about it. Get something else you can do."

"I can't walk much."

"Get a boat. Fish musky. Fish salmon."

He thought a minute. "Fishermen gotta fish," he said finally. "Don't they?"

"And probably painters gotta paint," I added. "I wonder if your wife just couldn't get back upstream of the Amish place, where she needed to be. That's pretty rough ground in there, and I expect she felt she had to wade up the stream, given what I heard about trespassing from the Kussmauls last night. Maybe she took a pass. She was younger than you, but she wasn't young."

"Yeah," he sighed heavily. "Yeah. That's probably it. I know her hip was bothering her."

We stood silently in a blizzard of September's last insects. Howard Adams began to nod and mumble to himself. "I'll get you another drink," I said at last, and I hobbled inside, cut him a little short on the vodka this time. When I brought back his cup, Howard Adams was saying, "Barns, barns, barns. Nothing but barns. She claimed she had to sleep in the goddamn things before she could paint them. Understand the soul, some shit like that."

His eyes wallowed up to me. "So…she doesn't come home last night, right?"

A bit startled, I said, "No?"

He bent his neck, waved a gnarled hand over the painting between his legs, trying to discourage the insects, which were somehow attracted to the gleam of oil paint under yard light.

"That meant she was into something new. And once she was into something new, a new barn, a new cause," he said, "forget about it. I might as well be furniture. But we were working on it, you know? You work at things. You hope to get a little better before you die." He sighed. "So, Annie doesn't come home last night…and she knows I don't care for that…but…then this…"

He was wavering. He was coming up on something that hurt him.

"This…"

He was shaking so hard I thought he was going to drop the painting. He leaned it against the inside of his right leg. He reached down into his baggy trouser pocket and brought out his wife's small, hard-backed sketchbook, the one she had intended me to look at on the morning I had found her dead. He shucked its clear plastic bag.

"But...then the detective gives me this...and...and I realize...I realize she did care...She...she..." he gasped finally, "...she sketched this in here...for me."

I didn't see that coming. I was thinking about sketches of the Amish barn, about a nice big canvas for Harvey, in place of the rocking chair. But Howard Adams thought something in the sketchbook was for him. I took a breath and looked away for a moment. Death did that—put the self at the bottom of a pile, every detail weighing down. Then I looked at the page Howard Adams held out. It was a sketch of a fly fishing knot in stages, like an instructional diagram. No—I looked closer—the sketches looked like copies of the instructional diagram I had sketched for her when I was teaching Annie the blood knot. You overlapped the tippet strands about four inches. Then you wound one tag end around the other line strand, six times in each direction. Then you tucked the tags back through the center of the knot—in opposite directions, one tag up, one tag down—before you widened your grip, wet the knot with spit, and pulled it tight. The blood knot was strong as wire, and a pretty thing to look at when done correctly. But Annie Adams couldn't—or wouldn't—get the opposite part right. She kept pushing both tags down through the bottom of the knot, or up through the top, or tying them around each other—doing it any way but the right way—and I kept taking the resultant mutation and stressing it, stretching it, snapping it. The slightest flaw, I tried to make her see, was fatal. But the Barn Lady had been a stubborn student—an "alternative learner," she kept proudly telling me. She had to attempt the blood knot every way other than the one I showed her, and she liked to watch me squirm while she did it. Now, nailing me from beyond death, I saw that Annie Adams had sketched the blood knot with both tag ends down. My eyes twitched. Wrong.

I said to her husband: "That's a blood knot. Sort of."

"Yeah?…oh, right…that's right…I was trying to remember the name of the damn thing…"

"You mean," I said, "you think your wife drew this to help you?"

"I know she did."

"Help you tie your own knots?"

"Yes. That's Annie."

Like she, herself, wouldn't be around to help? I wondered. Like the Barn Lady knew her time was up? But I resisted the thought, and I let it go—forget it, Dog—turning my attention to the buzzing of a small engine as the new sound leapt out of the darkness. Howard Adams' head snapped up at the racket, and he looked long and hard toward the field across the creek, where a pair of small headlights bounced through the black landscape. The old man stood stiffly, alert as a deer—and I closed my eyes. The Dog knew that moment. For Howard Adams, life had suddenly become a horrible dream, and any sound might be the one that woke him and allowed his real life to pour back in. The all-terrain four-wheeler—its engine redlined and backfiring—had to fade to nothing into the northern reaches of the coulee before Howard Adams could again face the fact that his wife was dead. When he looked back at me, his rheumy eyes were fierce.

"Those goddamn four-wheelers," he said. "Everybody around here's got one. Or two. Chewing up the ground. Buzzing around here day and night."

"Come on," I said. "Let's sit down, have another drink."

But Howard Adams stood his shaky ground.

"Naw," he said, "I'm bothering you."

"You're not."

"Hell," he said, "you been saving my butt on the creek all week. I gotta have some pride. I'm going to bed now." Then he spoke to himself. "Go on, Howard," he told himself. "Just tie up the teepee and wait for tomorrow."

I didn't know what to say. I looked purposefully away toward the dark cleft of the West Fork and had a moment of clarity with myself. *Dog, you can't help this man.*

"But just one more thing," said Howard Adams.

He held the sketchbook up for me and tried to wave the insects off.

"Yeah?" I said.

"Tell me what it is, this fly Annie drew, on the next page..."

I looked at it. It was a trico—a miniscule mayfly resembling a tiny black ant with angel wings. The imitation was a fly that I had shown her, one that we had talked about as being a staple, in certain spring creeks, of a trout's fall diet. But it was also a fly, I had warned Annie Adams, that was far too small for her near-sighted husband to handle. She had asked about the fly's name—where the name trico came from—and when I said I didn't know, she was abruptly delighted. "When that happens," she told me, her eyes twinkling with old-lady thrill and mischief, "you get to make up your own meaning!"

Now Howard Adams grew impatient and wobbled the sketchbook in front of me. "The fly?" I said, shaking myself. "It's a trico."

"Okay, then," said Howard Adams.

Okay then what? I asked him.

"Annie picked my flies," he told me. "She must want me to use this fly. Probably it's a real killer fly. I should use it. This...this..."

"Trico. Trico spinner."

"What the hell is a trico spinner?"

I told him. The trico spinner was a tiny spent mayfly, its eggs laid, ready to hit the water and die as its life cycle ended. I told him I hadn't seen a single trico in six days on the West Fork. Maybe there were tricos upstream, I told him, where I hadn't fished yet. But Howard Adams was back in the numb zone. He wasn't hearing.

"That trico fly's gotta be the ticket," he said instead. "Annie must have figured it out. She's got a sharp eye for that kind of stuff. Sees the small things. You got any tricos?"

I told him sure.

"You'll tie one on for me?"

I told him sure.

"With one of these whatzits? Blood knots?"

"Um...yeah...sure."

"First thing in the morning?"

I patted my Glock pocket. Beaver, I reminded myself. I nodded.

"You promise?" said Howard Adams. He put his hand on my arm, tugged my shirt sleeve a little. "I'm going catch a big goddamned brown trout for Annie in the morning. That's what I'm going to do. You'll bring me a fly and tie it on in the morning. You promise?"

Bad Dog.

Bad, *bad* Dog.

I would be gone in the morning. Shoot the beaver. Drop it off at the state health lab. Big-Two Hearted by sundown.

But I said, "Sure."

And Howard Adams tottered halfway back to his camp before he listed left and boomeranged slowly back. "And why do you think," he asked me, shaking open the sketchbook again, "on the very last page here, right after the blood knot and the trico, she draws me a picture of a dog?"

It's always hunting season in Kussmaul country

Hell if I knew why his wife would sketch a dog, I told Howard Adams. Because he might want a new companion?

Then I limped down to the creek with my Glock and my flashlight.

Hell if I know, I repeated.

After a few steps away from the campground light, the world shrank to black water, brown grass, and the beam. My breath shortened. Hell if I knew anything, I swore, except that there was only one place that I wanted to be after dark: in my sleeping bag, in my bunk, dog-tired and dead-drunk, in a full-brain lockdown. No sounds. No ghosts. No nagging ruminations. No dreams even. But first I had to nail that beaver.

I hunted downstream, shakily. The night was full of noise. Migrating birds had clustered in the first line of cottonwoods, and as I hobbled beneath they worried themselves in a feathery, rustling wave. Then a possum, or a coon—some heavy creature—crashed clumsily ahead of my beam through a thicket of nettles. I listened for a splash. None. Not a beaver. Then a cow began to bawl from King Kussmaul's pasture—and bawl, and bawl, and bawl, and the sound kinked and writhed and wrenched through darkness until it infected me—why in hell did the Barn Lady draw a blood knot, a trico, and a canine?—and I had to stop, had to talk to myself: *Breathe, Dog, breathe.*

Focus.

How in hell did one hunt beaver? That was the issue.

With a pistol, a gimp leg, and a flashlight?

I didn't think so. But I could find the beaver lodge. I could stake it out. I could park my ass on a piece of dry ground and wait for old buck-tooth to foray out, or foray back. Then I could shine my beam on those black-marble eyes, wait for the torso to porpoise up, and *blam!* The state health lab would need the head. Brain tissue. Immunofluorescence. Not a flattering thing to know—but Oglivie Secure, after my disaster, had fallen from its corporate platform all the way down to animal control and pest removal.

But there was no beaver lodge downstream. I hobbled back up, into a new set of noises. Howard Adams snored atrociously from inside the teepee. Then, beneath the County Y bridge, terrified barn swallows peeped from mud nests as I stumbled through the slippery rip-rap, my curses echoing weirdly over the fat black water where Barn Lady had landed.

It was hard going, and before I could clear the bridge, I had to rest my leg. I sat down uncomfortably on a sharp chunk of concrete. I turned off the flashlight. I let my breathing slow, and that was when I heard…what was it?…horses? Hoof beats. Shod horses on gravel. And fluttering around the hard noises, the music of happy voices, the whole package of sounds not hurrying, but ambling down the west flank of the coulee on the gravel road that draped itself over into to Norwegian Hollow.

I listened as the travelers passed overhead—*clip-clop, clop-clop*, young voices, teenage girls and boys, speaking…laughing…in German.

I crawled up the bridge berm as they passed. Amish kids—silhouetted now in the buttery light outside the Avalanche Mercantile. I lit a match over my watch: just after midnight. The group—there were three horses, five kids—paused outside the store. Somebody whistled. King Midas Kussmaul emerged, a beer in one hand, a thirty-six pack under the other arm. A tall, lean boy in a wide-brimmed hat slid off the back of a dark horse and took the beer box. A stocky girl in dark skirts and white kapp jumped from a spotted horse and took King by the hand. The six of them proceeded around behind the Avalanche Mercantile and into the two-story bank barn with the snug-dutch roof. After a moment, light sprayed out through the wall boards of the threshing floor. Vaguely recognizable power guitar chords tore from the mouth of a cheap sound system. King Midas screeched *whoop-a!* and the sound echoed across the creek, bounced off the Cruise Master, bounced off the bathrooms, stirred birds inside the Avalanche Oak.

Move on, I told myself. *You saw what you saw.* The kid shot Annie Adams. Somehow—and who cares how?—she knew it was coming. She was telling her husband to tie blood knots, fish tricos, and get himself a puppy.

I stumbled upstream, following the jerky path of my flashlight beam. And she was communicating her loving goodbyes, I told myself, in code, in pictures, instead of telling him straight, instead of telling someone she was going to die, because…?

But because wasn't my problem. Right? I turned off the flashlight. Because Annie Adams was an artist, I decided. Like René Magritte. And artists did weird things. I fumbled through pockets and lit a dried-out Swisher Sweet, one of my so-called cigars. I let the foul smoke, the bully nicotine, cure me of the need to protect other people, cure me of my fond and fatal old Oglivie Secure illusion that protection should, and could, be offered.

Beaver. Kill the beaver. Take its head north in bag. Drop it off. Call back later. Fish the Hemingway water. Take care of the Dog. That kept me focused.

But I found no beaver lodge for a good quarter mile upstream, either. I turned my light off. I didn't need its weakening beam to shine on what was now flat, tightly grazed pasture. I ducked under the Amish fence. I worked easy, beaverless ground up to the edge of a cornfield, where I ducked a second fence. Beavers ate corn, and I was working up the streamside row, looking for telltale damage, when from across the creek a spotlight leapt through the darkness and hit me in the face. I froze. A rifle barrel extended through the white-hot hole of light.

"It's that guy," hissed a voice, and the rifle lowered. "The guy the beaver bit."

"God damn, it is."

The spotlight went out, and for a moment I could see nothing, not even my own hands. Then, slowly, shapes re-evolved: two men, hunkered in a tree-stand across the creek, about fifteen feet off the ground, one with a spotlight, one with a rifle. Deer shiners. I put my own light on them. I recognized two faces from the blur of the surgical theater the night before. I stared long enough to match them with names. Uncle Roundy —the Kussmaul with the crooked cap, unzipped fly, and tree-root hands. And Cousin Lightning Rod— the birdy, high-strung Kussmaul with the ladyfriend and the meth kitchen in his barn. I switched the light off.

"Nearly shot ya," grunted Uncle Roundy. "There's a big buck crosses here sometimes."

"Fucking rack on him," Lightning Rod informed me.

"Thought you was him," said Uncle Roundy.

I caught my breath. I tried for calm. But I was jumpy, irritated. "I didn't think it was hunting season."

Uncle Roundy loosened a bit, chuckled. "It's always hunting season in Kussmaul country."

"I thought I was in Vernon County. Or one of the other counties that meet up right around here."

"Don't be a smartass," shot back Lightning Rod.

"Easy boy." Uncle Roundy gave the kid a tree-root shove. "He ain't done nothing." Uncle Roundy said down to me, "See, we Kussmauls don't quite agree with the government on every little thing. That's all. So goddamn many deer in here you could nuke the place and miss half of them. Ain't nothing to take a few."

No logic, I told myself. No debate. But I went ahead and said, "No. I guess not. Not unless everybody does it."

"We ain't just everybody—" Uncle Roundy started before Lightning Rod jumped in.

"We fucking been here, man. And who are you? Who was she? We been here a hundred years." The tree stand rattled as Lightning Rod lunged up. "We fucking broke this land."

Right there, my own brain startled me. The Barn Lady, Annie Adams, was in my head. We were hearing this together. The two of us were joined at the smart-ass bone, and I heard her say back to Lightning Rod, *You sure did break this land...*

As if I had spoken out loud, Lightning Rod snarled back, "All this crap about soil erosion and overgrazing. I've heard enough of that shit." The tree was swaying back and forth. He was groping for the ladder rungs on the back side. "Like you goddamn crybabies don't put no fucking milk in your fancy coffees. Let me ask you something. And you tell me. Who puts the butter on your goddamn craw...crass..." he tried to say croissant but had to backtrack "—on your goddamn waffles, asshole?"

Fair enough, I was thinking. Fair enough words for your average fly fisherman. Of course, the Dog was different. The Dog drank instant, with creamer swiped from Kwik-Stop tables. The Dog ate watercress for breakfast. But the words were fair enough. I tried to change the subject.

"Anyway...you fellas see a beaver up here?"

Lightning Rod seethed down at me. He cooked some strong meth, I could tell. "Not yet," said Uncle Roundy, cocking his ear beneath the slant of his hat brim as a chainsaw started up somewhere south. "But we see one, we'll pop him for you."

"Who the hell is that?" snapped Lightning Rod, jerking his head toward the chainsaw noise. "That Half-Tim?"

"Naw," said Uncle Roundy. "King don't ever tune his chainsaw, so that's gotta be him. Down at the campground. 'Nother tree musta fell, and I guess Half-Tim's busy these days. That's King's chainsaw."

"He's gotta saw like that in the middle of the night?"

"Guess his party's over. Musta got his hand slapped by one of them cute little Stoltzfus girls."

"Damn him," cursed Lightning Rod. "We're trying to hunt out here."

"Easy boy," said Uncle Roundy a second time. He stuck a dirty tree-root fist into a pocket of his hunting jacket. He withdrew a flask and passed it to Lightning Rod. "Doctor Jack says take some medicine."

Uncle Roundy called over to me, "Just go ahead with your business, fella." Then I heard that wet little chuckle again. "Of course, we was real glad to visit with you tonight," he told me, "or we wasn't all that glad. You know what I mean?"

I guessed I knew. I guessed Annie Adams might have known too. But I guessed she might have spoken up about poaching anyway—or told those two she would. But it was the kid who shot her, I reminded myself. I had seen it.

I began to move back toward the campground, toward the chainsaw sound. I was ten yards down the bank when Uncle Roundy's light scorched up through the grass and shined me in the side of the head. I froze again. I guess that's what deer do.

Their heads empty.

Their legs lock.

Then you shoot them.

She was taking down the Avalanche Oak

Back at the Cruise Master, I tried to ignore the chainsaw snorting raggedly near the top of the campground drive. A chainsaw at midnight? So what? Given what I had seen so far, what was so strange about that? I did my best to ignore as well the guilty possibility that Howard Adams, based on his dead wife's sketchbook, might attempt to heal his grief by fishing an impossible fly on flawed blood knots, while a new puppy thrashed the water all to hell. For a fly fisherman, of course, this was a combination that would promptly induce a rather messy suicide, but I ignored it.

Instead I dropped the awning, stowed the wheel chocks, and strapped my lawn chair above the rear license plate. By dim flashlight I checked oil and radiator fluid. Good enough to go. It also bothered me, of course, that away from the noise of the stream I could tell that Uncle Roundy had been wrong about the action in the red barn. King Midas' party was clearly not over. In the gaps of chainsaw quiet, over messy rock-and-roll, the man's drunken voice pierced the barn walls and brayed over the creek—which meant it wasn't King Midas on the midnight saw. He hadn't been slapped yet, if that's how it worked. The Stoltzfus girls were still game. Someone else was cutting wood by moonlight. That was dangerous, I allowed myself to think. Using a chainsaw in the dark. I lit a nervous Swisher and spewed smoke, talking to myself. *So go, Dog, go. Forget the beaver. Forget the Barn Lady. Get out of Avalanche, while you still can…*

And that's when it hit me.

Get out of Avalanche…*while you still can.*

If not King Midas, on midnight chainsaw duty…then who else?

Hadn't I, refusing her in the store that morning, seen the look in Eve Kussmaul's eye? Like she wasn't done with me?

I stepped on the Swisher. *Shit.*

And what else was there for Eve to take down with a chainsaw…up above the campground…up where the drive met the road? What else was there to do but finish the unfinished work of the 1913 Avalanche?

Shit.

I yanked open the Cruise Master door and reached for the headlight knob. It was a despairingly simple matter, after my half hour of willful ignorance, to turn on the high beams and check.

Yes. It was Eve Kussmaul. Yes. She was taking down the Avalanche Oak. And yes. It was nearly too late to stop her.

I hobbled hard up the drive, shouting curses. But the chainsaw roared over my voice, and I could see Eve making fast progress. I could see the directional-cut—down, then in—and I watched a pale disk of tree flesh clatter to the road. Then she went after the bulk of the oak in long, looping waves of chainsaw teeth, the saw shrieking up and down as she twisted it into the huge trunk—*damn it, Dog, hurry!*

But as I neared the top of the drive, the chainsaw sputtered and stopped. I heard it clatter to the pavement. In another two steps, I could see Eve's white kapp as she ran beneath the trembling tree for cover on the high side, across the road. Then the tree cracked—and cracked again—like lightning had struck it twice. It was still for a long moment. Finally, slowly, the Avalanche Oak crashed down across the campground drive, shaking the earth.

There followed a long patch of quiet. The whoops and music

from the barn stopped. After a few moments, the white of Eve's kapp reemerged from the stand of roadside sumac, and she re-started the chainsaw. I watched her through the gnarled, skyward limbs. Working with vicious efficiency, she sawed off any branches that stuck out into the roadway. Skirts swirling, the dirty red Chuck Taylor high tops lashing out, she kicked them aside.

I limped up when she finally finished. She dropped the saw. She stepped over the trunk to my side. She fished in her apron pocket. It *was* Drum tobacco I had seen in there. And a battered corncob pipe. I double-took on it. A damn pipe. As if Magritte and Digman were now following me around. Eve Kussmaul packed the cob bowl, lit up, and leaned on the ten-ton object that now blocked my exit from the campground.

"I told you I was going to Hell," she said around the pipe stem.

She pulled herself up to sit on the oak's fallen trunk. She smoothed her skirt and puffed. She blew smoke. She swung her Chuckies.

"I warned you," she said, looking past me. "I told you I didn't care what happened to me."

She puffed again. She stared off toward the barn, where the music had resumed.

"And I told you I needed help."

Psychiatric evaluation

She puffed a while longer.

"And though I may be going to Hell," she said finally, "that doesn't mean my little boy has to go there, too."

She kicked her feet against the tree trunk.

"As a matter of fact, Deucey won't go to Hell. Forget me and where I go. Him I care about."

I watched her: tense neck, cheeks sucked in around the pipe, hard, pinprick eyes staring off toward the party in the barn.

"Where is he?"

"Psychiatric evaluation."

I stayed quiet. The air around us was still raw from the collision of tree and earth. I had done an occasional juvenile background job with Oglivie Secure—a welcome break from the corporate stuff—hired by parents trying to balance out whatever dirt the cops had against their kids, parents trying to spread blame to friends, teachers, drug dealers, so on. I could have told Eve that state-paid shrinks were the worst kind, the kind that yawned their way through the motions for easy government money, but I didn't guess it mattered.

"He tried to fight with the sheriff's deputies. He kicked one in the eye because they wouldn't let him take Wally along—"

I stopped her right there. "Wally?"

"His puppy. He loves that puppy."

Some love, I thought. But I said, "I didn't see the puppy with him this morning."

"Freeman Yoder brought Wally down later. Wally was upstream chasing his lambs." She filled her cheeks and shot smoke toward her husband's barn. "Freeman Yoder is an Amish bishop too, just like my father. When Freeman Yoder brought Wally back this morning, Deuce grabbed him up and wouldn't let him go. I think he hurt Wally's ribs. So then King whipped Deuce, because King paid a lot of money for Wally, and by the time the detectives talked to him, Deuce was a real mess. So now they're keeping him overnight. They've already got a bunch of stuff from the public school he got kicked out of last year. Something about his sleep energy, his brain waves." She swung her heels a little faster. "I'm picking him up in the morning."

I nodded. I wrestled with what to say, what not to say. This was not a mess the Dog could put his arms around, so *Get this damn tree out my way* seemed like the leading option. But Eve spoke again.

"You don't have to tell me I'm simple minded," she began. "I know that. I don't believe in dinosaurs, and I don't believe in outer space. Deuce tries to convince me, but I just can't think that way. I believe God made the earth in six days, and I believe in Heaven and Hell, and I believe my son didn't kill anybody."

She sucked on the pipe stem and blew out a long stream of smoke. Flecks of bark rained out as her heels banged rhythmically against the tree trunk. I shoved aside a headful of doubts.

"I'm sorry," I said stubbornly. "But I saw what I saw."

She didn't reply for a long time. She filled and smoked another bowl. She said eventually, "You want to know my theory?"

"No. I don't."

"Then why are you still here? You can walk away. You don't have to listen to me."

"You sawed a tree down in my way."

"It fell the wrong direction. I'm sorry."

"You're lying."

"They like that kind of thing in Hell."

"But that's why I'm here—you're stopping me. You've trapped me."

"And now you're listening to me."

She had me—*she had me*—and in a such a direct, childlike way. Damn it. It was true. I was listening.

"So here's my theory: I believe you didn't see what you thought you saw."

Don't start, I muttered to myself. *I've got Magritte and Digman on my case. I don't need you.* But she kept going. "I think you saw Deuce. And I think you saw Deuce shoot Annie. But you didn't see him kill her. That's what I think."

"Right. And I suppose that's not a pipe."

She squinted at me through a cloud of smoke. She was puzzled, but she was too intense to be deterred.

"I think Annie was already dead."

"They have medical examiners for that," I said. "Professionals who determine how and when a person died. Scientists who are not the mother of the suspect."

"Yes."

Abruptly, she rapped the pipe out and dropped it back in the apron pocket.

"Yes, I know. Nothing I say is going to matter to anyone. This is why I need help. Deuce wouldn't kill Annie. I know it. If you got acquainted with him, you would know it too."

"He's cruel to that puppy," I said.

She shot an unbalanced glance at me. "No. No, he's not cruel. He's just—"

"He gets into my Cruise Master."

"I..." She was fishing for the pipe again. "I told him not to...but he just...he thinks you're so..."

"He throws apples into the creek where I'm trying to fish."

"I'm sorry. He just wants your attention."

I looked off toward the King Midas barn. The music had started back up. Christ—now I recognized the mess of it. It was Black Sabbath. Sabbath Bloody Sabbath.

"He's got a father."

"His father is busy."

"So his son is accused of murder, and he throws a party?"

"That's how King deals with stress. Plus he says Deuce is a minor, so the law can't touch him."

I held my tongue: King Midas might be very surprised what the law could do, to minors and otherwise, without necessarily even intending to. That was one reason why people hired Oglivie Secure, back when I had it all together—to get the right thing done, privately, before the law came around. But Eve Kussmaul didn't need to know that.

"So is that how you met King Midas? Partying in that barn? About what...ten years ago?"

Her hand moved restlessly in the pipe pocket.

"I told you. I'm going to Hell for the choices I've made. I accept that. I hear that once a week, by U.S. mail from Kentucky, from my father and my brothers. But before I go, I'm going to accomplish one thing."

She stopped there. A four-wheeler engine snarled through the distant dark. Eve cocked her kapped head and listened to it discerningly. I strained with rusty professionalism to pick out the fine points of an engine signature, wondering if it was the same four-wheeler I had heard a few hours before with Howard Adams. I couldn't tell. Then Eve looked at me. Out came the pipe.

"I'm going to raise that boy," she said. "He's going to make it. He's going to be okay."

She packed, tamped, lit and held the pipe out to me. Like a peace pipe. Like we had anything to agree on.

"No thanks. I don't smoke."

"You smoke," she retorted. "I've seen you."

"A-socially," I said. "Period." I waited a moment, thinking. "And where have you seen me smoke?"

"I hang laundry in the morning. I see your fishing line catch the light. Sometimes I see your rod bending. Usually after your rod bends, I see smoke rising above the weeds around the stream bank." She kept the pipe out for me. "Plus," she said, "Deuce tells me all about you."

"Yeah?"

"He admires you. He thinks your camper is neat. He thinks fly fishing is cool. He wants to fish with you."

"Yeah? Is that why he spoils the water for me?" I had a rant prepared. "Rotten apples, splash, right where I'm trying to—"

"Last summer he tagged after Robin Adams, Annie's son. High school kid. This summer it's you."

"Yeah?"

"He tells me you bathe naked in the stream," she said, "with your face all scrunched up like it hurts. You hold onto your jewels like they're going to swim away. And when you get out, you shake and pant like a dog. Then you light one up."

I slid a glance at her. "That's a cigar," I said.

She kept the pipe extended.

"Come on. Going to Hell is not contagious."

I looked off at the black shape of the big bank barn with the snug-dutch roof. "Yeah?" I said. I wasn't so sure. It seemed that she and Deuce might have caught something from the man in the barn. "Really?" I said. "So who's in there with King Midas right now?"

She shrugged. "Some of the Stoltzfus kids, Amish from Norwegian Hollow."

"Minors?"

"Of course."

"Illegal drugs?"

"I don't know, lately. King got busted this spring. He's on probation. But he believes people should follow their own rules. If he's up to giving those kids meth again, and Annie caught him at it, that might explain a few things..."

After a long, silent stew—the Dog gnawing over a *few things*—I said, "And who's that?" I pointed down across the campground toward the Avalanche Mercantile. A man on a one-speed bicycle coasted into the yard light. He let the bike fall with a crash and tried to open the store door. Finding it locked, he pounded.

"You know that woman yesterday in the store with Lightning Rod...?"

I nodded. The meth head with the kabuki face. Real nice gal. "Yeah?"

But Eve shook her kapp strings, and she backed up, as if a different explanation would work better. "You know the illegal room I told you about in Salt Box's barn? That Salt Box rents out and doesn't pay tax on? That man rents it. He's Salt Box's milker. Abe Borntrager. She and him, Philly and Abe, they got divorced because Abe doesn't believe in drugs. So now Philly lives with Lightening Rod. But Abe lost his driver's license. So he bikes down for his beer every night. He'll be mad I'm not there."

"It's one o'clock in the morning."

"They wake me up."

"Who does?"

"Anybody who wants beer."

The milker kicked the door. He got on the bike and pedaled hard back up the coulee.

"So if not your son, who would kill the Barn Lady? Would King? If she were going to rat on him?"

Eve Kussmaul exhaled smoke. "Maybe. Then again, practically anybody named Kussmaul could have the same reason."

"And why would your son lie about it?"

"Somebody made him."

"How? How could someone make him do something that wrong?"

She changed her posture on the log. Upright, alert. "Oh, we're going to figure that out," she said. "You can bet we will."

I kicked at the Avalanche Oak, knocking bark off, pondering her *we* silently, the insanity of it. The absurdity. The posture. The sheer psychopathic grit.

We...?

I was leaving Avalanche, I told her. Within the hour. And I

would leave on foot if I had to. I would limp out of here. Injury aside, I was good to go, I claimed. And just like that, Eve Kussmaul shot out a dirty red tennis shoe and nailed me, smashed the stiff rubber toe of the Chuckie right into my beaver bite. I gasped in pain, ahead of a surge of deep panic.

Talk about needing psychiatric evaluation.

"Hey," she said, reading me perfectly. "You think I'm scary now, you should see me on some of Lightning Rod's crystal meth..."

I stared at her. She wasn't kidding. She held the pipe out again, curled in her grape-tipped fingers.

"You know what?" she asked me.

"What."

"You look like you've been to Hell and back yourself."

"I—"

But I couldn't finish. I couldn't even start. She bumped the pipe against my arm, urging me to take it. "You look just how I would look," she said. "I mean, if I lost Deuce and..." Her voice faltered. Then she went on unsteadily. "If I lost Deuce...and somehow I managed to survive it."

She pulled the pipe back and puffed. Her eyes were teary and caught the pipe's brief orange glow. I nodded at her. I wanted the Avalanche Kid's mother to keep talking. I wanted to follow her back to solid ground. I wanted to remember the passion, the fight before the loss.

"I'm sorry," she continued finally. She stiffened her slender spine against the cold night. "I'm sorry, Dog, for whatever happened to you. But I just won't lose Deuce. It's not going to happen."

Suddenly I couldn't take my eyes off her. She dragged a wrist across her face. She held the pipe out—Hell-bound Eve Kussmaul, in her apron and kapp, starting to swing her dirty red shoes again— and she smiled at me.

"I'll dig out that madstone," she said. "And we'll do the rabies treatment. Okay? And you see if King is back to pushing meth in the barn." She kept her eyes brightly on me. "And tomorrow, you take Deuce to the stream."

She pushed out the pipe.

"Okay, Dog? Please?"

I shivered. My stomach flopped, my wound throbbed, and my legs trembled. But I accepted the pipe. Or the not-pipe. And now I was saying it.

Dog, this is not a fishing trip.

I felt the madstone grab me

"So I took your advice," Eve told me hoarsely, midway through the next morning. "I did what you told me outside your camper last night."

I had just hobbled into her kitchen, exhausted and stiff from three hours of bad sleep after a night of barn surveillance. Through cracks in the threshing floor walls, I had watched King Midas broker out beer and bourbon—but no methamphetamine that I could tell—to the Stoltzfus kids from Norwegian Hollow. Two hours before dawn, shivering behind a pile of feed sacks, I had watched him work his way up to the shoulder beneath an Amish girl's dress, before her brother weaved drunkenly in and put a stop to the King Midas touch.

"Like you said," Eve told me, "I searched Deuce's room before the county services people dropped him off."

She lowered the flame on a pot of fresh milk. In the next room, Deuce stared numbly at satellite TV cartoons as he mashed through a bowl of Cocoa Puffs. Wally wriggled and snapped in his lap. The kid's skin, normally Kussmaul pink, looked pale and chalky, and his wide-set blue eyes sulked deep in the shadowy, muddy crescents that hung beneath them. I watched long enough to recognize the program: Roadrunner. Then I twisted cautiously. Deuce's old man,

King Midas, slouched outside, beyond the kitchen window, smoking behind the dew drops that trickled off the bent tin awning. His lips moved. His non-smoking hand gripped the cord above a hummingbird feeder. His body swayed and jerked around the cord, as if the pieces of the new day wouldn't yet come to balance.

Eve cleared her throat and set the pot of boiling milk on the table.

"I found something under his bed."

She reached to the tips of her Chuckies and opened the cupboard above the stove. She set a Nike shoe box on the table. The box bumped and scrabbled on its own.

"Take a look."

I lifted the lid off. Four tiny, orange-rimmed, black eyes blinked up at me. Four eyes—on two heads—on one neck—trying vainly to retract into one green-black shell.

I murmured my surprise. "A two-headed turtle…"

"You can only imagine," Eve said roughly, "what Deuce would do for a thing like that."

I had been a little boy. I had even, fairly recently, been raising a little boy. But still I didn't believe it. "Deuce would shoot someone? For a turtle?"

"Maybe," she said. "Maybe…someone he knew was already dead."

"So who gave it to him?"

We both glanced into the living room. *Beep-beep!* Coyote was inflicting yet another anvil wound upon himself, but Deuce didn't seem to find it funny.

"Deuce's Great Uncle Roundy," Eve whispered, "deals in this kind of stuff. Trophies. Bizarre wildlife. Poached eagles. He shot the albino deer that had my madstone inside. I got it out of the guts he left behind. Here…let me show you something…"

She motioned me to the other side of the kitchen, where she pushed open a hollow-core door with a fist-hole through it. The room inside was lightless, wood-stove hot, and the air smelled like bodies. She pushed a light switch and quickly spun down the dimmer. As if through fog, I peered in at her bedroom—hers and King's—at a waterbed under tangled sheets, at clothes heaped everywhere, at a kind of shrine on Eve's side with pictures of folks in Amish dress, and at a stuffed black panther over the bed, its glass eyes and bared fangs glowing yellow in the dim light. Eve closed the door.

"Uncle Roundy is how King got that panther. It's King's prized possession."

A door opened somewhere, lingered open, then shut hard. Eve steered me quickly back to the table and sat me down. "Put your leg up here," she told me.

I swung my injured leg up on the chair between us. Eve pushed up my pants. My wound gaped open, purplish and gummy between Half-Tim's stitches. She shook her kapp strings. "This would have been a whole lot easier," she said, "if you had let me do this yesterday."

Alongside the pan of hot milk, she set down a straight razor on a clean white hand towel. She poured rubbing alcohol into a butter dish and moved the razor over into it.

I asked her, "So what did King do for his Uncle Roundy, to get that panther?"

"Nothing."

I looked at her. So what was her theory, then, with Deuce?

"I mean, King just keeps quiet. He leaves Roundy alone. Lets him hunt whatever, wherever. That's the deal. King's big brother Salt Box wears these python skin boots whenever he and Rachel go out to the Pine Tree Supper Club. Those are from Roundy."

I pictured Uncle Roundy—the short, round, unzipped Kussmaul with the tree-root hands.

"And King's great uncle Tater Kussmaul has a grizzly skin rug, because Uncle Tater feeds minerals so he gets the biggest bucks up in those hickory woods…"

She stopped. Feet scuffed across the gritty kitchen floor behind me. I waited. Then I tipped my head back to find King Midas right above me, mouth-breathing.

"Fucker's rabid," he said.

"Then leave him alone," Eve answered, "before he bites you."

I stared at Eve. Before he...*me*? But Eve scorched a look at King Midas, her acorn eyes afire in the light from the window. Grumbling, King Midas stumbled away to stare at the Roadrunner. *Beep-beep!* The falling anvil again. The mangled Coyote again. Deuce guffawed falsely.

"I was just kidding about you," Eve whispered, and she lifted the straight razor from the butter dish. With a single motion, she flicked off alcohol and brought the blade to my leg.

"I've never heard of a rabid beaver," she said. "My father called last night to remind me that I'm going to Hell, and I got my mother on the phone for a minute. Mother never heard of a rabid beaver, either. But if by some chance that beaver is sick, then the poison's moved up your leg by now, and she said we'll have to catch it up here."

Before I could stop her, she had snicked up a half-dollar-sized flap of skin from my inside-upper calf, about six inches above the beaver bite. I inhaled sharply as the alcohol sting set in. Tears sprang to my eyes.

"My midwife mother would tell you, right now," Eve said, "that men feel childbirth a little bit at a time, in a thousand tiny pieces. It's what she says to men, to kill the pain."

"Yeah," I muttered. "Thanks. I feel a lot better."

"Amish medicine," Eve deadpanned. "Works every time."

She dipped tongs into the milk pan. Her madstone came out between them. It was an amorphous gray mass, knobby and porous, steaming and dripping milk and looking every bit like the calcified hair ball of an albino deer that she had told me it was.

"Can I ask you," I managed, "why, if you got kicked out of the Amish, you still do things the Amish way? I mean, the dress, the bonnet, the rabies treatment...?"

"I didn't get kicked out on purpose," she said. "I just made a bad move, and then I had to choose one family or the other. I stuck by Deuce. And Deuce's father. I'd still be Amish if I could be. I love my other family, too, and there's a lot of good in Amish ways."

"But your bonnet, your dress...the Amish don't mind if you wear—"

"Of course the Amish mind. But I don't exist to them. So they can't say anything to me about it."

Frowning now, she tipped the madstone inside the tongs. Though not much larger than my thumb, the stone released an impressive gout of steaming milk.

"But I dress like I do because I have good memories that I want to keep, good Amish values that I cherish. A big part of me will always be Amish, and I want Deuce to know that."

I looked away, suddenly struggling with the image of her husband with his arm up an Amish girl's dress. Nothing could have been further from my image of an Amish girl's midnight comportment. "But the parties," I stammered, "the drugs..." I was confused as hell now about what it meant to be Amish. They were old-world, simple people of the earth—right? No cars, no electricity, no smoke or drink, no buttons even. To the Dog, the Amish had always been some kind of beacon, the place from whence modern man had come, and the place to which he ought to hie his ass back, asap. The Amish, I always thought, were smart enough to leave all the dark doors shut, and thus avoid the mistakes, the seven deadlies, that tormented the rest of us. But the Stoltzfus kids in King Midas's barn seemed free to make all the worst kind of mistakes, for which they could end up, like Eve Kussmaul, in exile for life. I didn't get it. As I watched the shunned woman before me, waiting for an answer, Eve tilted the dripping madstone and worked at the roughness in her throat. Her face had flushed and her frown had deepened. The parties...the drugs...I had touched a nerve—of course.

"What makes Amish different," she said finally, "is that baptism doesn't come until adulthood. You get a chance, before that, to be something else. Whatever you want, supposedly. You get a choice." She sighed painfully, and then she glanced at me over the madstone. "Of course, having been brought up Amish, you're completely in the dark about what kinds of choices you might be making. And the world outside the Amish moves so fast that the elders have no idea what's out there. A lot of kids that experiment, the ones that try to live a little, get blindsided. They do damage that can't be undone."

I shook my head so suddenly and so hard that it hurt. "Then," I said, "your husband...King...he's...he's a..."

I stopped, half-glancing toward the TV room, not sure how to finish.

"He's a predatory English bastard?"

That startled a painful coughing fit out of me. Patiently, Eve shook more milk out of the madstone. She caught me looking at her. "I learned the word 'bastard' in the Bible," she offered dryly after a moment, "so it's okay."

Now I glanced fully into the TV room. King snored face-down on the sofa. Deuce had crossed the room to sit with his dad, rooting between the comatose man's legs to create as much body contact as possible. The kid looked exhausted and scared again, staring blankly at the Technicolor chaos on the TV. Wally lapped from the cereal bowl Deuce had left on the floor.

I said, "At least King wasn't passing out meth last night."

"He must be running low."

Then Eve leaned in, lifting the flap of skin she had razored up. "So this morning," she told me quietly, "after I found that poor turtle, while King was asleep the first time and Deuce wasn't back yet, I took King's four-wheeler over the ridge and down the backside to Uncle Roundy's barn. I waited until he was done milking."

She rotated the madstone to a fresh angle, shaking more milk out.

"Uncle Roundy guts poached bucks in his calf pens. There were a couple of twelve-pointers hanging up. Maybe, if Roundy killed Annie, that's why. Because she was after him about that. She trespassed in the barns she liked. Snooped around, sketched stuff. She admitted that. And Annie really hated to see animals mistreated. But there was something else strange, too. A round barn always has a real nice silo right down the middle. That makes it easy to feed in winter. But all of Uncle Roundy's cut corn was blown into plastic tubes this year, and there was a big old padlock on the silo's feed door. I banged the silo with a shovel. It sounded hollow."

I watched the madstone's angle change in her chewed fingers. I wasn't a farm boy, so I had to ask her. "The silo sounded hollow...meaning...?"

"Maybe there's something besides silage inside Roundy's silo. Maybe Annie snuck a peek. Maybe Roundy caught her, waited for a chance, then found her yesterday morning out painting Yoder's barn from the bridge—"

"I don't think so."

Eve blinked at me. I said, "That painting was the wrong one. It was the north side of Yoder's barn, and the bridge is south. Howard Adams pointed that out. I think someone set that painting up on the bridge by mistake, someone in a hurry."

"You mean..." Eve fiddled with a kapp string "...someone set it up to look like she was painting on the bridge, after killing Annie elsewhere...?"

"Maybe. Maybe she was supposed to have fallen off the bridge by accident. And Deuce stumbled in on the set up. Which makes me ask the same question Uncle Tater was asking the night before she died."

She tipped the madstone a new way. Its pores were apparently labyrinthine. More milk dripped out. She nodded, remembering.

"Uncle Tater wanted to know where Annie was going with those candles..."

"Right."

Eve stared at me, suddenly angry, her eyes narrowed. "And you're saying that this son of mine accepts a...damn...mutant... turtle...to cover up someone else's murder?"

"Hey," I said. "It's your theory. It's your kid."

She looked down at the madstone. Her kapp strings dangled over her collarbones. Yes—I observed—that was a tattoo around her neck. A tattooed wreath of undoubtedly blasphemous, Christ-like thorns, in dirty tattoo green. Eve took a long, raspy, I'm-going-to-Hell kind of breath.

"Soon as you take Deuce out fishing," she said at last, "I'm going back over to Roundy's and climb that silo, look down the filler-pipe window."

"Shouldn't you wait—"

"No," she interrupted. "I shouldn't wait."

"Roundy could be dangerous. One person might be dead already because of—"

But the look in her eye stopped me. I saw the look of a woman who had reached some kind of turning point, who was not going to spend one more second of her life taking direction from a man. "The county will take Deuce away from me," she said, her voice abruptly flat and cold. She stuck her chin at me. "They've been down here before, the county social people, because King claims he's home schooling, even though he doesn't do a damn thing. They'll take Deuce away this time. I won't survive that, and neither will Deuce. So stop telling me what's dangerous."

I nodded. Okay. I leaned back. I looked into the TV room. Wally had finished the cereal and joined the big boys on the sofa. Blankly, Deuce grabbed the puppy by the forelegs and began twisting him around, forcing him to boogie to the hard-rock jingle from a toy advertisement. The puppy whined and fought. King Midas twitched and snarled vaguely in his sleep.

Then Eve sighed. "I'm sorry..."

She tipped the madstone back and forth, shook a final few drips of milk from it. "You didn't deserve that," she said. "Not yet, anyway." She matched up the stone with the seeping patch of skin, and when she was satisfied with the angle, she set it on my new wound.

Bizarrely, and quickly, I felt the madstone grab me, as if with the mouthparts of a leech.

"Oh, dear," Eve muttered, watching this. "Maybe I wasn't kidding."

"What...?"

She poked her finger at it, but the madstone had stuck fast.

"Well, if it sticks like that..."

Deuce was over my shoulder suddenly. "You got rabies, man!" he cried out. "Dad! Dad! The dog-dude's got rabies!"

King Midas, from flat on his face, moaned, "Told ya."

"Dad, come on, you gotta see this—"

Deuce jumped up and down, waiting for his dad, who didn't move from the sofa. "Dad! Dad! Dad!" the kid kept yelling. "Why don't you ever do what I want?" He stomped his foot. "Dad!"

"Deuce," Eve said finally, evenly, "Jesus wants you to be quiet."

Deuce hung his head. Wally was still senseless enough to wander by, and the kid lunged out, picked the puppy up by a back leg. Wally yipped and snapped, squirming desperately. "Honey, let him rest," Eve said. Then she nudged the knobby hair-ball again and said to me, "It's stuck, all right. Now it will suck the poison out. Don't worry. You'll be just fine. And as for fishing with Deucey today, I think that Uncle Salt Box's stretch—upstream a mile—might be the best for—"

"I can't take the kid fishing now," I protested. "I've got rabies."

"It's not contagious—unless, after all, you do bite."

"But…isn't this stone going to fall off?"

"Only on it's own time," she said. "That's how it works."

She pulled my pant leg roughly down over the madstone—and, amazingly, the stone hung on, rigid to my flesh as a barnacle. Eve gave me a told-you-so kind of look.

"My mother taught me that Abraham Lincoln's boy got bit by a rabid dog," she said, "and they put a madstone on him from someone called Missus Taylor and that boy walked all over Terre Haute for two days and had sodas and ice cream everything. Missus Taylor's madstone never fell off until it was ready."

I felt a swell of panic. Steal a car, I told myself. Steal a four-wheeler. Get out of Avalanche. Find a real doctor. But Eve fished a stout rubber band out of her apron pocket and snapped it around the cuff of my pants.

"We'll catch the stone when it falls," she said matter-of-factly. "And we'll boil the poison out."

She took the Cocoa Puffs box away from Deuce as he was about to shove his hand down into it.

"Now," she told me, "Salt Box fences the creek off up there, and he posts it for no trespassing, and sometimes he shoots a deer rifle over the heads of fishermen who try to wade through. But you're with Deucey," she said, "and he's a Kussmaul, so that's different."

She took the Cocoa Puffs box away a second time. "You're done," she said. "Take Wally along if you want to. Drive the four-wheeler. Wear your barn boots. Don't let this man out of your sight."

Behind his back she gave me a different look. "And vice versa," she whispered at me sternly. "He acts big sometimes, but he's ten years old. He's a baby. Don't you dare lose him."

Then she shoved Deuce. "Go."

I limped dizzily to the door and turned. I suddenly felt as if Eve had dropped the Avalanche Oak right on me. I didn't think I could speak. But I forced out words.

"What happens next?" I asked her.

I wasn't sure what I meant—what my topic was, but Eve said, patiently now, "When the stone falls off, we boil it in milk again. If the milk turns green, then we got all the poison out of your system."

"Yeah…I see…okay…" I shifted the weight off my injured leg and felt it throb. "And how long will it be, you think, before all the poison is out of my system?"

As she studied me, she fished the corncob pipe from her apron pocket. She glanced behind her, toward King on the sofa, and then she came forward, close to me, so close I could smell lavender shampoo through her kapp—so close I wondered suddenly what color her hair was—and she tipped my own hat brim up. She looked in my eyes a long time.

"In your case, Dog," she said finally, just barely smiling, "probably ten or so years."

She stepped back and filled the pipe. Tobacco crumbs scattered about her red Chuckies, blending into the mess on the floor.

I managed a deepish, almost forward-looking breath. "You've got a wicked sense of humor," I told Eve Kussmaul.

She snapped her lighter.

"I'm going to need it," she told me, "in Hell."

The law can't touch me

The kid drove his father's all-terrain four-wheeler. I scrunched up in the tiny cargo box, puppy in my lap, protecting the madstone and trying to make out an engine signature for King's battered and mud-spattered John Deere. The Dog was into off-road, in another life, and I had King's machine pegged for an old Trail Buck, about three-hundred cc, untuned in years. Meanwhile I watched the coulee pass by backwards. Leaves scattered. A ragged V of Canada geese honked overhead. The kid blew the four-wheeler's tinny horn, swerved hard and accelerated—and into my rear view slung a black Amish buggy, closed up against the chill, pulled by a balky brown gelding. I watched the buggy grow small in the distance, then turn down the drive toward the big whitewashed barn that Annie Adams had been working on. King Kussmaul's four-wheeler, I decided, had a high, oil-burning fizz-sound in fourth gear—at least when the kid drove it.

In a half mile more, Deuce turned us in where a large mailbox said: *Kussmaul's, Salt Box and Rachel, Kelly, Kirby, and Kirsten.* A sign behind the mailbox, on a taller pole, orange on black, said: N*o Trespassing.* A third sign, handmade, was wired to the post below: *fisherman, this means you.*

I leaned my rod against one of the big, knobby wheels. Wally bounded out across a broad green lawn and raced among ceramic ducks and geese. He peed on a plywood cutout of a little boy peeing on a border of real tiger lilies. Deuce stepped off the seat and squinted at the tidy, two-story, white house. I followed stiffly, my twice-injured leg not wanting to straighten.

"Nobody's home?" I asked the kid.

"Naw," he said. His voice was hoarse. In bright sunlight, his eyelids were red-rimmed and crusty from lack of sleep. "My uncle Salt Box is cutting corn. Aunt Rachel just shops all day up in La-Crosse. My cousins go to school."

"But not you?"

He turned his big, white-blond head away from me, scowled across the yard beneath the Kussmaulian brow. I spent a second thinking about, and understanding finally, the odd way the kid was dressed: shapeless, rough-cut, black cotton pants, held up Amish-style by suspenders strapped awkwardly over a Green Bay Packers Super Bowl sweatshirt. The Avalanche Kid, like his mother, was half of one thing, half another.

"Not me what?"

"You don't go to school?"

He snatched up Wally by the puppy's neck skin. He scuffed away toward the creek. "My dad's home schooling me," he rasped back. "My ma says, okay then going fishing with you is home schooling too and he'd better shut up and let me do it, because anyway she was making me."

He got about thirty yards away, between the salt box barn and the house.

"They're always making me do stuff. Everybody is. And they're always fighting about who's going to make me do what. Amish stuff, or English stuff, or whatever." He stuck the puppy under his arm. "So...are we going fishing, or not?"

I limped after him and his struggling, gagging puppy. "Yeah..." I said, distantly, dizzily, feeling the madstone wobble but hang on. "Yeah...only this is not exactly a fishing trip."

I soon saw that Salt Box's whole spread was aged beyond its prime but exquisitely groomed. We left the yard through a gateway flanked by obsequious clay Dutch boys and walked out on a wide path mowed through asters and goldenrod and popping joe-pye weeds. The path curved gracefully afield, then back on itself, then ended at a nifty wire-loop gate into a pasture, close cropped by black-and-white Holstein milk cows. Monarchs flitted between the milkweed, and the thistles were head-high and starting to brown. I asked the kid, "So have you ever seen a trico hatch?"

He didn't answer me. We navigated silently between munching, steaming, head-swinging bossies. The kid hung on to Wally.

"I'll bet you have," I said. "I'll bet you've seen a zillion tricos and didn't know it. The trico is a tiny mayfly, about the size of a question mark on a page in a book, with these two crazy tail strands about five times longer than the body, and perfect, see-through wings that—"

The kid stopped. "I hate bugs."

I kept walking, gimping right on past him. "—wings that stand up like sails on a sail boat. Did you know there are millions of times as many insects as people on the earth?"

"Whatever. That's why I hate them."

"You hate them all?"

Catching up: "Yup."

"Even monarchs?"

The kid passed me and looked back blankly. I filled him in: monarchs were the butterflies fluttering all around us, the orange-and-black ones landing on the milkweed.

"I had this pellet gun once," he said over his shoulder, cutting between two cows. "That's how I learned to shoot it. Them orange butterflies."

"You ever hit one?"

"Hell yeah."

"So you're quite the sharpshooter."

"I shoot bettern' my dad. I shoot almost as good as my Uncle Roundy."

"And now you finally got your own rifle. That a .22 I saw you with on the bridge the other day?"

"Nice try," he said. "But I ain't talking about what I did on the bridge."

"What—you've got a lawyer now?"

I was kidding. I thought. And then I thought I shouldn't kid the kid. He was only ten. He wouldn't even know what a lawyer was. But the boy said, "My dad says he'll be my lawyer. He says he's smarter than any lawyer or cop. He says the law can't touch me."

We were halfway to the stream, and suddenly I was thinking for real about lawyers. From a hump in the meadow I could see down to the Amish farm. I could see the beaver tails nailed to the north side of the barn. But the bridge where Annie Adams was painting—where she had died—was about three hundred yards south. So...the crime scene didn't match up. A good lawyer, I thought, could do something with that. Suddenly I limped hard, feeling the madstone wobble. I caught the back of the boy's shirt and dragged him to a stop.

"Kid," I panted. "Deuce, listen. I know you shot the Barn Lady. I saw you. But you didn't kill her. She was dead already. Right? And somebody made you take the blame?"

He yanked out of my grip.

"Right?"

"I ain't talking about it."

"You won't go free," I told him. "I know you're a kid, but you won't go free. You'll go away somewhere, away from your mom and dad. You'll go to school every day. Your mom and dad will be hurt. They'll feel a lot of pain."

"That sounds about right to me," he said, dropping Wally and stomping churlishly away.

I pushed after through a stand of crispy, seed-flinging wild parsnip. Inside that ring of dying vegetation, the West Fork glistened and gurgled over a bed of cress and limestone, then plunged into a deep, green-black pool that cornered neatly under high grass and tag willow. On force of habit, I stared beyond the kid, following an oak leaf as it made the ride. Nice drift, I murmured. Fish rising.

I told myself to focus. Not a fishing trip, I told myself. But then, after six days of searching and hoping, I saw them: tricos. Not a hatch. Better. A spinner fall.

"Kid," I hissed. "Stop."

He didn't.

"Stop!" I begged him. "Get down! Grab the puppy!"

He heard the last command. Wally yelped as the kid corralled him. I waved my arm. Get down. Be quiet. I pointed. Deuce swung his big, angry head in the direction of my finger.

"Rising fish," I hissed. "On tricos."

He looked blankly back at me.

"Be totally still," I told him. "The trout can see you, but they're on the tricos. If you don't move they'll forget about you. Sit down slowly. Stay put. Stay low and still. I'll crawl up."

He looked at me like I was mad, or dumb, or both—and a faint wiggle of the madstone on my leg made me weak for a moment. Mad. Dumb. What besides the dementia of rabies could explain why I wasn't, right then, about two hundred miles north, stopping for gas and coffee on my way up to the Big Two-Hearted River?

But self-flagellation could come later. These were fish on tricos and I had to stay focused. By the way the trout slashed and popped along the foamy seam of the big hole, I figured I was looking at the early edge of the hatch. I glanced upstream and down—riffle, corner, and pool, both directions—but the spinner fall was on this hole only. Hatching tricos, I knew, were like that: finicky to within a tenth of a degree on water temperature. Five minutes of sun, or cloud, could make all the difference. And sometime later, some-where no human could predict, these same ten thousand tiny insects would swarm, mate, and fall—a spinner fall—and a few dozen trout would eat until their gills leaked. And that's what Deuce and I had right here.

I tried to slow my breathing. I hadn't felt energy like this since the previous fall in Montana—the thrill of being on a little pocket of stream about to erupt.

"Deuce," I whispered, kneeing up beside him. Wally wriggled and gagged in his arms. "This is the moment that fly fishermen live for. The rest of the time, we're just out there waiting for this."

Deuce whacked the puppy sharply on the nose. Wally yelped and dug his feet against the kid's chest.

"I don't see nothing."

I pointed to the foam seam that snaked along the bank side of the deep hole. Noses...tails...porpoise rises...the seam was full of moving fish. "Deuce...those are trout."

"Little ones," he grumped. I saw he had a rotten apple ready in his fist. I grabbed at him, but he chucked the apple anyway. Sploosh! The hole went still.

I swallowed about three dozen choice dirty words. What I said finally was, "Your mom says that means you like me."

"Screw her."

"She says you liked Annie Adams, too, and that Annie was nice to you."

"Nobody's nice to me."

"But you were friends with Annie and Howard's son. Right? A high school kid? And you're upset your friend didn't come back this summer?"

"His name is Robin. They make him do stuff he doesn't want to, just like me."

"What kind of stuff do you have to do?"

"None of your business."

As I straightened my leg and felt it pulse, I understood the horrible privacy of pain, the loneliness of it. No one else could know your pain. No one else could know Deuce Kussmaul. Probably, the kid was just beginning to comprehend that. So I let him grip his puppy's neck and stew silently—and, little by little, the trout came back.

"You never know about big or little fish," I said, returning his attention to the stream. "Usually the big fish are the careful ones. That's how they got big. Pick one out," I said. "Watch it."

In despair—or maybe just to prove me wrong—Deuce Kussmaul half-tried. But the trout were on a different clock than an angry boy with a restless puppy, and the kid was now holding Wally in a two-handed grip around the dog's nose. Wally's back end wriggled and spewed clawed-up grass, like he was digging a hole. The kid missed several good, plump rises. I whispered, "Look—let's deal with the puppy. You can't really fly fish with a puppy. It doesn't work. Not for you, not for the puppy."

He twisted away. "Wally stays with me from now on. All the time."

"Let's give him a break."

"He don't need a break."

I ignored that, unzipping my vest. "I've got...let's see..." In an out-of-the-way pocket I kept three boot strings knotted together in a kind of trout-leash, for when I kept a fish to eat it. And in my back vest pocket—down at the junky bottom—I found half of a peanut butter-sugar sandwich.

"Hey!" protested the Avalanche Kid as I slipped my trout-leash under the puppy's collar. I wrapped the other end through my hand. "He'll get away. He'll get under Uncle Salt's fences, and then..."

I let Wally sniff the sandwich, then whipped it into the weeds behind us. Wally lunged out of the kid's hands and came up short on the leash. I crawled toward him, tied him up to a crumbling fence post where he could reach the sandwich, and crawled back. "There. He's fine."

"He'll get away," sulked the kid. "He always gets away. He'll get under the fences, and Uncle Salt fences the crap out of the crick up here so nobody can get in. I won't be able to catch him, and..."

I waited.

"He might get hurt. Somebody might hurt him."

"He's fine," I said. "Let's fish."

"He'll get hurt."

"Hey…Deuce…the little guy is indestructible. Obviously. Now come on. Turn around. Let's fish."

I rigged my rod and tied down to 7X. "These are blood knots," I told him, and he focused for a moment, bending his head to watch as I overlapped tippet ends and wound them around each other, six times, each direction. At the center I made a pivot point, with two tiny monofilament windows, upstairs and downstairs, and—shaking my head, muttering a little as I remembered how this was the moment when Annie Adams always went "alternative" on me—I tucked the right tag end through the upstairs window, the left tag end through the downstairs window. I licked the knot and pulled it tight. Correct. Precise. Perfect.

"Why is it called a blood knot?"

"I have no idea."

"Do you use blood?"

"No."

"It's stupid if you don't know why it's called that." He looked away, his interest gone, but back into my mind jumped Annie's happy, impish squeal: *then you can make up your own story for the name!*

"But it's a strong knot," I said. "Maybe that's why. When you tie it properly, it won't break, and you know what people say about blood, as in family blood, how those kinds of connections just can't be undone…"

He wasn't listening. A four-wheeler—this one well-tuned—was buzzing in the near distance, and Deuce was hearing that now, looking for it. My hands began to tremble as I traced my way to the end of my 7X and started a clinch knot, trying to attach a size 22 trico dry fly with an eyelet the size of a pinprick.

"So I think you shot Annie," I told the Avalanche Kid, squinting at the shifting minutia between my finger tips. "But you didn't kill her. That's what I think. And somebody in your family convinced you that it was a good idea to take the credit."

The kid was silent. I looked up to find the buzzing four-wheeler—coming closer, but still not in view—and I lost the damn knot.

I lowered my hands. "But see, kid, here's how it works. The sheriff takes the body to someone called a medical examiner. That person uses scientific methods to determine exactly how Annie died. By tomorrow or so, they'll know, for example, if all the bullets in her body came from your rifle, or whether at some point there was a different gun involved."

The boy remained silent, while the engine noise grew louder. I restarted my elusive clinch knot.

"They'll know, too, if she died of something else, like drowning, like a blow to the head, and then you came along and shot her later."

At last I threaded the tiny hook. I let a breath out.

"And lying to police," I said, "that's a crime too."

The kid twisted to glare at me. "I did it," he assured me. "I killed her."

We met eyes for a long moment while the four-wheeler rooted closer along the opposite stream bank. His dull-blue, deep-set eyes were suddenly flush to the edge of tears. Then he twisted away.

"Wally!" he bawled, and he jerked to his feet. Excited by the four-wheeler's approach, the puppy had tugged the rotten fence post in half. He was dragging it. The kid lunged, caught the post, but the rotten wood crumbled through the loop in the leash and the little dog was free. Wally crashed enthusiastically through the creek—I felt a wave of remorse for the ruined trico action—and then the puppy wriggled up the far bank to greet the four-wheeler as it bulled through a nettle thicket.

"Wally!"

The kid smashed the creek to hell a second time in pursuit. I should have guessed it would be Uncle Salt Box Kussmaul arriving on the four-wheeler—but as Wally jumped to greet him, the burliest Kussmaul surprised me by shooting out a boot that caught the puppy in the rib cage.

Wally sprawled away and streaked downstream, yelping.

"Wally!" bawled the kid and charged after. Salt Box's bellow pursued them both: "What the hell are you doing up here?"

He wrenched his handle bars, reversed direction, and spurted after the kid, mashing back through the nettles.

I sat back on my heels and released a moan.

For Christ's sake, Dog.

Mad.

Dumb.

My leg pounded. I had lost the trico fly in the grass. The kid was gone. The fishing was ruined.

And now Salt Box Kussmaul was revving the engine, spinning a donut in the nettle patch, crashing the creek to hell a third time and then rooting up the near bank, driving himself right into my face.

Riparian rights don't apply here

"Eve," was my answer to the big man's angry accusation. "Eve said I could fish up here."

The four-wheeler's engine still ticked and snapped. This machine was brand new, a Yamaha Grizzly, with black mud stuck in startled globs to its glossy, realtree finish. Creek water ran down through the maze of its knobby tire treads. Salt Box hitched his ass forward in the cushy saddle and stuck his jaw out. "Eve, huh?"

"She said if I was with Deuce, it was okay."

"But you ain't with Deuce."

"I was."

"But you ain't now. And let me tell you something about Eve. I know about Eve, seeing as I'm married to her sister. Eve does drugs. She and that dumb-ass brother of mine. And then she wears that Amish kapp like she's a goody-two-shoes. So you take what Eve says and you wash it, real good, and you see what's left. Wash your hands after, too. Then you tell me what Eve says."

I paused, heart-thumping, to choose my words. I hadn't liked Salt Box Kussmaul very much the night before, in my surgical haze, but now the big brother of King Midas had tripped my snarl trigger.

"You own the creek?" I decided to say, stepping into the West Fork. "Is that how it is?"

He squeezed his brake levers with big, leather-gloved hands. He pulled himself up another quarter inch. He was a tidy shit, right down to the knots on his boot laces.

"Because a while back when I first pulled into Wisconsin," I said, "I was doing a little reading. Pretty good book, too. Called *State of Wisconsin Fishing Regulations*. I learned that when I bought a license, I bought riparian rights. When I'm standing in the water, I'm standing on public land, not Kussmaul land."

Salt Box answered that volley with a mean little grin. He was so much like his brother, I thought, yet so different and so opposed. Salt Box had fifty pounds on King Midas. Another predatory English bastard, he had knocked up and married the Amish sister who went in for yard ornaments and shopping. I was guessing Salt Box Kussmaul also had a positive credit rating, and probably another day or two of self-control.

"And you know," I said, "it just occurred to me that maybe the dead lady read that same book. Matter of fact, I'm sure she did. She knew she could legally walk the West Fork within the high water marks. I don't know how else she would get up in here to paint that north view of the Amish barn."

I nodded toward the Yoder farm. There it was, framed perfectly under the bluely handsome monitor roof: the vast, white barn side with the beaver tails nailed to it, exactly as represented on the canvas Annie Adams had set up opposite on the bridge, to the south, where I had found her body.

"Funny thing," I said, "that she would paint the north view from the south side. Being the kind of woman that I gather she was."

Salt Box squinted down at his Amish neighbor's barn. He looked back at me. Heavy fencing pliers yawned from his left jacket pocket, and he seemed to notice them when I did. He tucked them down.

"Riparian rights," he said, "don't apply here. This is Kussmaul country."

"So you guys make your own rules."

"Yup."

"Fish and game?"

"Yup."

"Speed limits. Septic. Burning. Dumping. All that?"

"All that."

He was tucking at the pliers again, and I was wondering just exactly how many people had passports to Kussmaul country—how many Kussmauls, exactly, Eve and I had to worry about—but I was suddenly distracted by something yellow in the stream before me. As Salt Box Kussmaul began to speak, I kicked at the West Fork's pretty limestone rubble, and the yellow object broke free and tumbled away downstream. Stepping after, I roiled the water. Now I couldn't see.

"...the West Fork ain't navigable up here anyway," he was telling me. "Can't float a log down it at high water anyway, so it ain't navigable and riparian don't apply. You people want to get legal on me, you want to play fine print on me, then it's as simple as that. The West Fork ain't navigable."

I kept my eyes down, waiting for the water to clear. I had read the fine print too. High water meant peak spring flow. Anybody could see where the West Fork's high water had been. A piece of Salt Box's farm trash—a long shred of blue-plastic tarp—hung from a willow thicket about head-high on the Dog. That was six feet plus. I was sure I didn't need to tell Salt Box that the both of us could drown, right where we were standing, at the right moment in April. You could float a whole raft of logs down the West Fork at the right moment.

I said to Salt Box, "I heard from Deuce you fence off the creek."

He didn't answer. I suppose we both wondered suddenly where Deuce had gone. But Wally's goofy yelp—up in the hardwoods on the coulee wall—told us the boy had caught the puppy up there.

"I got cattle. That's why I fence the creek."

"Sounds like more fence than cattle need."

He looked over his shoulder toward the Amish barn. He tucked at the fencing pliers again.

"So somebody cut you out?"

"What makes you say that?"

"Roll of wire in the cargo box there, pliers in your pocket. Looks like you're out fixing fences."

Salt Box scooted up once more. His breath steamed and now the sun caught the amber lenses of his sunglasses, caught in the bristly gray fibers atop his square, sun-burned head. I figured I would have to back off him any second. I figured I would have to come back for the yellow object. I looked around to mark my spot. I was precisely triangulated between Salt Box's tall blue silo, the Amish barn, and a limestone outcrop on the eastern bluff.

While the oldest Kussmaul brother stared me down, I re-checked the spot where the object had disappeared under silt. Then I made my triangle again, for good measure. But this time, when I looked up at the limestone bluff, someone was standing on it. Salt Box squinted that way too—but the vain bastard needed real glasses and couldn't see.

"The hell's that?" he said.

I unsnapped a vest pocket. I put binoculars on the outcrop. I saw a tall Amish girl, in full morning sunshine, shaking out a pink-and-turquoise beach towel. She flared the towel out square and tight and floated it down onto the rock—then her kapp came off and long ringlets of reddish-blonde hair flowed out—and then, as she lowered herself, unfastening her plain dark clothes, the angles cut her off and she vanished. I stared another few seconds. Nothing but sandy-orange rock and autumn hardwood forest, struck by a late September sun.

"Dunno," I lied to Salt Box.

"That's my land. You tell me what that was."

"What I see," I said, "belongs to me. That sound familiar?"

He grunted, inched up on his seat, and when I glanced down at my feet, meaning to walk away, I saw that the water had cleared. The object was still there, rolling in the current behind a stone, bright yellow and linear, thin as a grass stalk, with a little hairy head. The clear view surprised me, like seeing a big trout suddenly, right at your feet, and I blurted to Salt Box, "So you're an artist?"

I felt his head jerk.

"Or a patron of the arts?"

I had him guessing now. I had me guessing. But I had seen the object in the bib pocket of Barn Lady's overalls, as she had tucked in the candles and the jumbo Snickers bar beside it. It had tickled her plump little chin.

"Or did Annie Adams break the laws of Kussmaul country?"

"Say what...?

"Annie Adams. She painted that Amish barn from up here. Right about here would be perfect. And then somehow that painting got set up in an easel on the opposite side, on the bridge."

Deuce was jogging back, trying to cut wide around his uncle, smashing through the nettle patch, Wally captured around his fat little gut.

"Fellah," said Salt Box, "what in hell are you talking about?"

"I'm talking about fixing fences. And Annie Adams' riparian rights. Or maybe the lack thereof."

I reached into the West Fork. With the bubbles and the motion and the parallax, the object was hard to grasp at first—such a tiny thing, a tool to draw the finest lines—but then I got my fingers on it.

"I'm talking about this," I said. "In Kussmaul water."

And I showed him Barn Lady's little yellow paint brush.

There has to be some explanation

"She ain't been up here," said Salt Box Kussmaul.

The big man glared at his nephew as the kid sloshed across the West Fork. "Probably that goddamn little hoodlum right there who cut my fence."

I gave them a moment. I watched them closely. I don't need to tell you that Deuce was a kid off the rails, a boy who didn't quite know where his best interests lay. But even so, the Avalanche Kid surprised me. He nailed his Uncle Salt Box square in the neck with a rotten apple.

"That's for kicking my puppy."

"Git home," his uncle snarled, hurling the sloppy apple back. "Go brush your momma's teeth."

I watched Deuce's face. He flinched. The apple missed, but the insult to Eve nearly crumpled him. He turned away, stomped away through the black-and-white cattle, spooking them on purpose. Salt Box, wiping at his neck, turned in disgust and said to me, "All that nutty painter bitch had to do was ask my permission."

Poker-faced, I nodded. But I was thinking that it was guys like Salt Box Kussmaul who made America great. All the barn lady had to do was ask his permission to exercise rights she already had.

"All she had to do," continued Salt Box, "was come right down my driveway and ring the doorbell."

Right, I thought. Come right down the driveway marked: *No Trespassing, this means you.*

"Heck, my wife mighta even bought a painting. She mighta paid for a portrait of the kids. She wasn't allowed no graven images growing up Amish, so now that she's English with the rest of us, she loves that kind of junk." He cracked his mean little smile. "You getting my drift here? There's a way to do things."

I nodded slowly. Drift.

Drift.

It was an interesting word to use with a fly fisherman. A fly fisherman floated something down the stream—an artifice, a lie, basically—and hoped for a take. A drift, it was called. A drift—a good drift—was a perfect falsehood. I could imagine, suddenly, Annie Adam's death as the result of a team effort—brothers, nephews, and uncles—a well-coordinated, regime-sponsored hit-job in defense of Kussmaul country.

Maybe Salt Box saw that coming. "We Kussmaul's ain't political people," he told me. "We just believe in freedom. We keep it simple."

I stashed the thought for later. I held up the little yellow brush, let the bastard take a good, long look.

"Simple is good for me," I said. "So how'd this get here?"

"She—hell if I know."

He reached for it. I pulled it back.

"There has to be some explanation," I told him. "A simple one."

Salt Box stepped closer to me. "You got a point. She might have been up here a month or two ago. Someone did cut me out back then, now that I think about it. I did do a patch about a month ago. I'll turn that in to the sheriff and them," he offered suddenly, like we were working for truth and justice together. He held his hand out for the little yellow brush.

I couldn't stop a hot little snort. I told him I could handle the transfer myself. I told him I didn't think Annie Adams' brush had been in the West Fork for more than a day or two—certainly not a month. "And it won't be hard," I said, "to figure out the last time you patched your fence over the creek."

He looked around—his land, his farm buildings, his fences. "Okay," he said. "Off. Get the hell off my land."

"I'm not on your land. I'm in the stream."

"Don't give me that shit."

I tucked the brush into a vest pocket and zipped it.

"And I'll let myself out," I said. "I'll just navigate right on down the public thoroughfare. I remember reading that the law gives me the right to deal with obstacles in my path. You block me, I can deal with the blockage."

I turned my back to him. I waded downstream into my own mud, stepping slowly because I couldn't see.

"This is Kussmaul country," he bawled after me. "You hear?"

Wading slowly, guarding the leg, feeling the madstone wobble but stay fast in the current, I felt his words climb up on my shoulders and stay there. I felt a destabilizing wave of trepidation.

"You pay to play in Kussmaul country. Fella? You hear?"

But I kept my course, having no other, and when I reached the downstream fence, Salt Box's patch was obvious. The new wire was tight and shiny, an expert four-strand splice across the stream, its barbs pricking sunlight out of air. The rusty wires at the sides had collected flotsam from high water.

I took a long and steadying breath. Then I lit a Swisher, nipping the nasty smoke into my lungs, waiting for the nicotine. When it hit, I tossed my rod over the fence. I took off my vest and dug into the back pocket, down deep beneath the bread crumbs. I lifted out my wire cutters and I got busy.

The 'what next' phase

A Vernon County Sheriff's deputy waited for me at the County Y bridge. He leaned on the rail, drinking a can of Sun Drop from the machine outside the Avalanche Mercantile. As I sloshed closer, I could tell he was the same young guy, Deputy Austin Vossteig, who had been in charge of loose ends the day before on the Annie Adams crime scene investigation. Nice kid, I had noted. Controlled and polite. Asking the right questions. Keeping me comfortable. Keeping his cards close. The kind of young man I had preferred to employ at Oglivie Secure.

Deputy Vossteig called down, "How's fishing?"

"I never tied a fly on."

"I'm sorry to hear that." Courteous. Genuine. "What happened?"

"I got Kussmauled."

"Yeah." He smiled. "I heard. Mister Kussmaul gave dispatch quite an earful. Since I was down here on a trespassing already, I got the call."

"I wasn't trespassing. I can legally walk in the stream."

Deputy Vossteig raised the green-and-yellow Sun Drop can and drained it.

"Well," he said, "folks can disagree, and that's what we're here for." A barn swallow shot chittering past me into its bridge-bottom nest. The deputy crushed the can and added, "If you don't mind, Mister Oglivie, I need you to come up to the car."

He was twenty feet above me. The West Fork was shoving me in the ass. The madstone wobbled hard. "I can quote you the law," I said. "There's not much to disagree about. The land inside the high-water mark is public, if you can float a log down the waterway."

"Yeah," said Vossteig. "I looked it up too. I picked up a copy of the fishing regs in the Mercantile. You want to come up here a minute, sit down in the car with me?"

Well-mannered, I thought. And stubborn, too. Good cop. "I wasn't trespassing," I told Vossteig again. "Deuce Kussmaul took me in across his uncle's land, and then I was in the stream. That's a public thoroughfare. You can't block it. And by the way," I told him, unzipping my vest pocket and bringing up the little yellow brush, "I found this."

The deputy didn't say anything, didn't negotiate or break from his message. He just waited for me to come up. And the irritating truth was, I was getting out at the bridge anyway. Grasshoppers sprayed out around me, and I emerged onto the road puffing, limping badly. Madstone, I thought again. *Stone mad* was more like it. I was dying. Maybe. And this young buck wanted to bother me with a phony trespassing. His cruiser was parked about fifty yards west, off the bridge. I could make out a white head in the back seat.

"It's true that Salt Box can't block a public thoroughfare," Deputy Vossteig said, steering me toward the vehicle, "but you also can't destroy his property."

"I can do what's reasonable to maintain my progress."

"But when you carry wire cutters," said Vossteig, "it looks a little more militant, I guess." I had stopped. He put his hand on my elbow. "So let's go sit down in the car. You won't mind, I hope, that I already have someone in there."

"Kussmaul is the militant," I said back. "I'm just a fisherman. The stream is mine. It's your law here in Wisconsin."

"If the stream is navigable. That's what the law says."

"It's navigable if you can float a log down it at high water."

Vossteig shrugged. He gave me a very subtle shove. "But what is a log?"

That irked me. The guy was good. He was immovable. "Damn it, we all know what a log is."

Again, the faint pressure at my elbow. "Well, when he called, Mister Kussmaul told me he dropped a log in the crick a couple of springs ago, and it spun around and stuck about a hundred feet from where he dropped it."

"The law says *float*." I was running out of patience. "Not drop and let go randomly. *Float*, as in guide it down, as in use the waterway as a mode of transport." I pulled strongly out of his grip, resisting-arrest-style. *Mad, dumb.* "To move timber," I said. "As in commerce, community, people working together—those are the things you're supposed to protect. Not some frontier-psycho like Kussmaul."

Vossteig shrugged again, less smoothly this time. His hand left my elbow and arrived at my back, on my wader belt, on the spot where sumo wrestlers leveraged one another's quarter-ton bodies. I felt myself grow lighter.

"Well, I guess it's always funny," the officer said, clearing his throat uncomfortably, "how different folks can see different things."

I braced my legs and closed my eyes. I tried to remember how to steer a young and nervous cop who had over-burdened himself with all the right intentions. I had to harness those intentions. There was a very good chance that Annie Adams, in the last couple of days, had been painting up on Salt Box Kussmaul's land. That ought to matter. Vossteig ought to care. He ought to take that fact back to the people in charge, get credit for coming up with it.

"I found this up there," I repeated, holding out the little yellow paint brush. "In the creek," I said, "on Salt Box's place. It belonged to Annie Adams."

That softened him up a bit. He let go of my belt. He pushed his sunglasses up atop his close-cropped bronze hair. He took the brush, pinched its tip, played out its sparse hog-hair bristles.

"And Salt Box just fixed his fence," I said. "Plus the painting on the bridge where the woman died—it was of that side of the Amish barn. The north side. The side you see from Salt Box's place. Not the south side."

Vossteig gave me the brush back. He blinked at me. His eyes were pale blue and deep in his suntanned face, and he shoved a thumb and a forefinger into them, pushing them deeper.

"Look," he sighed heavily. "This is a very sad thing. Very hard to accept. And I appreciate your concern. But like I just told the child's mother, I can give you a couple of facts to help you move on. We now have the medical examiner's preliminary report, with time-of-death corroboration and an airtight ballistics match. We have the kid's confession. And most important of all, Mister Oglivie, we have your eye-witness testimony to back it all up. To be honest with you, the concerns of the sheriff's department and the district attorney's office are now in the 'what next' phase."

He watched me closely, to see how I was taking it.

I wasn't taking it. Not a bit.

"Meaning," he explained, "how to deal with a ten-year-old homicide suspect. What kind of charges are appropriate? What social services are appropriate for a family in this kind of trouble? Do we rule the parents incompetent? That kind of thing. It's a tremendous challenge for us."

Now he took my elbow again.

"And meanwhile," he said, "you and I have this trespassing thing to talk about."

"I wasn't trespassing."

"Excuse me," he corrected himself, his grip tightening, "destruction of property."

"If Salt Box Kussmaul put a fence across this road"—I spumed out the words—"would you arrest me for cutting it to get through?"

"Mister Oglivie, come with me to the car."

"Dog," I snarled.

He looked at me.

"Dog. The name is Dog."

Deputy Vossteig gnawed his bottom lip a minute—and one half of my brain, perhaps the uninfected half, was thinking, Damn, he really is solid. Patient. Worth his weight in gold—while the other half wanted to cock back and smack his big, clean head.

"Here is what I'm working on now," he told me. "I mean today, at this moment. The dead woman had a son. A teenage boy. He was hers with a previous husband. We can't find him."

Okay…well…a son…that was something…that slowed me down just a little…*she had a son*…who needed to know his mother was dead…and while my brain was busy with that, Deputy Vossteig moved me twenty feet toward the car before I got heavy again.

"I take back my statement," I said. "I didn't see anything."

"It doesn't work that way."

"I didn't say he killed her. I said he shot her. And I only saw one shot hit the body."

"The DA is moving forward," Vossteig told me firmly. "A kid's mom has been murdered and he doesn't know about it. He's at summer camp, up north somewhere, and the new husband, Howard Adams, doesn't have the phone number and can't remember the name of the camp."

I looked off toward Annie Adams' damn teepee. I could see Half-Timber Kussmaul over there, unloading the last few pieces of firewood from his ancient red Chevy pickup. He had delivered Howard Adams way too much wood, I saw, as if in sympathy.

"The poor husband is helpless," Vossteig was saying. "He's frantic. He can't touch his ass with both hands. So I need to find that kid and let him know. And right now, Mister Oglivie, I need you to get into the vehicle. I have another passenger, but this is all minor stuff if we can let it be that way."

Get in! a part of me shrieked. But I said, "Somebody set the kid up. And he agreed. He thinks since he's a minor nothing bad can happen to him. Somebody made some kind of deal with him."

Vossteig had begun to sweat.

"I just heard the same from the mother—"

"Which doesn't make it wrong."

Vossteig's cheeks filled out and shrank back. His gave me a sturdy little shove. "You're concerned about the family," he said. "I appreciate that. Looking ahead, in the event that the child is guilty—whenever we have to come down here and deal with him—our major concern is the reaction of his family—"

"King Midas."

"Correct."

"Armed and dangerous."

"Absolutely. Record of violent behavior. Full of substances as well. And then there's the mother—"

"She's just trying to take care of her kid."

"We all are."

"But you won't talk to Salt Box about how the dead lady's paint brush got in the creek on his property."

"Mister Oglivie," he said, "I *have* talked to Salt Box and Rachel Kussmaul. They have been interviewed thoroughly. They are very concerned about all of this. The sheriff and the DA met with them and social services last evening. The Kussmauls have offered to foster their nephew Deuce for a while…you know, create some stability and distance for everybody while this thing goes through the courts…now you've gone and cut their fence, just when I'm going to need their cooperation—"

I twisted away. "Damn it!" I blurted at the deputy. "You're fucking this up!"

He had a taser on his belt. He unsnapped it and showed it to me—just so we both knew the future. Then he took my arm again.

"Mister Oglivie, you're under arrest."

"Let me go."

"Mister Oglivie…"

"Dog," I said. "And let me go."

"Mister Oglivie, I was hoping to leave this fact out of it. But you've been in trouble before. Your DL came up on the computer in several states. You tend to have trouble behaving yourself. Just a couple weeks ago in Black Earth—"

"She and I were friends. Good friends. Then her old man came at me out of nowhere with a shovel. I defended myself, but she thought I started it. She wouldn't believe me."

I felt pathetic suddenly, and the young deputy shook his head as if to confirm it. "Always a lot of high emotions," he said through gritted teeth, "when family blood is involved."

My feet were moving toward the cruiser. I wrenched at his grip.

"Don't be an idiot," I began. "You can't let Salt Box and Rachel—"

Suddenly I thought my arm would break. I landed on the cruiser's back seat like a heap of wet clay. My rod came in after, bent almost double. The door slammed behind me. That's when I noticed that Deputy Vossteig had done more than pick up fishing regs at the Mercantile. Eve was his other passenger. He had busted her too.

"Hey," I said stupidly. "Funny meeting you here."

She wouldn't look at me.

"Trespassing too? At Uncle Roundy's barn?"

She stared straight ahead, chewing angrily on a kapp string.

"Where's Deuce?" she demanded.

"I—"

"You promised," she cut me off. "You promised not to lose him."

She was the one on meth

Eve's look-away anger lasted all the way to Viroqua. It lasted all the way through the booking and bail process. At the bailiff's desk, she sulkily opened her little denim Gap purse and paid us both out with two hundred and seventy-nine bucks' worth of egg and pumpkin money. I followed her out to the pay phone in the county courthouse lobby. "Eve," I said, "now both of us are limping. What happened?" She turned away. She plugged quarters. I listened while she called her brother-in-law Half-Tim. Find Deuce, she told him. And then come get us.

She hung the phone up. "At least there's one English," she muttered, "that you can count on. More or less."

"Look," I said. "I'm sorry. The fishing lesson was a disaster. I couldn't even get your son next to the stream. He threw apples at the fish. Then Salt Box kicked the puppy and they both took off—"

"You told me that in the car. Twice."

So I had. Rod in hand, I followed her out to the courthouse steps, where she chopped her skirt between her knees and sat down heavily. She packed and lit her pipe. My waders hissed out smelly air as I eased down beside her. She moved a foot farther away. She wasn't going to talk to me. Maybe never again. That was the message. And the Dog was a sucker for that. Cold shoulder the Dog and watch him squirm.

"I'll try again," I said finally. "I promise I'll teach him to fish."

I watched Eve's face unscrew just a little. I noticed then that her eyes were dilated, her acorn-brown almost occluded by an intense, jumpy black. And she was chewing her right thumb nail—chewing the hell out of it. I showed her the little yellow paint brush. "And I found this in the creek."

"That looks like Annie's…"

"It is. It was in her pocket when she came in the store the other night."

"Right." Eve startled me by snatching it, dropping it in her little purse. She was lead detective, I guess. Or she was the one on meth. "Thank you," she said.

"You're welcome," I said.

I waited a minute, watching her tobacco smoke waft out over the sidewalk. We drew stares—the surly, punky, somewhat-Amish woman and the Dog, mangy and stiff, in vest and waders. Finally I asked, "So how did your silo climbing go?"

Nothing. Gnawing. Tapping her red Chuckies. Her knees darting in and out beneath her dress.

"If you don't talk to me…then who do you talk to? At this point?"

She switched to her left index finger, picking at it with her small gray teeth.

"Bastard," she called me finally.

"Fine. I'm a bastard. So tell me."

Eve sighed out smoke. Her knotted shoulders went up and down. "Uncle Roundy had the top of the silo locked too. He saw me up there and took the ladder away from the bottom so I couldn't get down. By the time I jumped and sprained my damn knee, that cop was coming down the drive."

I nodded sympathetically. Tough outings for both of us, then.

"But Uncle Roundy's got horseshoe league this evening," she

went on, "and his wife goes with him, so I'm going back. He's got a good reason for locking his silo up like that. And Annie loved that round barn, so I bet she snooped in it. I bet she knew why the silo is locked."

"So how would that fit," I asked her, "with Annie's paint brush up on Salt Box's place?"

Eve thought about it, and I could almost see the brain sparks flying. Funny thing about meth—you could think on it—even if sometimes the thoughts came out a little too nasty and fast, like arrows off a crossbow. "If Roundy killed Annie," she said, "then he set up the wrong painting on the bridge, right?"

I nodded. "Maybe."

She asked me, "You think Uncle Roundy would make a mistake like that?"

"I don't know him."

"I do. The man's about as careless as a fox with a good piece of meat. He's sneaky, and he's smart."

"So he sets up the wrong painting, on purpose?"

"Of course," she meth-sparked. I had to wait for her to explain. "He sets up the wrong painting to move people's thinking up to Salt's place. To make it clear that Annie was up there, and she needed to go back. Then people look up there, and they find the paintbrush. Salt Box gets the heat."

"But the cops never..."

"That's because you came along and saw Deuce. You said he shot her. That's all they needed to hear."

"So Uncle Roundy kills her, brings her to the bridge, and tries to set up Salt?"

"They all hate each other—all Kussmauls—deep inside. They hate everybody."

"But what about Deuce? You thought Deuce was in bed."

The kid's mother dropped her head. She fiddled with her kapp strings. They were soiled, I noticed, frayed—no, chewed—at the tips. "No. I knew he wasn't. When his daddy doesn't come home at night, he doesn't sleep well. I knew Deucey was up and out of the house. I just didn't know where he was until those gunshots started. I figured he was out hunting crows. But then you walked in with that look on your face…"

"So Uncle Roundy sees Deuce—"

"They're real close. They're a lot alike. Deuce worships his Uncle Roundy."

"—and, just to complicate things, Roundy has the kid pump her with lead? In exchange for a two-headed turtle?"

Eve blew smoke at her kapp strings. Then she reached down, scratched her leg, and twirled a dirty finger in the laces of her red Chuckies.

"That's pretty fantastic," I said.

"Welcome to Avalanche," she replied.

A school bus rolled by, kids on a field trip, and the children on our side pointed and pounded the windows. What else could they do—seeing a guy in chest waders on the courthouse steps, beside a woman smoking a pipe? I touched the madstone. Tenacious as a leech. Eve straightened her right leg partway out beneath the skirt—no socks under the red Chuckies, fine brown hairs on her shin—and pulled it back in.

"So what's the Amish cure for a sprained knee?" I said, trying to lighten things. "Eye of newt?"

She blew smoke, pretending to ignore me.

"No," I went on. "I know. Raccoon liver. And duct tape."

Puff…puff…

"Ice," she said finally. "And time," she said. "Just like everybody else. And you're a smartass bastard. You'll be a big hit in Hell too."

We sat a while more. Eventually, after loading a fresh bowl, she passed me the pipe. The stem was slightly damp. I dragged it discretely over my sleeve and took a pull. But she caught me.

"Amish germs," she said, "or girl germs? Which one bothers you?"

"Both—" I coughed out, starting to laugh.

She took the pipe back and gave it a thorough wiping with her apron.

"English germs or boy germs?" I asked her.

Eve eyed me sideways, puffing. "Try rabies," she said.

We were quiet again and strangely close until Half-Timber Kussmaul sputtered up in his old Chevy. Deuce and Wally rode with firewood in the bed, and Half-Tim carried two passengers in the cab. "Son of a..." cussed Eve softly beside me as she sized up the situation. Then she warned me: "Half-Tim brought Ma Kussmaul. No doubt she's got errands."

Staring from the passenger window, tracking my gimpy approach with beady eyes, was an old woman with random tracts of plywood-colored hair on her broad, pale scalp. Half-Tim leaned over and waved a little sheepishly at me. I heard him say, "Don't stare a hole in him, Ma."

"I know a sick man when I see one," the old woman snapped.

"Ma—"

Then the middle passenger, a tall, teenaged Amish girl, leaned around the vast old woman and smiled shyly.

I nodded back.

"That's Dorcas Yoder," Eve told me. "She helps Half-Tim...with Ma."

"I saw her this morning up on—" I began, but thought the better of it when I received a sharp-knuckled jab from Eve. She helped me up, and we sat side-by-side on rolling, sliding sticks of firewood as the truck pulled away.

"—up on the rock, sunbathing?" Eve finished into my ear. Then louder: "Sit down, Deuce."

"Yes. On a rock over Salt Box's place. I think it was her."

"That was Dorrie, all right." I felt Eve's body jerk awkwardly close, her breath hot against my ear. "Isn't she gorgeous?"

Well...I had noticed, up close, the perfect peaches-and-cream skin, the deep brown eyes, the cute nose. And in the circle of my binocs, earlier, I had seen the height and wide-shoulders, and, even through the Amish dress, the kind of insistent bust-line only a six-teen-year-old could have.

"Is that…" I stammered, "…is sunbathing…an Amish prac-tice…?"

Eve marked my evasion with narrowed lids around her dilated eyes. "Of course not."

"But then…"

"We're people too. Sun and skin feel good together. Don't they?" She gave me half a second. "Don't they?" Then she snapped again, "Sit down, Deuce."

Half-Tim Kussmaul swung a U-turn. Logs rolled and our shoul-ders jostled. Eve's thoughts jumped. "I think I'll do some shopping too, then. I need a few things. But Dorrie's father would kill her for sunbathing. She's on the verge of getting the ban, just like me and my sister. Dorrie looks at me and Rachel," Eve said, "and she thinks the ban looks like fun."

"The ban…"

"Excommunication. Yes—I need a few things. Deuce, sit down."

Half-Tim pulled out onto U.S. 14 and I clamped my hat against my skull. Deuce's fat brown puppy clambered messily all over us. The Avalanche Kid tweaked his mother by kneeling down, rather than sitting, and—while his mother stared at him and gnawed her fingers, appearing to forget me—the kid sailed mud clods over the tail gate, landing them like bombs on the highway.

"Where are we going?" I asked finally.

"Hmm?"

I let it go. I would see. We rattled between car lots and mo-tels, a Country Kitchen, the county fairgrounds. Then we were turning, bouncing through some road work, and coasting across a seemingly immeasurable parking lot. I twisted around. Now I saw. Wal-Mart.

"Deuce," Eve commanded, "Wally stays in the truck."

But Deuce had already dumped the puppy into the grid of parking lot lines, and Wally raced away. "No way!" Deuce hollered back, zigzagging after the puppy.

Eve closed her eyes a moment. Then she climbed over the tailgate and left me. Exuberant Dorrie had exited from Half-Tim's door, and the long-legged girl was nearly to the Wal-Mart doors, Wally nipping at her flying black skirts.

"Wally! Wait up!" Deuce howled.

When I managed to get grounded beyond the tailgate, sluggish Half-Tim was gently easing his mother out of the cab. Ma Kussmaul had ankles like empty sacks. Her lemon-chiffon house dress was grimy, packed with flesh. She glared at me.

"Like to see you try that fly fishing up on my place—"

Half-Tim cut her off with, "Ma...*please*..." and steered her away toward the store.

Eve shut the pickup door. "This time," she said as they moved away, "you think you can not lose Deuce?"

I glanced up and saw Wally bolt through sliding exit doors into Wal-Mart. Deuce, on the puppy's heels, grabbed the doors as they started to close.

"Wally! Come back!"

"You think," Eve repeated, tight-lipped, "you can keep track of him this time?"

I glanced at her. She was re-loading her meth, nipping a small white tablet into her mouth. I felt my gut drop. *Mad. Dumb.* The Avalanche Kid strained, and strained, and finally checked the Wal-Mart exit doors to squeeze in after his puppy.

"But what the hell am I supposed to do with him?"

Eve had already headed off toward the big box.

"Remember?" she said over her shoulder. "You're teaching him to fly fish."

Which brings us to Wally trout

I swear—limping in chest waders after Eve Kussmaul across that Wal-Mart parking lot—I swear I heard the voice of my tax guy, Harvey Digman.

Of course, an oracular visitation from Harvey was not in itself an unusual event inside the head of the Dog. The strange thing was that—even as I followed her into the damn store—I heard Eve's voice too. Talking to Harvey Digman. Like they were together on the *This is not a fishing trip* thing. Like they were co-conspirators in a plot to push the Dog a little deeper. Then I heard, even dizzily *saw*, the two of them, chatting in Harvey's Boston office, across Harvey's big walnut desk, smoking their damn pipes.

Or their damn not-pipes.

Or whatever. Ask the Belgian guy, the smartass artiste, Magritte.

Teach a kid to fly fish? In Wal-Mart?

And they ganged up. They chorused back at me.

All three of them.

Why not?

So, "Kid," I panted.

He turned. He was in Automotive. He was flushed, teary-eyed, gasping for air, furious that I had stopped him.

"How's it working, chasing the puppy like that?"

"It's not!" He glowered. "I can't catch him!"

"How about throwing something at him? Have you tried that?"

"I—" He looked around.

"There he is," I said, as Wally frisked past a stack of tires at the far end of the aisle. The puppy paused to sit and nip at his belly, and Deuce grabbed the nearest thing. The pack of air fresheners whiffled hard through the air. Wally heard the sound. He never had to look. He knew. The little dog's instincts engaged, and he was gone.

"Hmm…" I said.

The kid whined, "That was a stupid idea. Now I'll never catch him!"

Beep-beep—we had to scatter as Ma Kussmaul cruised through in an electric shopping buggy. Half-Tim trundled sheepishly after, pushing a cart. "I just saw Wally over by—"

And then the puppy appeared again directly in Ma Kussmaul's right-of-way—*beeeeep!*—and he tumbled, yelping, and streaked toward the far back corner of the store.

"—over by Men's Wear," Half-Tim continued, in a ponderous way that made me feel my stitches suddenly. "But I guess he's not there anymore."

No shit. I reached down, touched the madstone. Intact. Connected.

"Thanks," I told Half-Tim.

"Sorry about Ma," he said. "She's not real easy around strangers. You gotta know her a few years before she, you know—before she can relax and feel friendly."

I nodded. I edged away. But Half-Tim fixed me with a mournful look and dropped anchor.

"Mental issues," he said. "Though what those issues may be, who knows, because we got no insurance. All we got is these damn old farms—you know, the land, the animals, the creaky old barns.

We got no cash. So we can eat, or we can go to the doctor, but we can't do both. And you can see what Ma prefers to do."

I said I was sorry—meaning sorry I couldn't stop right there and chat—but Half-Tim misunderstood.

"Oh, don't be sorry for us. We survive," he said. "We do things ourselves. That's why I'm in, you know, kind-of-like medical school. We've got medical needs, no insurance. And I'm not exactly gonna be a doctor with just a GED."

I nodded. "I'd love to talk sometime—"

"Me too," he said. "I love to talk." And while I searched aisles for a glimpse of Deuce, off went Half-Tim, behind me, talking, working his way through Byzantine and seemingly endless difficulties with his father's health, his parents' marriage, his brothers' legal affairs...

I lost the thread—or I never had it. I heard a *clang!* a few aisles over. Deuce was chasing. He was throwing things again.

"Look—sorry—Half-Tim—but right now I'm a little preoccupied..."

The youngest Kussmaul worked up a brave smile.

"You know," he said, "I don't like that name. I don't like Half-Tim. I don't go by that anymore, except in Avalanche."

I nodded warily.

"I'm just like you," he said, alarming me. "I made up my own name, a name that suits me better."

I scratched underneath my hat. "Dog...just kind of made itself up...it was kind of just there all along..."

"Me too," he said excitedly. "My name is Timothy, and in the middle of that is 'Moth.' Get it? That's what I'm called at school. Because...I mean, don't you think moths get a bad rap? And like, they're actually beautiful and complex...but they come out at night so nobody really sees them?"

He was scaring me. "You're scaring me," I said. But I felt a friendly smile come on as I said it. He was right about moths. And Half-Tim wasn't a name I would want either. And he was pudgebodied and grungily ornate in that peculiar way of moths. He could call himself whatever he wanted. Who was the Dog to argue?

"Okay," I said. "Moth. You got it."

"Thanks, man. You got enough wood at the campground?" he asked me.

"Plenty. Thanks."

"I got more up at Ma's and my place. I cut wood for three whole years solid after I quit high school. I cut about five hundred cords. Some people say that must be a record. But I don't care. It's just wood. So holler if you need more."

"I'll let you know."

"How's the leg?"

"I think it's going to be all right. Thanks."

He was staring at the leg now, his big Kussmaul brow aimed down around the faint madstone lump in my waders. His greasy corn-silk hair stuck out in twin tufts around his big, soft shoulders.

"Maybe I should see the wound? See how it's doing?"

"Uh…sure…that's a good idea…sometime."

"Ma says I shouldn't have helped you like that. She says you could sue us. She thinks that's what you're trying to do."

Clang! again, from a few aisles over. "Listen, Moth, I—"

"Annie talked about suing us," he went on. "Last summer. When Ma said something about finally tearing down that old half-timber barn. Annie talked about some group taking legal action to preserve the place."

"I'm not going to sue you."

He nodded eagerly. "Right."

"Okay?" I said. "So thanks. Come by the campground later and we'll look at the leg. Right now I'm teaching your nephew to fly fish…"

Beep-beep went Ma Kussmaul's electric shopping buggy from the end of the Housewares aisle.

Beep!

Beeeeeep!

She had waited for Moth long enough.

"Kid," I puffed anew. "Deuce..."

His voice came back surly and exasperated, from inside Women's Wear: "What?"

"Give me the report. How's it going?"

"I can't catch him. He's too scared. And he's too quick."

Deuce pushed out through a rack of ladies fall blazers, rage and despair etched on his wide, pink Kussmaul face. Lovely Dorcas Yoder—over in Lingerie—swung her tightly kapped head to smile bashfully at us. Then she headed for a fitting room.

"So what have you tried?"

Deuce shrugged.

"Anything new? Different?"

Another shrug.

"Hmm. Same old approach. Chasing. Throwing. You bump into anybody from Wal-Mart yet?"

"Some fat lady standing on a ladder. She said dogs weren't allowed. She said she was going to call security."

I did the hmm thing again. "So what do you think happens next?"

"Some guy?" he said, lip trembling, "with a gun...shoots Wally?"

"Well..."

I appeared to consider the possibility. And the possibility did exist. Some hungover loser with a pistol, in a rent-a-cop suit, ready to go off on a puppy—that guy was out there, that was for sure. At one low point, the Dog had hired that guy. Hell, for a week or two, at the very bottom, when Oglivie Secure was history and I was a temp, guarding paint at a paint factory, the Dog *was* that guy. But the odds were long, and instead I told the kid that someone from Wal-Mart would probably call Animal Control—another old version of the Dog—and Animal Control would probably impound—

Deuce leapt up. "There he goes!"

I snatched the kid so hard out of mid-stride that he whiplashed at the end of my arm, and he looked at me, stunned and empty-headed, opening a brief window for the Dog.

"Not the same old thing," I said. "No more chasing and throwing. It doesn't work. You've proved that to yourself."

Deuce nodded, blinking.

"So what else is there?"

He looked around at the forest of ladies' autumn fashions. He looked back at me, warily shaking his head, stumped. I patted through my vest pockets. I found half a Milky Way bar, an ancient box of Lemonheads, and an untapped rod of beef jerky. I unclipped the water bottle from my wader belt.

"Let's sit down," I said. "Let's think it over."

I shoved him firmly, and down we went, cross-legged on the waxy tile, our heads brushed by the frilled limbs of long-sleeved rayon blouses. The kid hunched red-faced over his share of the Milky Way, picking at it, breathing loudly through his nose. Around us, the mid-day doings of a small-town Wal-Mart gurgled and flowed. A fitting room door opened. Dorcas Yoder called out, "Eve…Eve?…Where'd you go?"

I asked the kid, "You know anything about brook trout?"

"Nope."

"Easily spooked. Quick as light. Eat anything. About as much memory as a blade of grass."

"So?"

I shrugged. "It's just interesting, that's all." I glugged a little stale water and set the bottle between us. "You wouldn't think so, but brook trout are very different from brown trout."

I leaned back, looked up into the beamy, fluorescent sky. "Yeah," I said, "it's not that brown trout aren't spooky. Any trout is spooky. That's their survival instinct. One sudden cloud crosses the sun, and they're gone—any kind of trout."

He said crankily, "Trout are afraid of clouds?"

"No. They're afraid of herons. But there's no time in a trout's life to figure out the difference between cloud and heron. Movement is movement. Movement is danger. Period."

"Then how are brown trout different?"

"Oh, well, let's see…" A shopper behind us twirled the blouse rack. The fabrics twisted and tossed like branches in a breeze. A price check call went out on the PA system. The kid picked up a Lemonhead and tried to pinch it flat. It wouldn't budge.

"…a brown trout is more of a gourmet eater. Picky. Gets obsessed with one thing. And that means he gets in a good spot and wants to stay there. You can make a tiny bit of noise around a brown trout, risk a tiny bit of movement, as long as you fish exactly what he's eating, and fish it perfectly."

Skreee! went hangers on a rod. Aisle signs swayed gently under the air handler. Ma Kussmaul, surly as a beaver, plowed her buggy past us down a horizontal current, swiveling her patchy, plywood-haired head for a baleful look before she motored on into Frozen Foods. "Eve?" called Dorcas Yoder. "Eve? Eve?"

I looked around for the kid's mother. I had last seen her headed for Hunting and Fishing.

"Whereas," I said, peeling open the beef jerky stick, "assuming you stalk perfectly and don't spook a brook trout, you could toss Cheetos on the water and probably get a strike. But either way, you don't chase trout. You don't attack them."

Now the kid squirmed impatiently, crunching the Lemonhead.

"Which brings us to Wally trout."

He looked up at me, his face scrunched into a question. I nearly laughed at myself—Wally trout?—but Deuce was listening. I tossed the beef stick out beyond his reach, out near a tarn of discount shoes.

"Is Wally more like brook?" I asked him. "Or brown?"

"He ain't that spooky," Deuce said. "More like playful. But he eats anything. So, I guess…" He was confused. "I don't know. All this stupid talking…we could have caught him by now…"

"Really? How?"

"I don't know. Not sitting here talking."

"What happens when you yell and chase Wally?"

"He runs away."

"What happens when you sit still and relax, have a snack?"

The kid sulked. He hammered in another Lemonhead. He dropped his head and chewed. "This is stupid. Nothing happens."

I reached over and raised his chin. I pointed up a deep and shadowy feeder aisle, bulked tight with stacks of moss-green plastic garbage cans. There was Wally, watching us, sitting in his little puppy-slump, tail thumping, pink tongue hanging out, his wet little nose keen to the scent of jerky.

"No!" I whispered, grabbing Deuce by the back of the pants as he tried to lurch up. "No…You did it. He's coming. You caught him."

"I caught him!" Deuce bragged to his mother as we left the big box behind and crossed the parking lot toward Moth's pickup. He kept Wally solidly under his arm as the puppy gummed the last of the jerky.

Eve's packages were large and awkward. She walked fast and spoke distractedly. "I knew you would…"

Dorrie skipped, her skirts and kapp strings dancing. Ma Kussmaul zoomed ahead and did a clicking-humming U-turn by the tailgate, where she waited for Moth to arrive with the loaded cart.

A few minutes later, from my vantage in the bed of the pickup, I made a survey of our respective takings. Ma Kussmaul had scored a case of macaroni-and-cheese, a case of tube socks, several packs of Wal-ka-Seltzer, and a half dozen paperback romances—plus a rare twelve-pack of Mr. Pibb. Moth's bag had men's boxers, men's boxer-briefs, Vaseline, and Wal-bu-profin. Dorrie's things were private—but they were also, I could tell, lacy, colorful, and pink. The Dog, looking ahead to the next fishing lesson, had acquired a rawhide bone large enough to keep Wally off the stream for a week.

Then Eve tried to sneak her purchases under the radar. Long, awkward, heavy—she laid them in last, tucked them against the sidewall against a stack of split oak and behind the other bags. But as Moth Kussmaul pulled out onto the highway, I pried a hand in there and looked. Eve had bought bolt-cutters. And she had bought a Snake Charmer shotgun, a cute little thing with a plastic stock, stainless steel barrel, and break-open breech, plus a box of .410 shells.

"Eve—" I began discreetly. "I really don't—"

She shut me up with a meth-high, Hell-bent look.

"You do your job," she hissed, "and I'll do mine."

When you kill someone, you need a reason

"You ready to try it on the stream?"

"Whatever. I mean, sure Dog. Yeah."

Wally sprawled in the tall grass, fifty feet back from the West Fork, happily working the rawhide bone. The Avalanche Kid and I crawled up on a hole that was short, deep, and fast—and clear in the backcasting lane.

"I can't see any trout," he whispered.

"That's good. Most likely then, they can't see you either."

He crawled right into the water and sat back on his heels. I watched his jeans darken to the waist. Immediately he shivered.

"Now what?" he whispered.

I glanced up. We had sun for maybe five more minutes. I figured with the late-afternoon rays strong on his back, the kid could stay out of hypothermia for that long, at which point, under the sliding cloud cover, he could land a fly on fast water.

"Let's choose a fly," I said.

Staying carefully off the madstone, I kneed up beside him and opened my autumn fly box. There is always a moment here—over the open fly box—an epiphany for the non-fly fisherman, and I saw the kid have it. My autumn box was lined with neat rows of grass-hoppers, beetles, crickets, crayfish patterns, tiny mayflies, tricos, nymphs…my fly box was the one and only thing the Dog was neat about…and the kid sucked a breath in and moved his face closer. "That," he said after a long look. He pointed at a size twelve Stimulator. "I want to use that."

I tied on the Stimulator—green body, golden deer-hair wing—gaudy, but not a bad choice for a non-descript afternoon in late fall. The kid could probably cast it. He could probably see it on the water.

"I'll bet you like the Packers," I said, and he smiled, knowing I meant the colors of the fly.

"Yeah. Me and my dad. But my dad says he oughta be the general manager. He says they trade all the wrong guys, and they pay some guys too much."

A kingfisher chittered through the still air. We were halfway up the Yoder farm, and a dinner bell rang.

"You think trout like the Packers?"

He made a shivery little grin. "I hope so."

"Okay," I said, as the West Fork made a slow dissolve into shadow. "Like we practiced on the grass. Let's chuck that sucker up there."

Deuce Kussmaul took the rod from me and stripped out line. He raised the rod and worked it back and forth, spilling line out the tip, snagging water on both ends. "Elbow in," I said, "and stop the rod at ten and two o'clock."

Crudely, tongue bit between his bent front teeth, he got a false cast going. "Now drop it," I told him, and he slapped the rod to the water.

The fly lunged up and out at a crazy angle and landed in a dense patch of jewelweed on the opposite bank, and the kid muttered, "Crap…I never do anything right…"

"No," I whispered. "No, that's perfect. Wait a few seconds, then gently tug it off into the water."

The kid shivered hard. "Now?"

"Sure."

He raised the rod and tugged. The Stimulator crawled through the jewelweed like a fat, cold grasshopper, snagging up, pulling free, determined to end it all with a silly little plop! off the last jewelweed stem into fast, deep water.

Wham!—a little brookie took it.

The kid yelled and staggered to his feet, unsure what to do. The brookie raced around in a similar confusion, leaping and twisting in the top of the hole.

"Take the slack up," I told Deuce.

"How?" he begged me desperately.

"Grab the line with your left hand and pull it in."

Clumsily, he got tight to the fish. But then he kept stripping in. When the trout came to the end of the rod, he raised the rod and the fish thrashed madly a foot beyond the rod tip, while Deuce swung the whole situation into my face and yelled, "Get him, Dog! Get him!"

I had not before netted a seven-inch brook trout out of mid-air at head height with a defensive backhand swipe. But I did it for the Avalanche Kid. And for Eve, I guess. And for Annie Adams—and whoever really killed her.

The kid glowed as we sat on the bank, crunching the Funyuns and guzzling the Sun Drop Orange Eve had given us from the store before she had dropped us off and gone back to break into Uncle Roundy's silo. The brave little brook trout, tethered to a chunk of limestone, gasped and finned at our feet.

"So who *does* like trout," I was saying to Deuce, "since you want to kill him, but you don't want to eat him?"

"My mom."

"She does? How do you know?"

"She buys farm trout at the supermarket."

"You're kidding…"

"Because she says her brothers used to catch trout all the time in the creek. And she liked to eat what her brothers caught. But her family's in Kentucky now—because she had me. She don't ever see them."

Sensing an opening, I stepped a little further into his world, a little tighter to the bone. "But your mom's a part of your dad's family now, right? She's a Kussmaul?"

Deuce shrugged.

"And her sister's right here, in Avalanche, with your Uncle Salt Box. That must be nice for her."

Another shrug. I couldn't tell if he was bothered, or just ten years old and without the interest and vocabulary to discuss family issues.

"Does she talk to Rachel much?"

Wally brought his rawhide bone over—but not too close. Gnawing, he kept an eye on me.

"Naw," Deuce said. "Never. They yell at each other sometimes, when Rachel comes into the store because she forgot to buy something in town."

"What do they yell about?"

Shrug. "Rachel don't like our store's prices. She don't like the way my mom wears Amish stuff, when she ain't accepted in the Amish anymore. But then my mom says Aunt Rachel's got a big English mouth. And a big English butt."

He grinned.

"My mom's funny sometimes."

"Yeah," I said. "I noticed that."

We sat a while, crunching Funyuns and watching the little brookie get his spunk back.

"Okay. Well…but anyway, Deuce, do you know why your Uncle Half-Tim had to come into town and get me and your mom today? Do you know why we were in town in the first place? At the sheriff's office?"

"No."

"But you wondered?"

"Yeah. A little."

"I cut your Uncle Salt Box's fence. After you and Wally took off on me. I got charged with destroying property. And your mom climbed Uncle Roundy's silo to see what he's hiding inside. He nailed her for trespassing. We both got busted. We had to go and pay money to stay out of jail. We're supposed to go to court later."

I let that drift a little.

"See…Deuce…your mom and I were both trying to figure out why you did what you did with Annie."

No reply.

"Because when you kill someone, you need a reason. And you don't seem to have one. I'm sure," I said, though I wasn't, "that the sheriff's detectives are all thinking about that. Thinking about what could be your reason."

He stared at a half-Funyun in his dirty fingers. "Nobody liked her anyway."

"You did."

"That's a lie. I threw apples at her."

"That's what I mean. You liked her. And you liked her son. What's his name?"

"Robin. Robin hated her."

"He told you that? Last summer?"

Deuce shrugged and went silent for a long, cold stretch. He was shivering hard, but he would not let go of his pop can. I unpacked my rain coat and put it over his shoulders.

"You're a tough kid," I told him finally, meaning it. I saw him nearly look at me. "And I think you're honest too. I just don't know if you're tough and honest enough to tell the truth."

He flopped over suddenly and grabbed Wally by the leg. He pulled the puppy roughly into his lap and hung on while Wally, separated from his rawhide, whined and fought. I stood up. I got the bone. I settled things and sat back down beside the boy.

"What's in your Uncle Roundy's silo, Deuce?"

Sniffling, from under the raincoat: "Nothing."

"Just tell me the simple truth. I'll be careful with it. I promise. There's gotta be something in there."

"Pigeons."

"And?"

"Nothing."

"Then why is he keeping his silage on the ground this year?"

No answer.

"Why is the silo locked, top and bottom?"

Another shrug.

"That's where your mom is now, Deuce. At that silo. Cutting the locks off. She's got a shotgun with her. I think she might be a little...um...high, too, if you know what I mean."

"Of course I do," he said angrily. "She pops meth when she's uptight."

"She cares about you more than anything, Deuce. She thinks you're covering up for your Uncle Roundy. She's risking jail to find out what's in his silo."

"Nothing!"

His face had gone patchy with pale and hot streaks. His eyes sprung fierce tears.

"Nothing, I told you. Uncle Roundy closed it off because after my dad gave me that rifle, I was climbing up inside there, shooting pigeons, even though Uncle Roundy said it was too dangerous. So he locked it. He didn't want me to fall." He glared wetly at me. "That's it."

"I don't know if I believe that."

"I don't care if you believe it."

"Where'd you get the two-headed turtle?"

"Uncle Roundy."

"For what?"

"For nothing. Because nobody else ever gives me nothing."

"Your mom's there now. At Roundy's silo. We'll know soon if you're telling the truth."

"I am."

We sat there silently as late September afternoon fell in a hard, cold heap. I wondered what Eve would find in Uncle Roundy's silo. I wondered how well, how far, the kid could lie. How much savvy did he have? And why exert himself like this?

"So what's your reason then?" I asked him finally. "When people ask you why you shot Annie Adams, what do you tell them?"

Shrug.

"You mean you don't know?"

Shrug.

"You don't know…because you didn't kill her, Deuce. And who-ever is making you tell this lie didn't think to give you a reason to tell people. And you can't think of a good one on your own."

That hit something. The kid slid a glance at me. He grabbed the end of his trout leash and swished the little brookie back and forth. The fish, fully alive now, fought for its life, and Wally plunged in after it. Deuce caught the puppy up by the tail, hauled him out, whacked him hard.

"I did it to be one of the boys," he said finally, looking like he had just recalled something from the churning upset of his brain. "I wanted to be one of the Kussmaul boys. And I did it because killing Annie is what my dad and my uncles wanted me to do."

I challenged him: "That the shrink's idea."

"The hell's a shrink?"

"The doctor. The one the sheriff took you to see. That's what he said."

The boy flashed me a surly glare: "It wasn't a he."

"I'll take that as a—"

But some distant memory of fatherhood stopped the words in my throat. I would take that as a yes. The county's shrink gave him the "Kussmaul boys" idea. So be it. It was an enchanting idea, too. It was the kind of idea that tied up grad school loose ends and made the student loans seem worthwhile. I skipped ahead.

"Deuce…whatever offer, or threat, somebody's made you, I think you should give your mother a chance to match it. She's a strong woman. She's going to fight for you."

He made a snort.

"She believes in you, Deuce. She believes you're going to Heaven some day."

He raised his big Kussmaul brow and, fighting through a shiver, he fixed me with a heartfelt sneer of derision.

"Yeah. And she believes in Noah's Ark, too. And angels. And God made the world in six days."

"And you don't?"

"Hell no."

"Then how did the world get made?"

No answer. An Amish buggy clip-clopped in the distance. Up on the coulee wall ahead of us, a tree cracked, and something rustled through the cold slush of fallen leaves. The sky above us was woolen, moving fast.

"So how many days," I asked Deuce, "did it take to make the world?"

"About a gazillion. The world evolved."

"From what?"

"From dirt."

"But where'd the dirt come from?"

"From planets."

"Where'd the planets come from?"

"From asteroids. They collided with each other."

"What were the asteroids made of?"

"Rocks."

"Where did the rocks come from?"

He gave me a pitying look. "From *dirt*."

I nodded.

"Okay," I said. "But where did the dirt come from?"

He sat there a long time while the buggy clip-clopped and the leaves rustled in the dark. His final answer made my heart kink with a weird and tricky kind of joy.

"We gonna fly fish any more," the Avalanche Kid grouched at me, "or just sit here and talk about nothing?"

We worked upstream, casting into the cold, flowing slabs of cloud-gray water. I tied on my biggest, whitest fly, and the kid slung it every which way, stumbling over limestone riffles, slogging through weed beds, scrambling up the bank around dead-fall box elders and deep holes. Wally fervently worked the bank ahead of us, spooking any trout that might still be out feeding on a cold fall afternoon.

But that didn't matter. We moved. We covered water. We were there, and the kid began to lean on me in iffy water, let me hold him up through slippery patches, let me re-tie his fly, re-build his leader, re-tuck his elbow. But he needed all that less and less as we went.

"Here," I whispered, and on the deep, slow hole just short of Salt Box's fence, I tied on a sinking leech pattern called a Wooly Bugger. I shot it upstream for him. I helped him strip it back. When the big trout struck, I raised his arms to set the hook.

The kid whooped and staggered back. Wally yipped and worked his hind legs on the high bank, spraying grass. The fish made one of those big-trout tours of the hole, but Deuce had enough sense—and just enough arm strength—to set limits. "Oh, man," he kept muttering. "Oh, man."

"You're doing fine."

"Oh, man."

"Rod tip up."

"Oh, man."

"There you go."

"You gotta help me."

"You don't need help."

"Oh—"

And then, in mid-breath, in mid-joy, the line abruptly went slack. The big trout had broken off.

The kid stood there dripping, draped in sprung and useless line. I heard a choked sob.

"Nice job, Deuce…well done…"

He was suddenly furious. "Sonofabitch! You could have helped me!"

"No. You didn't need help. You were perfect. There was nothing you could have done different…"

"Yeah sure," he hissed through his teeth, and he hurled my rod to the bank. "I could never be born. Or I could be dead like Annie is."

For a long, dark moment, even Wally was still. Then, growing out of the distance, an ill-tuned four-wheeler approached. Soon the engine was revving behind us, the vehicle rooting, smashing through weeds. In a moment more, Eve pulled up on King's John Deere.

She cut the engine and stood, straddling the four-wheeler, scowling from me to the shivering child I had led into deep water. The four-wheeler ticked, overheated. From the smudge of defeat on Eve's face, I could tell she had found nothing in Uncle Roundy's silo. From the angry set of her jaw, I could see she was frustrated.

"Empty," she said. "I talked to his help. Roundy locked it to keep Deuce from falling inside there."

Teeth chattering, head down, Deuce sloshed out.

"Told you," he muttered as he shivered past me.

"Get your mom's fish," I said.

The kid wheeled angrily back. He rooted in the dark cold water for the string that held his brookie.

While we waited, Eve said, "Looks like you almost killed my son."

"No. No, I don't think so."

I stood my ground while she tried to meth-glare me down. I wouldn't go. "I don't think so," I said again. "I think he's more alive right now than ever."

Eve let out an exasperated sigh and lowered her shoulders. She reached into the cargo box behind her.

"It's about time for this," she said, and she held out a quart of whole milk in a carton.

I took it. I understood. For the madstone.

Then the three of us faced each other, silent, exhausted. But I felt we had won something. We had built something. We had hammered out one truth between us. We had narrowed things, scratched one Kussmaul off the list. We could work this out together—sort of. Maybe.

"Deuce," Eve said blankly. "Supper."

He grabbed Wally. He climbed on behind his mother, and as they ripped away across the Amish pasture, I felt something.

I felt the madstone drop off.

The wrong beaver

And the milk, with the madstone in it, boiled up a dull but certain green, just like Eve said it would.

So I *had* had rabies—an hour ago. And now I didn't.

I celebrated with a peanut butter-and-sugar sandwich on white bread and a heavy vodka-Tang. I ate outside, around a hot fire made out of Moth's free wood, thinking and watching frigid clouds pinken above the western coulee wall. I marveled that a kid as young as Deuce could lie so sturdily, could keep his channels straight. Of course there was one easy way to explain the tenacity of Deuce's story: the kid wasn't lying at all. As with his Uncle Roundy's silo, he was telling the truth. He *had* killed Annie Adams.

I still couldn't buy the idea.

Yet if I did buy it, I could leave.

Right?

I could be on the Big Two-Hearted by morning.

But what about Eve, and the trouble she was sinking into? And what about the little yellow brush up on Salt Box's place? And what about the wrong painting up on the bridge? How did these factors weigh-in against the kid's new credibility? And…what about Eve's credibility? Had I really had rabies? Was I really okay now?

So went my celebration.

I kicked my too-high fire, feeling cold sweat and heartburn. But after all, I decided, if I couldn't swallow the idea of Deuce telling the truth, I could at least, as an exercise, try to work it through. If Deuce, then, had shot Annie Adams off the bridge, there would be no surefire way of deciding precisely what had killed her: the fall, the bullets, and the water in Annie's lungs would all run together in the medical examiner's biochemical record. In that case—I mean, if the biochemical record was blurry—then the shooting and the death were simultaneous, and I had seen it, and no one was there to set up the phony painting scene on the bridge. The scene wasn't phony then. Deuce's story could be true.

But that still left the major question of why Annie Adams was painting the north side of the Amish barn from a bridge to the south—in the foggy dawn, yet. And the major additional question of why I had found her little yellow paintbrush upstream, on Salt Box's place. And why Salt Box's fence was cut. And why Annie's barn-painting sketchbook had suddenly turned to a blood knot, a fishing fly, and a dog.

The question rebounded, and an answer suddenly stiffened me in my chair: because the dead woman was talking, not to her husband, but...to me.

Like I hadn't known that already. Like I hadn't looked the other way.

I stood and circled my fire. Stick to the facts, I commanded myself. I had seen Annie Adams with the little yellow brush in her pocket the night before she died. It was already dark. She had nothing on her, that I could see, with which to cut a fence. She was buying candles and a snack. Would she then wade upstream, cut a fence somehow, without proper tools, and try to paint a barn—in the dark?

No.

But did that have to be the same little yellow brush?

No.

But was it likely that it wasn't the same little yellow brush as the one missing from her bib pocket?

No. It was almost certainly the same brush.

Then…could Annie have gone up to Salt Box's place, at night, with candles, for some other reason?

Sure. For a hundred other reasons.

I felt confused suddenly, overwhelmed and almost angry. I felt dizzy and hot. I moved back from the fire. My leg throbbed strangely, and I imagined a virus dance, tricos and blood knots jittering madly, a Rhabdo rhumba in my veins.

When I was on my third—or so—vodka-Tang, Howard Adams wobbled over, in his own cups, clearing his throat—again, again, once more—pulling his wife's little red wagon.

"Guy dropped this off," he managed as he approached the back side of the fire. He wheeled the wagon over by my lawn chair. "Can't recall his name. Guy that milks for Salt Box."

I leaned over. The wagon contained a fat, dead beaver, glossy and gut shot, missing a hind leg, baring its long orange teeth. Nice gesture, I thought—but it was the wrong beaver. The beaver that nailed me was bigger and had broken teeth.

"Thanks," I told the old man. "But take it back. It's not mine."

"No…wait a minute," dithered Howard Adams, not hearing me. "No. Yes I do recall his name. Abe. Salt Box's milker fella. Abe said you'd be wanting it. Said to tell you it looked just fine. Healthy. Said you could be on your way any time."

The creature looked dead—that was all. I lifted my eyes from the beaver to the man who had delivered it for Abe—for this stranger, this sudden Abe, who mysteriously cared about the Dog, who could go now. I found it all very interesting, in an ornery, three-vodka-Tang kind of way.

So I waited. 'Let the players play' was an old mantra from my Oglivie Secure days. I looked silently up from my ratty lawn chair. Howard Adams was short of stature anyway, but he seemed to have shrunken overnight. Shocks of wild gray hair challenged the air

above his spotted head. He wheeled the beaver over, dumped it in
the grass beside my picnic table. His hands shook.

"You ever lose someone?" he eked out.

My leg itched now, at the crests of the throbbing. I sure had, I
told him. I sure had lost someone.

Howard Adams wasn't really asking. He said, "You ever lose
someone, let me give you a tip." He staggered a bit. He cleared his
throat.

"Drink clear booze, Dog. Not brown." He hacked and spit.
"Not whiskey."

He wobbled close and put a shaky hand on my arm. He looked
down at me, and he waited for my full attention. Then he said,
"Dog…my friend…here's what I have to say…"

I waited.

"…on the subject…of whiskey…"

He took a deep breath.

"…fuck whiskey, Dog. You hear me? Fuck whiskey."

I didn't bother to tell the poor guy that the Dog had already
fucked whiskey—about five years ago, somewhere below the midpoint of my own aftermath. Drink vodka-Tang, I wanted to advise
him. It was good for you. Astronauts drank it. Well, half of it. But
what came out instead was, "Say again about the guy who brought
the beaver?"

He clutched at my sleeve, confused.

"I said there were two guys…two guys stopped by…"

"You didn't say that. But what guy dropped the beaver off?"

"Guy milks cows for Salt Box Kussmaul. Abe something. Rides
a bicycle. Lanky guy. Filthy as hell. Said to tell you that beaver looks
all hunky-dory."

I stared at the creature dead beside the picnic table. Wrong
beaver, I thought again. But the milk had boiled up green. I was
fine. Right?

"Who was the other guy that stopped by?"

Howard Adams had lost the thread. He cleared his throat. As
he turned away from me, I asked him again.

"Who was the other guy?"

"I told you. Abe something..." he muttered.

His face had darkened suddenly, even in the fire light. "Can't you hear?" He turned—"Jesus Christ, nobody listens"—and he shambled back through the thick grass. When he neared his own campsite I watched him pick an awkward little bit of momentum— like the terrain had tipped downward, though it hadn't—and I was certain that Annie Adams' drunk and widowed husband was going to stumble and pitch forward into the lame little smolder of a fire he had managed to start.

But he was taking a run at something—taking a run like an ancient place kicker at the back of the canvas lawn chair set up around the fire—and with a sloppy roar he swung his foot into it—"Agghhhh!"—and kicked it over into the fire.

I stood.

Then, still roaring, Howard Adams kicked the chair out of the fire. Then back in. Then he picked the chair up—forest green canvas smoking at one corner now—and he hurled it against the side of the teepee. I had wondered, of course, about the teepee—where an old white lady got such a thing—the authenticity of it all—and I guess I got some kind of an answer when the impact of a single lawn chair collapsed the structure to the right, and then Howard Adams, with a drunken, elderly rhino-rush, forced the thing—soft aluminum poles crooking wildly—to the ground.

Having stood, I had trailed toward him, thinking he was going to hurt himself and need help. He swung around and glared at me.

"What? What the hell do you want?"

I didn't have an answer.

"You think that's funny? Huh? Me living in a goddamn Camper Jack's teepee all goddamn summer? And for what? Huh? Pal? You got a reason for me? Why did I do this?"

He panted at me.

"Thirty-nine years behind the wheel of a goddamn truck, sleeping in a goddamn cab. I retire, I meet a woman, and what do I get? A Camper Jack teepee. 'We'll make lots of money on my barn painting,' she says."

He stomped ineffectively across the surface of the toppled tee-pee, stumbling on the lumps of clothes and camp gear inside. He fell hard—but that mess was a good place to fall.

"Bullshit!" he croaked. "Turns out she's obsessed. She's gotta be perfect. Takes her a whole goddamn week to paint one barn and then she gets five hundred bucks for it. That's a lot of money? Five hundred a week? Huh? I can haul Ding-Dongs to Weewahitchka for that kind of money. Hell—if I want real money, I'll truck smack. I'll truck weed. I'll drive wetback apple-pickers up to Washington."

Then he went after what had tripped him. He went after the lump beneath the "hide" of the teepee. He caught a seam and pulled it open with his hands. He flung out a menagerie of women's things—bras, hairbrushes, a cute purple cell phone, neatly balled socks, and then out—its plastic bag flapping noisily through the air—came the sketchbook he had showed me, the one with the blood knot, the trico, and the dog.

I don't know what I was thinking then—the Dog wasn't *thinking*, really, so much as absorbing, processing—but the mood-shift of Howard Adams was bothering me, was informing me somehow, and I knew that in his rage he had lost track of where I was. So I picked up the sketchbook and stuck it under the waistband of my pants, in the back, and let my jacket down.

"You're still standing there," he grumbled at me eventually, head down. "So what the hell do you want?"

"You're going to be okay," I said.

"What the hell do you know about it?"

"Quite a bit."

That snapped his head up. His sunken eyes nearly disappeared as he squinted at me.

"Meaning what? I loved Annie. You're saying I didn't? I'm griev-ing. You're saying I shouldn't take care of business, take care of what I need anyway? I don't know whether to kick your ass or shoot myself."

I nodded. "Right," I said. "That's all the stuff I know."

"Then why are you still standing there? Why don't you leave me alone?"

"Who was the other guy?"

"Huh?"

"You said there were two guys. One beside Salt Box's milker."

"I never said—" He stopped.

"Two guys," I said. "Think about it. Please."

He turned away, dug through the teepee mess, looking for something. On a whim I salvaged Annie's little purple cell phone from the grass at my feet. I turned it on and hit the directory.

"Abe Borntrager," I said, reading from the display before I dropped the phone into my pocket.

Howard Adams looked up. "Huh?"

"The milker. Dropped off the beaver. His last name is Born-trager."

"Yeah. Yeah, that's it."

"He happen to know your wife?"

"Naw."

"You then?"

"Naw. Nothing to do with him."

I nodded. More than mood was shifting now.

"And this second guy, he came with Abe?"

"Okay…yeah…naw…let's see…the goddamn Humane Society of Vernon County…wasn't it? Some sissy kid, a while earlier, climbs over that fallen-down tree up there, telling me he got a call from Annie about animals abused around Avalanche and he was there to follow up. I said, 'Animals? My wife is dead, asshole.'"

He lurched up, suddenly purposeful. He found his tin whiskey cup in the grass and shook the ants out. Then he went looking for something else. But the Adams' were messy campers. Beneath the tin-roofed shelter, their Coleman stove was awash in cottonwood leaves. Howard Adams' fly rod was mixed into a bedlam of dirty dishes atop the picnic table. Their vast supply of firewood should have been neatly under the tin roof, where Moth Kussmaul had stacked it, but it was spilled out into the grass—and the erratically bereaved old man stumbled through it. He found their water jug finally, behind an overturned chair on the back corner of the shelter, but the jug had dripped itself empty, making a mud pit with two neat wagon tracks through it. Howard Adams cursed again—"Asshole…"—and staggered off toward the bathroom.

I stepped up, cautiously, into the remains of his ruined world. Annie's little painting wagon had been pulled through the mud puddle. But not today. Earlier enough that the mud had hardened. Maybe that was something. I looked further. Under the shelter, behind the first picnic table, on a second table, Annie Adams stored her painting gear. Stacked in a peach crate were a half-dozen paintings of the Amish barn. Quickly, I flipped through them. As far as I could tell, they were finished—*A. Adams* in the far corner, with a date. She kept her paint tubes in a Rubbermaid tub, and her brushes in Mason jars clogged with murky thinner.

I turned out toward the ruined teepee. Revealed now in the blank space behind it stood a trailer, retired from U-Haul and painted lavender, with *Annie Adams, Barn Painter* drawn in kitschy green script on the side. The trailer's tongue was propped on a chunk of firewood. The door was combination-locked.

I gimped over to the window of the couple's silver mini van. Another mess—and I felt abruptly saddened as I lifted out a rumpled handful of what turned out to be invoices for paintings. The paintings had names like *King Midas 45, Salt Box 270, Round Barn 90.* And Barn Lady was getting about five hundred apiece. Or he was. It was his name, Howard Adams, signing received on the invoices.

I set the papers back on the cluttered dash. One or both of the Adams smoked weed—a roach clip in the ashtray. Howard Adams had left his wallet on the dash too—a thing so fat with life-litter it weighed-in like a softball. I took few random pulls at the scraps inside. Business cards from framing shops. A Wal-Mart receipt for paper plates. A school photo of a boy, about ten, Deuce's age, in a Green Bay Packers jersey. *Robin, fifth grade*—written in ballpoint on the back. The kid was sixteen now, Detective Vossteig had told me. I wondered: had anyone reached Robin Adams yet?

And then, inside my pocket, Annie's cute purple cell phone began to warble. Maybe—hopefully—this was the son, I thought. Checking in with his mother finally. The phone call of the poor kid's life.

I pulled the phone out. But the digital letters jittering across the screen read *Borntrager...Abe*. And so the ground kept shifting. Annie did know the milker. Didn't she?

"Hello?"

The voice that came back was drawly, slow, and nasal—but Abe Borntrager was not the least bit surprised to hear a male voice answer Annie's number. Of course, I thought—because Annie was dead now. Abe Borntrager thinks I'm Howard.

"I got my oil, and now I'm up here looking at this darn oak like we talked about. I know you wanna stick with your own vehicle, but it's gonna be two-three days before I can cut you out."

"Hmmm," I stalled. Eve had felled the Avalanche Oak after Annie Adams had died.

"So," continued Abe Borntrager, the milker, "I ain't supposed to drive, and folks around here know my truck. I done drove it through enough of their fences." He made a little *heh-heh*. I gave it back. *Heh-heh*. "So what I'm saying is tomorrow sometime we just get Salt's or King's pickup and we transfer 'em."

"Hmmm."

"That a yes you're giving me, partner?"

"Yes."

"Hunky-dory, then," he said. "Heh-heh. Hunky. Plus dory. Get it?"

My leg itched like hell. "Got it," I lied. "Heh-heh."

Abe Borntrager hung up. A moment later, Howard Adams emerged from the bathroom smoking a cigarette, drinking water. I gave him a nod and limped off as quickly as I could.

Up at the top of the campground drive, I found the milker still standing there beside a spilled-over bicycle, sizing up the Avalanche Oak. Abe Borntrager was lanky and dirty. He must have ridden the balloon-tired bike with no hands, because he dangled a jug of chainsaw oil in one loose fist, a chainsaw in the other. He spat tobacco juice and smiled at me with sparse, unkempt teeth.

"Gotcher beaver now?"

"Yeah. Thanks."

"Heard a feller say once that trusting Amish medicine was like trusting an Amish auto mechanic. Get it?"

I nodded. I got it.

"That beaver looks real healthy and all, but I thought you oughta have him…"

"Thanks."

"Ain't nothing to shoot a rat the size of a god dang pig."

He spat brown juice into the tangle of the fallen Avalanche Oak.

"Thissun job here, though's, gonna be a bitch."

He swung an appraising steel-toe—*clunk*—at the trunk.

"Two-three days," he said. "On the short side. I get weather and all."

I looked the milker carefully up and down. He had barn all over him. He looked like barn, he smelled like barn, and he moved in fluidly among the oak limbs, big hands first, like he was going to milk a cow.

"Yep," he grunted. "See, the trunk's all buggy-whipped around in there. Grain's twisted. That's tough on a saw. And acourse people been nailing whatnot to her for about a hundred years. Must be dozens of iron spikes in there. So I'm gonna have to be all surgical if I ain't gonna ruin my saw."

I nodded, my mind elsewhere. Salt Box's milker, I was thinking. Ex-husband of the girlfriend of Cousin Lightning Rod. Concerned about my health. With the wrong beaver. With Annie Adams' cell phone number. With a cell phone of his own. Transferring something tomorrow. Referring to the trucks of Salt Box and King Kussmaul. Interesting guy—this Abe Borntrager. Connected. Busy. Eve and I needed to talk him over.

I said, "But you can get started with that chainsaw now?"

"Naw," he replied. "Not today. Losing light already. But I hadda just come down and look it over, study on it. That's just how I'm put together. I like to study on a thing. Now I gotta get back and milk."

I nodded. I would talk to Eve later, I had suddenly decided. I had my evening planned now. I had to shake off the vodka-Tang. I had to see inside Salt Box's barn. Inside Abe Borntrager's illegal barn apartment.

"Yeah?" I asked him. "And how long's the milking take you?"

Abe Borntrager studied up at the sky. The cloudy pinkness had leadened and slumped down behind the western bluff, setting ridge-top trees in sharp relief. The air had dropped ten degrees as we talked. He looked back at me, shot some Red Man juice to the side.

"Oh," drawled the milker. "'Til about dark-thirty."

About dark-thirty

I had a little under an hour, then, to penetrate the salt box barn, where Abe Borntrager stayed in his hayloft apartment—the apartment that broke housing code, I imagined, and snuck beneath the tax radar...though I couldn't imagine how those were things to kill over.

I loaded my Glock, dropped batteries into my flashlight, and grimaced my way back into frigid chest waders. Sneaking up the West Fork was the surest way. I would stay out of sight below the banks. At the line between the Amish place and Salt Box's land, I would cut the fence again. I would come up the creek side of the farm. I would slip past the milker—I pictured him with head down into a cow's flank, elbows cocked, hands deftly pumping teats—and into his upstairs room, where I would find...what? I couldn't guess, and the uncertainly hollowed me. I felt too alone as I shoved off from the Cruise Master. As I moved upstream away from the campground, I once more called up the directory on the dead woman's little cell phone, scrolled until I found the Avalanche Mercantile. I surprised Eve with a call, intending to tell her my plan. "Don't call me again," she broke in quickly, her voice low and breathless. "King had kind of a bad night at..."

There was a long pause, her palm squeaking like Styrofoam on the phone. Finally she came back. "But if the light is on in the top right window of the second floor, then King is...um...out...and it's okay to come over and talk to me."

The famous salt box barn was a lot less than I anticipated. I guess I expected the structure to punch me in the eye, the way Salt Box himself would have liked to do. But the barn was a long, simple, gable-roofed rectangle, its only design variation being the asymmetry caused by one roof line, on the northern side, having been extended nearly down to touch the hoof-chewed mud of the barnyard. Or no. I looked more closely at the roof extension and the barn space under it. No seams. No jump to new materials. Not extended. The barn was originally built, then, as a salt box in the first place, probably in anticipation of foul winter weather out of the north coulee. I guessed that this forethought in design meant a lot to the likes of barn fans like Annie Adams.

But I shrugged it off. I felt for a moment the impatience a Kussmaul might feel at all the hoopla around a simple, damn barn. It kept the hay dry, kept rain off cows' backs. They shit in it. I moved closer. I crouched below a window on the short, north side, looking in to get a second disillusionment. Salt Box's milker wasn't buried head-down in cow flanks, as I had imagined. As I saw him through the grimy window, Abe Borntrager was upright, moving clamps and hoses and shuffling cattle. He milked by a noisy machine. His mouth was moving too, chewing, spitting, talking back to callers on a fire-and-brimstone radio show emanating from a tiny transistor atop a hay bale.

His apartment was nothing to sneak into. The entrance was from the outside, by a 2x6 stairway nailed up parallel to the long-eaved east end, opposite the house. No one could see the milker come and go. And his door was wide open. His light was on. All I had to do was climb the steps...leg throbbing badly now...and I was in.

Habits are funny. I popped the fridge first. Miller Genuine Draft—one lonely can, opened and half-gone. Plus a pack of cold-cut head cheese, a jar of ranch dressing, a jar of barbeque sauce, and a carton of night crawlers.

The floor was filthy, barn-like. But above that level Abe Borntrager was exactingly neat. Beside the tautly made bed, on the up-turned crate he used for a night stand, he kept a Bible, and he hid a pistol on the floor, inside the left boot of a pair of green galoshes, lined up with the floor boards exactly where a man's hand could reach from the bed. I turned on his television, all spanking–new, thirty-five-inch, nine-hundred bucks worth of Panasonic brilliance. Salt Box's milker paid for full-channel satellite. I pumped through a half-dozen porn channels, and then, for a long, strange moment, I hesitated over a guy gutting a deer, speaking what could have been Russian. I turned the TV off. The milker's desk was clean except for a cell phone charger.

I pulled a drawer. Locked. And the Dog was rusty. It took me a whole fifteen seconds to spring the latch, and during those fifteen seconds I felt an equally rusty hunch that Abe Borntrager studied on more than fallen trees. The peculiar evidence of his life, neat and dirty at the same time, gave off a feeling I recognized. And the contents of the first drawer only strengthened my hunch: bro-chures, advertisements, research—Abe Borntrager was looking into digital. Cameras, zooms, printers, laptops, software. But he hadn't gone there yet.

As the second drawer popped open, I caught a whiff of photo paper, and I saw I was right.

Abe Borntrager studied on a thing all right. Oglivie Secure had nailed a dozen studiers like him. Abe Borntrager was a peeper.

I widened the drawer. He had the old-school, basic poor-man's tools: binoculars and a Polaroid camera, which used together made a cheap telephoto. The self-developing Polaroids, of course, bypassed the need for photo-shop processing. And Borntrager displayed the peeper's classically exact version of library science. His photos were organized in a shoe box inside the drawer. His first and favorite subject was unmistakably—though I hadn't met her—Eve's sister,

Salt Box's wife, the woman living conveniently in the house next to the barn. He studied on her quite a bit: Rachel Kussmaul.

Traces of both her sister Eve and her husband Salt Box jumped from the thin-faced, intense-eyed, over-fed young woman whom the milker had secretly photographed. And Abe Borntrager had a bit of talent, as talent runs in peepers. He had caught Rachel Kussmaul bending over to water store-bought flowers; and straining with split skirt, with too many packages, out of a new, forest-green Ford Ranger; and in sweatshirt and underpants, tiptoeing to nail up a gaudy painting to the living room wall; and tank-topped, fleshy and sweating, steering a John Deere mower through a green slalom of ceramic buck, doe, and fawn.

I raised up, listened for the milking machines. Still going, clanking and hissing over the faint buzz of the radio talk show. Something nagged me. I knew peepers. I knew their tenacity. Their obsession. Their perfectionism. I knew Abe Borntrager could do better.

I turned back to the drawer. To the rhythm of the milk machines beneath me, I flipped onward through the milker's gallery of sordid, half-assed photos. Poor Rachel Kussmaul didn't fit with English ways. Her hips and bust had exploded, her complexion veered to an exacerbated, sun-burned rash, and her sexuality, as she wrestled with it, kept lunging out of her control and into the cheap lens of Abe Borntrager's camera. Cleavage at the wrong time. Butt sweat from the mower seat. A forgotten button after breastfeeding. All of it building a kind of painful tension in me, a rage at Borntrager coupled with a wish that Eve's big sister could just break through, get comfortable, show the creep who lurked in her barn a moment of womanly grace and beauty...

And then the floor fell out on Rachel Kussmaul. Toward the back of the shoebox file, Abe Borntrager, in his grimy, molesting diligence, had scored big. And I wondered, suddenly, what kind of peeper he was. There were kinds, I remembered. Different impulsions.

I moved the photo into better light. From the squat shadows on the patio stones, I could tell that the scene was early afternoon, mid-summer. Rachel Kussmaul, packed into a blue bikini, sunned herself on a white wicker chair. Her wine cooler sweated on a white wicker table. The angle on her was a peeper's dream, the kind of inelegant angle that makes you wince and croak the word *crotch*. But the photo's incriminations spread much wider than Rachel's chubby, sun-burned thighs. Her cigarette was the fat kind, the illegal kind, with twists at both ends, and her brother-in-law King Midas stood over her, in cutoffs and t-shirt, reaching down with a lighter to spark the joint, his spine curved like a guy landing a trout. The hand of Salt Box's wife went up, as if to steady King Midas, grabbing him by the...and again that word...by the *crotch*.

I looked up and tried for a cleansing breath. Incrimination— that was one of the peeper types. The peeper who peeped and then leaked what he had on file, wanted something in order to keep things secret. That felt like a long shot, but the way the Rachel-King collection ended right there gave me an equally certain feeling. Abe Borntrager had stopped there. Why? Needing nothing else? Having enough leverage? For what?

I put the picture back in its shoe-box Dewey Decimal position. Salt Box's milking machines throbbed through the floor. I checked the sky beyond the open door. It was dark-fifteen. I ought to go.

But I had to see what else the milker was up to. Rushing, I pawed ahead through the dozens—the hundreds—of cheap, stiff photographs. Abe Borntrager got around. He studied on a lot of things. He spent a lot of time around the campground bathroom, catching bare feet under the door of the shower stall. But that went nowhere. He had stalked Ma Kussmaul out of a slumping clapboard farm house to a chipboard-sided privy—and there, feeling far too squeamish, I grabbed a chunk of photos and lunged ahead...to find Annie Adams, painting from a little hump of sand, mid-stream in the West Fork, the Amish barn in the distance. So she had been up on Salt Box's land, painting south toward the Amish barn. In the milker's picture, Annie had the little yellow paint brush tucked behind her left ear. I hesitated a moment—did I dare remove an item from the collection?—then I slipped the picture into my pocket. So Annie would and could and did defy Salt Box and go up there. She wasn't the kind of person to suddenly slack off, paint a north view from the south. Not Annie Adams. Everything mattered to Annie. Her husband had been right.

The milking machines still thrummed downstairs. I ticked forward through the photographs. The milker liked Annie Adams, too. On hot days, she was generous with her wobbly old flesh. And the milker, I imagined, had the cover of stream noise. And, probably, Annie painted with incredible focus—no less dialed-in than a fly fisherman—in a state of mind nothing like the bubbly, wise-ass awareness she carried around for her dealings with the Kussmauls. Nothing like the goofy, child-like provocateur who kept messing up the blood knot and watching for the Dog's reaction.

But what—now—was Annie painting? I flipped back. She was turned away from the Amish barn. The milker now studied on Annie's humped little back, through angelica stalks, at some remote place beside the West Fork, and her subject was obscured by the angle and the streamside brush.

I flipped forward—more photos. Abe Borntrager and his Polaroid had pried at Annie's subject over a long period of days, trying to get around the painter's back and into the little copse of dogwood and Virginia creeper that sheltered the subject she put to canvas. For a long moment I started at an oddly streaked series of Polaroids—until I realized that a breeze had whipped them over into brush before they could dry. But Borntrager had hung in there. Eventually he tried for a Norman Rockwell—tried to get the painter's subject from the canvas itself—but Annie's head, arms, shoulders, and shadows…he never got more than a black-and-pink blur, framed in green. In one ruined photo, the peeper's fist had come down in the gel, spreading the unfixed chemicals in frustration.

But I was getting a vague, uncomfortable sense of Borntrager's research topic. In one picture, a lamb tottered toward the milker. In the inadvertent foreground of another, a white Amish kapp lay in the ground ivy beside a delicate and dusty pair of black hook-and-eye boots.

I kept that picture too. I closed the drawer.

In the final drawer, the bottom one, the milker had a single shot of Barn Lady's lavender trailer, padlocked. He had three business cards paperclipped to the photo. I laid them out. I had thrown away the first card once myself, my first day or so in Avalanche, frustrated after shopping for Harvey's bent-hickory rocking chair. The second card was for Kussmaul Farms, Salt Box's place. Abe Borntrager had clipped beneath that a fancy card, thick and buff:

RIVERSIDE GALLERY
FINE CONTEMPORIES
317 W. RIVER RD.
SAINT PAUL, MN
RAUL LUNDQUIST, PRESIDENT
612-555-2346

I flipped it over. The back of the card said, in ballpoint: *Rachel, I'm interested, call me anytime.*

I turned the card over, and over again. *Rachel, I'm interested.* I found a pen and copied the dealer's name and number. Now I had to see Eve. I closed and locked the drawers. I stepped back outside.

The West Fork murmured quietly through the deep, still coulee. Cattle sighed in the barn below. I heard Borntrager move beneath me into a far corner of the barn. A door closed and water ran. It was just dark-thirty.

And she was blocking my way down the stairs: Eve's big sister, Abe Borntrager's model, Salt Box's wife...Rachel Kussmaul.

Nasty Dog

"You're lucky Salty's at horseshoes," was the first thing Eve's big sister told me. She looked up with a half-scowl, half-tremor, the way people do when they're outraged and frightened at the same time.

"Whoever you are, you're lucky all the Kussmaul boys are at horseshoes."

She held some kind of a dessert on a small white plate. Scrunch, we used to call it: oatmeal and brown sugar, baked on top of apples, or peaches, or rhubarb. I could smell the butter and cinnamon. From above, looking down on her, I could see that Rachel had scrunched herself up to about twice Eve's weight. But this dessert had been headed for Abe Borntrager, Rachel's personal photographer. And that made a small and sick kind of sense. If he was bribing her, maybe that would shut him up for a while. *Dessert.*

"Abe's not in," I lied. "He must have gone down to get his beer."

This threw her off balance. I watched her struggle to respond.

"You came across our property," was her eventual answer. "There's no vehicle in the driveway, and you've got waders on. You just waltzed in here across our pasture."

"I don't dance," I said. "I especially don't waltz."

"And you don't make me laugh, either. You don't know how lucky you are that Salty's not here."

I nodded at her gift for Abe. "You too," I said, "is my guess."

That blushed her. Bringing dessert to a man's room—her husband gone—a man who had a secret on her. Now she was all scowl and fury. She looked more like Eve—except for the chubby cheeks and overstuffed pants. I tried to picture Eve's hair as the same wavy, buttery blonde, but it didn't work.

"That looks like scrunch," I said.

"It's Razzle Dazzle Dessert."

"Amish recipe?"

"I don't have to tell you anything." She glared at me. "What do you want?"

I took a few steps down to see if she would move aside. She didn't. For a moment I thought to show her my Glock. Sometimes fear pressed just the right buttons, shook loose all the answers. Maybe I could point a pistol at Rachel Kussmaul and she would tell me everything—whatever everything was—and my confusion and ignorance and obligation would all drop away in one magical moment and I would be on my way up north to the Big Two-Hearted.

But maybe, I reconsidered, the Glock was way too much. Maybe—as it often was—the everything she had to tell was nothing. I didn't know enough to know. But Rachel Kussmaul could be toyed with. Abe knew that. She thought she could tuck and smooth and ride things out. Wasn't that the meaning of the dessert?

Instead of the Glock, then, I put this out: "I just had a message for Abe."

She waited. I worried Borntrager would finish washing up and find me on his stairway.

"Tell him to tell the other guy, the art guy, that I'm interested too."

I watched her face. As bluffs go, mine was technically a weak one, but I could tell I had read Rachel Kussmaul correctly. Abe's picture of her and whatever the art dealer wanted were linked. Rachel was furious that I seemed to know that. But while she had Eve's nose for a fight, she didn't know what came next. She hadn't been there a hundred times before, like Eve had. Rachel Kussmaul had left the Amish to be comfortable. And she almost was.

"Oh...you..." she began to splutter. She backed off the steps and fumbled a cell phone from a back pocket. But apparently Salt Box, at horseshoes, was off the grid. "Oh...you...big...son of a...bull!"

"Ouch."

"You...nasty...ass!"

"Nasty Dog," I said.

She glared at me. Puffy, comfy, I thought, watching the young woman's face swell with all the poisons that scrawny Eve burned off in her meth jags. As some women could be, some wanna-be-cozy women with their true selves buried inside like land mines, Rachel Kussmaul was deadly.

"Oh," I said, "and tell Abe one more thing."

Rachel Kussmaul waited. I had a hunch—more than a hunch— that a woman like Rachel Kussmaul would hate a woman like Annie Adams. For the moment, for the Dog, as Eve's big sister stood in the barn yard below me, Rachel Kussmaul might as well have been naked. And I saw it was soft and messy in there. It was treacherous.

I gave her the message as I passed.

"Tell Abe," I said, "wrong beaver."

Action in the dark Amish barn

Wading back, heading for Eve at the Avalanche Mercantile, I noticed that the lanterns were snuffed out inside Freeman Yoder's house. From the stream bed, the Amish home looked dark and cold and silent—and the barn beside it looked twice as desolate. The Amish got a lot of things right, I thought. No cars. No phones. No credit cards. No televisions. No late night show. The sun went down, and the Amish went to bed.

Except for the light I saw suddenly flicker high in the haymow of the barn. I steered, sore-legged, to the bank of the stream and lit a Swisher. My news and questions for Eve could wait a little while—especially if there was action in the dark Amish barn.

I smoked and watched. The light was weak and variable, but it stayed on. It flickered, I thought, like firelight.

I doused the Swisher. I sat and took my waders off. On Amish land, I figured, even under cover of night, there was no room for the *swish-swish* of Gore-Tex. I stashed the waders in a dogwood thicket. I put my wader boots back on. I headed for Yoder's barn.

But as I left the cold stream breeze into Yoder's pasture, I smelled something fetid. And then I heard something—the grunt and crash, I calculated, of a scuttling possum.

I turned. I shined my flashlight. Possum, all right, and the gore-jawed scavenger hadn't fled far. The hunk of carrion in the tall grass was too good to abandon. I trained my light over the bloody mass: a dead lamb.

I stared down the beam of my flashlight, piecing thoughts together, getting myself all worked up. But the farm world was full of lambs, I told myself. And coyotes. The scene before me meant nothing. Creatures died everyday, for a million reasons. Still, I couldn't shake the image of the lamb in the milker's picture, gamboling away from whatever subject Annie was putting on canvas. And I couldn't help making connections to the Kussmaul complaints of missing animals, and to Annie's plea to the Humane Society. Was this one of those creatures? How could I know?

Soon enough, the possum got over my light and waddled back in, showing its drooling, blood-flecked jaws. The creature rooted at the lamb's gut, stuck its snout inside a neat, hairless split that spilled a smear of entrails over matted vetch and clover. I studied that split a moment. It looked shaved. But maybe lambs were hairless there in the first place. City Dog—what did I know?

I turned the flashlight off. To get the taste out, I lit a second Swisher. I took three pulls and doused it.

Then I moved on, reviewing my approach. Freeman Yoder's was a straight-up, two-story bank barn, Norwegian style, with limestone stable walls, a drive-in, second-level threshing floor and, above that, a haymow on both ends. My friend in Black Earth, Melvina "Junior" O'Malley—the one who kicked me out for defending myself against her father's fit of Alzheimer's—had taught me all the terms. A farm girl, an original Black Earthling as she put it, Junior had romanced me with local history and rural architecture, in those blissful weeks before our collapse.

I slid the heavy door twelve inches and squeezed in, looking around, using the flashlight again, muted against my palm. Freeman Yoder made his furniture in a long, narrow room off the threshing floor. The room was fragrant with drying curls of planed hardwood. On the threshing floor around me sat neatly arranged burlap sacks of grain. I dipped a hand into an open sack and laughed silently at

myself. More city Dog. I couldn't say what grain it was. Below me—
I lifted a trap door and shined my flashlight down—Yoder's dairy
herd slumbered peacefully. There was a brief moment when I tipped
out of reason and yearned to be Amish. It had to be easier, somehow,
more pure and more peaceful, less fraught with the dissonance of
modern life. If I were Amish, I thought, I would be sleeping right
now, with my family. I would be dreaming of big pumpkins, full
pails of milk, and my Saturday night washtub bath on the kitchen
floor. Certain bad things could never have happened.

But I shook it off. That life, if it was real at all, was a million
turns ago. I stirred myself into action, and I was climbing the ladder
into the stream-side haymow toward the flickering light when the
scramble and clatter began.

Voices hissed. Straw chafed. *Bump-bump-bump* went something down the outside of the barn. I slipped my hand in my jacket
pocket. I touched my Glock and waited a long, still minute. Finally, far away—near the creek, I guessed—an engine started up,
idled precariously for a few moments, then skulked away—neither
a beater like King's John Deere, or a massive, fine-tuned beast like
Salt Box's Yamaha. Five speeds, modest engine size, with a body
rattle that the driver was trying to keep quiet by staying well under
the engine's red line.

On another hunch, remembering the pretty teenage girl who
sunbathed, who shopped in Lingerie, I called up, "Dorcas?"

Nothing. Straw shifting.

"It's Dog," I said. "We were at Wal-Mart together. I'm not here
to get you in trouble."

I took the last ten rungs through the square hole into the loft.
I smelled smoke. I turned my flashlight on.

"Oh!" said Dorcas Yoder.

And, from inside her cozy little cave of hay, she gave me a
big, false, gorgeous, hunky-dory smile. And wasn't that what Abe
Borntrager had said? Hunky-dory? I turned the light off. As a shifting piece of girl-shaped darkness around me, Dorcas was large and
fragrant. She smelled like crushed mint from the stream bank. She

had broad shoulders, was almost my height. I spoke to her calmly as she replaced the white kapp over her long hair.

"What are you doing, Dorrie?"

Out of the dark, voice quivering, she answered, "Now? Do you mean right now what am I doing?"

"Yeah, pretty much."

"Well…I…Why are you asking me?" Then her voice recovered. "What are *you* doing?"

"Picking up where Annie left off. I'm snooping in your barn."

"You'd better not let my Pa catch you in here without him knowing."

I hit her like I had just hit Rachel Kussmaul: "I'm guessing that makes two of us."

I turned the light back on and watched the blushing girl close the shutters around the point where her father had extended the hay fork track outside. Two candles smoked on a thick, sawed beam above her head. On a quilt at her feet was a can of lemon-lime Sun Drop, a Hostess cherry pie, and a pair of battery-operated hair clippers. I stared at those a long time, wondering. Then I noticed that the soda can, opened, rested wetly atop a fold of white papers that looked like internet printouts.

"Well," said Dorcas Yoder, "I don't mind telling you exactly what I'm doing. It's Thursday, so I work for Half-Tim up at the tri-county farm. I take care of Ma Kussmaul while he goes to school. It's pretty easy. I just adjust the TV antenna, cook stuff, help her go outside to potty. I do it three afternoons a week until nine o'clock, and I just now got home."

She acted like that settled it.

"Home to the hay loft?" I said. "That's where your Pa expects you to be? And you work until nine, but it's still not eight-thirty? You're telling me a story."

She gave me a sassy look. "You know, here's the story my friend Eve tells me about you." I let her go ahead. "My friend Eve says you wear the same clothes every day. She says you wear the same hat every day. She says you never take a hot shower."

She waited for the rise. I didn't give her one. I was guilty as charged. She would have to kick the Dog in a different spot.

"And now," she went on, "I find out that you think everything I do is your business, even though I'm sixteen. Are you sure you're not related to my father?"

Maybe I was, I told her.

The girl tried to make an unpretty face and nearly succeeded.

In some way, I said, I probably was like her father, in the way I was worried about her, at this particular moment.

She rolled her stunning brown eyes. "Why is everyone always worried about me?"

"Who else is worried?"

"Everybody…"

"Is Eve worried?"

"Especially Eve. She says I'm going to get the ban, just like her. Get shunned. But I don't really care. I want to drive a car. I want to go to college. The ban looks good to me. So why should I worry?"

I glanced around the loft—the candles, the snacks, the quilt. A lover, I guessed. But I still couldn't make sense of the hair clippers. "I think Eve misses her family," I said. "They only talk to her to tell her Deuce was an evil mistake and she's going to Hell. Does that sound like fun?"

"No." She glared down at the hay. "It sounds like Eve."

"You don't believe Eve?"

I gave Dorcas Yoder a minute to work this through. She twisted her slender fingers in the pleats of her black dress. She sighed.

"Yes," she said quietly. "I believe Eve. But have you heard of Rumspringen?"

I told her I hadn't.

"It's a time when Amish kids get to be a little wild and their parents look the other way. My brothers got to do it. But I'm a girl, so I don't. No Rumspringen for me. Working three part-time days a week with a crazy old English lady is enough for my father. So I'm making my own Rumspringen."

"Is that how Eve got mixed up with King Midas? Her own little Rumspringen?"

"Maybe…"

"There might be a reason that the rules are different for girls." She looked up at me. "We have babies?"

"Maybe."

"That's not fair."

"I didn't say it was."

"You are just like my father."

"I doubt it," I said this time. "Nobody loves like a father."

"Then you're just like Half-Tim," she said. "'You should think about this, Dorrie. You should think about that, Dorrie.' Like he's God almighty with all my answers and not some greasy-haired, twenty-two-year-old English lump, living with his mother and pooping in an outhouse."

I couldn't help a little grin. There were parallels. "You mean, like I'm a greasy-haired forty-something English lump, living in a trailer, pissing in the grass, and telling you what to do?"

"A little like that, yeah."

"I don't mean to tell you what to do, Dorrie. What I'm trying to do is help Eve, and Deuce."

She took that silently. I turned my flashlight down and put a Polaroid photo under it. She released a little gasp.

"Was that you, Dorrie, that Annie Adams was painting down by the creek?"

She shook her head, kapp strings flapping. No…Then, Yes. Yes, it was her. That was her kapp, her shoes in the grass.

"You took things off?"

"Just a little bit."

"Did your father find out?"

"Someone told him," she said weakly. "Some jerk tried to make him pay money to get the paintings back."

"*Paintings*…" I had to make sure she understood. "Not photographs, like this one?"

"We did six paintings."

"Because…?"

"I…we…Annie wanted to make gifts…for…people…she knows…"

"Did Annie know how much trouble you'd be in?"

"I didn't tell her."

"But someone told your father? Who?"

"I don't know."

"And your father…"

"Went straight to Annie. And Annie sassed him at first, the way she liked to do with bossy men. But then he explained about how Amish can't have pictures. She changed her mind and wanted to burn the paintings, but her husband wouldn't let her, because once he heard that paintings were against Amish rules, he figured they were worth money. Annie and Howard had a huge fight. My father started watching me closer, and Annie and I never talked again. Annie felt horrible. She started telling people she had ruined my life."

"Did she?"

Dorcas Yoder shrugged—beautifully—and the Dog, seeing the aching loneliness to the way she turned her palms out, felt a motion in the gut. "I don't care!" she cried. "Doesn't anybody get that? If my Amish life is ruined, I don't care. It's a big world out there!"

That was true enough, I thought. It was a big world out there. And yet it was totally false, too. The world was huge and tiny at the same moment. The Dog's trout bum world, ostensibly, was boundless and free, any middle-aged man's darkest and most thrilling fantasy—and yet it was no more spacious, no more disencumbered, than the cluttered confines of my skull. The world could narrow real fast. Just like it had narrowed for teenaged Eve…who must have thought, for at least at one small moment, that she could marry royalty, escape family, become Queen Midas.

So I didn't lecture Dorrie. Hunky-Dorrie. That was what Abe Borntrager meant. Dorrie as a hunk of forbidden, exotic meat. I didn't ask Dorrie who had thump-thumped down the side of the barn as I came up the loft ladder. Some young buck. I thought of

Eve ten years ago. I thought of Dorcas ten years hence. Was there a Kussmaul—the worldly and dashing Lighting Rod, for example—courting her? But I held my tongue, and Dorrie thanked me for the silence, reaching out to offer me a sip of her Sun Drop. We stood together, listening to the pigeons coo in the rafters and the mice rustle in the straw.

"I saw you this morning," I said after a while, "on that high rock over Salt Box's pasture, shaking out a beach towel."

"I was sunbathing. Up on the bluff. Ma Kussmaul's morning shows were on, and I had at least an hour."

"Sunbathing…" I mused. I tried to avoid seeing the picture—and I mostly succeeded. Instead I saw Dorrie's kapp bobbing through Women's Wear at Wal-Mart, her voice calling out of the fitting room door, *Eve-Eve*, and then my mouth moved again.

"So…um…"

She waited.

"So…does Eve sunbathe too?"

Dorcas Yoder giggled suddenly. I felt heat in the dark.

"Well…does she?"

"No," the Amish girl said, grinning perfect teeth at me. "But I'll be sure to tell her you asked."

"Don't—"

"It will make Eve's day."

And the girl was still tittering happily when the threshing room door rolled noisily open beneath us, wide beyond the crack I had slipped through. Footsteps crunched on the grain-strewn floor, and a voice roared, "Dorcas!"

We were silent—matched by an ominous silence from below.

"Dorcas?…Dorcas Yoder!"

She peeped at last, "Yes…" and this triggered a long, explosive train wreck of Amish German.

Dorrie shrank back as lantern light climbed the loft ladder. In a moment more a round black hat punched through into the loft, followed by the enraged face of Freeman Yoder, rimmed in his trembling white beard.

He knew me. I had asked him for a rocking chair. On a Sunday. He aimed a crooked finger at me.

"Devil!" he thundered at me. "Devil! Out!"

But he blocked the only way. Unless I went out—like the lover—via the hay fork track.

I hesitated. Freeman Yoder bulled through the hole. His daughter toppled back at the sheer force of his presence. He stepped toward her, thundering in German. Then he turned—"Devil! Out!"—and sent me down the ladder.

I went gladly. I had no desire to disturb the good man's family. But I fell the last six feet onto grain sacks. I thought I felt stitches pop open. A moment later, as I tried to stand, the Sun Drop and the Hostess pie came crashing down around my head. Then the electric hair clippers cracked down like a stone on my right shoulder. Next came the white papers, fluttering into my lap.

"Get out of *mein haus!*" roared Freeman Yoder.

Then the blanket darkened everything.

A new low in porno

Eve…now I really had to see Eve. And the light was on in the upper right, second-floor window of the Avalanche Mercantile. That meant I could stop in.

But my leg was a pulsing mess by the time I climbed out of the stream at the County Y bridge.

I felt feverish, too. Dizzy. Agitated. My God, I fretted. I still have rabies.

I hobbled past the Avalanche Mercantile. I dropped off my waders at the Cruise Master and dragged myself straight into the campground bathroom. The lights were on, the room was steamy, and I remember thinking that Howard Adams had at least seen his way clear to take a shower—and that was a good sign, I thought, grief-wise. I turned the hot water on in the sink. I peeled off waders, socks, pants.

I had two wounds now. The upper wound, where the madstone had dropped, was seepy-red and itchy. The lower wound had burst between Moth's 8X stitches. But it hadn't bled yet. The crust of pus was too thick.

I brought the leg up like a hurdler and stuck it in the sink, twisting my hips to get the water running over both wounds. I pumped foam soap out of the dispenser and smeared it on. I let the water get real hot, and then, to distract myself, I took Dorcas Yoder's papers out of my jacket pocket and unfolded them. They were damp and streaked with soda. I spread them on the counter beside the sink and stared through the steam, mildly aghast at the images.

What Dorrie had been looking at, up in the hayloft, with her pie and soda and hair clippers and blanket—with whatever friend had thumped down the outside of the barn—were pictures of naked men and women.

Normal enough, I thought at first, for a sixteen-year-old kid.

But then I waved through steam and leaned in, because something was off. This was not *Playgirl* or *Penthouse*. These were not whole naked men, or whole naked women. These naked men and women were not posed in erotic contortions. Nor were they even in color. Dorrie's pictures were grainy, black-and-white internet printouts, so graphic and raw I could take them only in glimpses before I had to look away, feeling too shy, too sad, for the subjects. A new low in porno, I was guessing.

I turned the water off but left my leg up in the sink to throb and drain. I picked up one Sun Drop-splattered printout and examined the human female body, caught square between the legs and completely off guard in all its fuzzy, droopy, damp retirement. Nothing I hadn't seen before. I set that paper down. I picked up another: the male piece, cockeyed, thrashed, and flaccid. Nothing new there either. But the next one had arrows and letters. Another had an alphabet on the folds and bumps. Others—I shuffled them quickly—looked simply off, weird somehow. Then came a photo with the tissues cut, folded back. Man…woman…God help me, the two were knotted up somehow…I couldn't tell…like gene strands had taken wrong turns…and the genders had climbed one on top of the other…

Rabies, Dog. Rabies. You're seeing things that aren't there. I pushed the papers away. Thinking things that can't be.

You're snapping.

And that's where I was, still seeing things, still thinking things, trying to snap back to normal, when King Midas Kussmaul barged into the bathroom, shotgun barrel first.

He was breathless. His momentum took him a little behind me, toward the toilet and shower, and I watched his red-plaid shirt become a blur in the steamy mirror. Somewhere back there, he got his feet under him and shoved the gun at me. I glared dizzily back. His trembling hands held a Remington pump.

"Not a good time, King. I'm in the rabid snapping phase. I don't give a shit about your bad night at horseshoes."

"Yeah..." he puffed back. "Fuck yeah...I figured it was you stealing from me. The big rip-off started about the time you rolled into Avalanche driving that—"

He stopped right there, in the midst of grasping for a way to describe the Cruise Master. He had noticed the pictures on the sink counter. There was a long, boozy pause where his interest was triggered...where he was sucked in...and then...very slowly...after several heavy breaths and a pair of inchoate mumblings...he saw the dismal strangeness of the photos and unglued himself.

"Get your dick out of the sink," he said, "and pay me up."

I brought my leg down. I hopped through my pant leg, and when I had both feet down, I told him, "I paid your wife in trade. For camping. I cut out a deadfall."

I looked him in the eyes, but there was nobody home. His pupils were pinpricks, and the surrounding Kussmaul blue seemed to vibrate and scatter.

"Oh, no, Brother. Maybe you paid for camping, but that don't come with all the LP gas you can burn."

I stared. LP gas? Where was I? KOA?

I tried nice. "King...I'm sorry. Can you put that thing down? I don't know what you're talking about."

He tilted his head sideways, and his smile took about three seconds to catch up. Man, he was ripped.

"LP..." he said. "Gas. I gotta thing on that shower in there that takes quarters. Six quarters getsya six minutes. Them LP tanks burn for about three hours straight time. You're here one week and the fucker's about empty." He lurched at me. "Do the math, mother-fuck."

I didn't know what math he meant. The Dog's brain was busy calculating body weight and blood alcohol level, factoring in meth, plus my split time in the forty with a bad leg, and dividing all that by the depth the Glock in my pocket and the lethal range of a shot-gun. I was pretty sure King Midas could do me. I was pretty sure he would.

"Help me out," I said. "I'm bad at math."

He stared at me a long moment, as if he were trying to remem-ber what we were talking about. Then he had it.

"When that hot water heater burns a full LP tank, quarter a minute, should be a hundred-eighty quarters in that box."

I nodded. Now I followed. *That* math.

"You know howmanysinum?"

Now I knew what he meant. How many quarters were in the money box on the shower? I shook my head: "No. You tell me."

"Twenty."

I said, "Damn. Wow."

"Anda buncha screwdriver marks, asshole. Somebody's stick-ing a screwdriver in there instead of that last quarter. Running that water forever. And now I got him."

I reoriented my hips slightly toward the door. I picked up Dor-cas Yoder's printouts and folded them back into my jacket. King's eyes did a weird flip-flop thing and followed my hand into the pocket.

"Not me, King. Sorry. I don't own a screwdriver. And I bathe in the stream. You can ask your kid. I guess he spies on me."

"Yeah? Then what's all this steam in here?"

"I washed my leg in the sink. I got that beaver bite, remember? Sink water comes with the camping fee, right? I mean, a fisherman can wash up, right? Shave and all that? Get prettied up before he goes home?"

"You going home then?" he grunted hopefully.

"Maybe," I said. "But can I ask you something?"

"Whaddya wanna know?"

"I wanna know why—or how—with your little boy accused of shooting one of your campers, you can be so damn worried about some quarters in a shower box. I don't get that, King. Can you tell me?"

"Live in Avalanche a while," he slurred, "you'll see."

"That an invitation?"

"Hell no."

"Then I guess you'll have to tell me."

He staggered slightly, and again I thought I saw him searching the folds of his blasted brain for the topic.

"Quarters," I said. "Versus son."

"My father…" he began, fixing me with a big-browed Kussmaul glare. "You're a smartass, huh?" I shrugged. I was waiting. "Me and Salt and Half-Tim," he slurred, "…we grew up…our father cut fire-wood with a hand saw, he picked mushrooms, he butchered deer, he fixed machinery, he drove a snowplow, he worked nights at a gas station in LaCrosse…he made corn whiskey…he sold pumpkins and watercress by the side of the goddamned highway…one spring we ate fucking possums…"

I watched the Remington barrel inch closer to me.

"Fucking possums," King Kussmaul snarled at me. "When you live in Avalanche," he said, "every…sonofabitch…quarter…counts…smartass." I nodded. "You got that?" I nodded again. "We get by down here…quarter by…quarter. Asshole. You got that?"

I nodded. Yeah. I got that.

"But your boy's in real trouble."

He shook his head and snarled again: "Leave it alone."

"Deuce has confessed to a murder. Your wife doesn't think he did it. Neither do I."

"Fuckers can't touch him. He's a minor."

"*Somebody* touched him, King. Somebody made him lie."

"Leave it alone, I said."

I backed off. King Midas had said more than he knew. There was an *it*, for one thing—an *it* that I was supposed to leave alone.

And I was forming an inchoate sense of what it was—and who it involved: Annie, art, Dorcas, Abe Borntrager, money, blackmail, the whole brutal hand-to-mouth ethos of the Kussmaul clan.

"Okay," I said. "You've got the shotgun. So I'll leave it alone. But you only get one chance to be a dad, King, and this is it. The county can take Deuce away."

He breathed through his mouth, wheels spinning now, looking for traction on something new and slippery. His pin-prick pupils jumped around, nicking my eyes and bounding away again.

"Naw. County can't touch him. Like to see the fuckers try."

But I had him on his heels now. I had the fuckers on his mind, in place of where I had been ten seconds ago. The shotgun was still pointed at my gut, but King Midas had forgotten it. I calculated. I reached for some old instincts. I decided his meth-and-booze-hopped mind was one little push from the kind of spacing I could use. And I had a trick for that, a final mental-judo move that I hadn't pulled on someone like King in a dozen years. I thought a second, sizing the man up, because the right dollar figure was important, it had to be believed, and it varied.

Finally, giving him the hand-to-mouth version, I said, "If I gave you a thousand dollars, King, right now, what would you do with it?"

He eyed me warily. I thought I had gone too high.

"You mean it?"

I nodded. "I'm dead serious. Think about it." King Midas wet his lips. He went somewhere inside his addled mind, and inside the space of his sudden greedy numbness, through the exit hole of his complete and eager belief in dumb-ass, thousand-dollar miracles, I stepped past the gun barrel and out the bathroom door.

"Wet bar!" he hollered after me.

I limped hard for freedom.

"Wet bar in the barn!"

"Draw up plans," I yelled over my shoulder. "Let me see them."

"Heineken!" he hollered. "On tap!"

Just as perfect as God could make us

"That would be so cool," said one of the black-hatted Amish boys milling between me and the Cruise Master, drinking beer.

"That would be *fürtzig*," said another.

A bespectacled girl in a white kapp whispered, "*der Hund...*" as I passed. I took them in only vaguely—the Stoltzfus kids, King's party posse—as I churned stiff-legged for my vehicle. Any second now King's thousand-dollar wet bar would go *poof!* and he would be back to stolen shower quarters. By then I would be tucked, my Glock drawn, behind the ten thousand pounds of rust, aluminum, and road-cheese that constituted the Cruise Master.

But he didn't come out...didn't come out...he couldn't break the spell I had cast over him...and then a voice behind me said, "Psst...Hey, Dog..."

Chicken breath. Familiar. Then the quick snap of a lighter to show a face. Moth Kussmaul was hiding back there, right behind me. His hands steamed slightly as he put his fingers to his lips.

"Shhh."

"What the—"

"I'm hiding," he whispered. "From my brother. I came down to see you. You remember? I need to look at your beaver bite. See how my surgery is holding up. I was sitting in your chair outside when

I saw King come across the crick with that old pump action. He sucked at horseshoes tonight. Too drunk. Then he got into some new batch of Lightning Rod's meth…"

I heard King Midas come out. He yelled in the direction of the Cruise Master, "This better not be you, leaving this sick shit in my shower!"

"Come on," I whispered to Moth. "Let's go in."

I sat down opposite the youngest Kussmaul at my galley table. I had a black-out curtain, for sleeping in parking lots. I pulled it down. I lit a candle.

"Those Amish kids," Moth said, his broad, red face flickering in the dim light. He gathered up his dampish, white-blonde hair and laid it back over his shoulders. "Thank God for them sometimes. They worship King. They kind of keep a leash on him. They look out for him a little bit."

"He'll ruin them," I said.

Moth shrugged. "Or make them more Amish than ever. It works that way sometimes too." He pulled a pen light from his pants pocket. "Here. I brought this. Put your leg up here."

I felt my shoulders come down an inch—maybe over the relief of finding myself in the presence of the one Kussmaul who wasn't about to tear my face off. Still, I felt dizzy, hot, and strangely exhausted as I stood, took my boot off, and eased my pants up over my right calf. I laid my leg across the galley table, showing him the stitches.

"Hmmmm," said Moth, bending over it.

"Not what you had in mind?"

"Well…I didn't cut you up here."

No, I told him. That was Eve. Making a spot for her madstone.

"Her what?"

I explained Eve's rabies treatment, expecting Moth—as a provider of modern medicine, however marginally—to scoff. But he didn't. He listened alertly. He nodded thoughtfully. He said, "See…

that's the way it is with folks outside the system. They deal with their medical issues one way or another. My grandparents on my Ma's side—they were Skinruds from down by the Bad Axe—they didn't believe in doctors at all. They believed everything went just as God designed it."

He leaned into candle light. I thought he was getting too close to it. But he had something important to share.

"Get this. My ma's family has one sister who's a retard. She has another brother that starved to death when he was a baby because he had some kind of diarrhea that didn't get better. They fed him chalk and he died. Ma talks about it like she's proud. Like that's a good thing. And her biggest sister died in childbirth, at home, not even a midwife present. The baby died too."

His soft chest wrapped the edge of my galley table. Bits of hair from the top of his head prickled up, curling in the candle's heat. His chicken breath came and went excitedly. "And get this too. When Ma was a teenager she broke both legs, both femurs, for Christ's sake, falling off a wagon, but she never saw a doctor for it. But she hasn't been able to keep the fat off ever since because she could never walk right. She can float like a boat, but that's about it. Then, get this too, when King was growing up—"

I stopped him.

"Hey…Moth…hold on. I'm standing here like a damn ballerina. My leg looks okay?"

His raised back up to see it better. What struck me now that the pus and crust had been washed off was how fine his stitching was: eleven perfect little straps of 8X tippet. The fact that the wound was swelling beneath them was another matter. My calf was starting to look like a small, red football. Moth said, "That fishing line worked fine. But I should have given you this stuff right away."

He reached gingerly into the same pocket the flashlight had come from and brought out three tiny sample bottles of amoxicillin.

"Little rip-off job," he winked, "from my clinical."

"So it's infected?

He gave a little laugh. "Not so bad," he said. "Just take two of those a day for a couple weeks. It's not bad at all. I've seen a lot worse. You want to see infected…" he began, but he trailed off. "No," he said. He laughed again. "You don't want to see infected."

I dropped my pant leg and stood on both feet. I reached across the narrow aisle and flipped the bungee cord off a cupboard door.

"Drink?" I asked him.

"Never," he said. "Not anymore."

"Tang then," I said. "You were telling me about when King was growing up…"

"Oh," he said. "Yeah."

I stirred orange powder into clean mugs. I sloshed vodka into mine. I moved my maps and set a mug down between Moth's hands.

"If you can say that King actually grew up," he said wistfully.

"Well…"

"He was about seven. He got sick with scarlet fever. There were Amish around here even then, the Zook family, and Ma wouldn't let our dad do nothing to help King, but Salty snuck out to get help. The Amish sent Sarah Zook, Eve's and Rachel's mother, but Ma wouldn't let the woman in the door. Instead, Ma made King strip naked and sit in the creek until his fever went away."

I stared. Moth sipped his Tang. His shoulders had collapsed as if from the weight of his story.

"He sat there all day and overnight."

I pushed out words.

"That kind of thing is hard on everybody."

He nodded over the mug rim. "King didn't say a damn word for about two years after that. But eventually he was good as ever. I mean…well, you know what I mean. Probably why he hates that creek so much though. Probably why he won't take Deuce fishing."

"So you take care of your ma? That's kind of a big job, isn't it? Why not Salt Box?"

Moth turned the Tang mug. He didn't answer me for a long

time. "Well," he said finally, "both my big brothers married the Zook sisters eventually, and Ma's not going to be taken care of Amish style, that's for damn sure."

"But Eve's sister, Rachel—"

"Yeah. I know. Rachel's more English than the English. But Ma and Salt have been mad at each other as long as I can remember."

"Yeah? Over the treatment of King?"

He shrugged. "Oh, that was just one thing. Basically, both Salt and King think Ma gives me special treatment. See, King got money when my uncle sold that middle farm and he bought the Mercantile and the King Midas barn. But Salty wanted the farm I got. The tri-county. There's this strange thing, because of the confusion over which of the three counties I'm in, where the property taxes get all mixed up, and I end up paying nothing. That's a real big deal to Salt—not giving money away to the government. But Ma wanted to stay where she had been all along, and she wanted me with her. So Salt hates her for favoring me."

"And your dad…?"

Moth heaved a big, buzzing sigh. He sucked down a bolt of Tang like it was the hard stuff. "My dad…our dad…Herman Kussmaul…when I was twelve years old, he and our ma had a huge fight that went on for like three days solid. Then one morning after milking we were having breakfast and our dad tied a rope around his neck in front of all of us. He was drunk and I guess we thought he was just trying to scare Ma. Anyway, I remember he took the rope off and threw it over his shoulders, and then he went for a walk."

He stopped. He tried to change subjects. He looked around the Cruise Master. "Privacy," he said. "Wow."

"All the privacy you can stand," I replied. "And then about ten times more. Plus no heat and no plumbing."

"I'll take it," he said. "Right next to the bathrooms anyway. All I got up at the tri-county is a pump and an outhouse."

He sipped Tang, still looking around.

"Hey. Cool. That's René Magritte. That postcard. The pipe picture."

I raised eyebrows. "You know that?"

"I guess I like the surreal."

I gave the poor young man a smile. "Go figure," I said. I nodded at Magritte's painting. "So can you explain how that's not a pipe?"

He was pleased. He leaned into the flame. "Pipe is just a sound you make with your brain and your mouth," he said. "That object exists no matter what you call it. So it can't be a pipe. It can just be called one."

I blinked at him. "You lost me. But you're into that stuff?"

"Yeah. I've been checking it out on the net, on the computers at school. Escher. Dali. That kind of stuff. Magritte really makes you think. I like to think. I was almost valedictorian at the high school, before I got all fucked up with my cousin Lightning Rod and quit school." He paused. "You know, it's funny how I can tell things to a stranger that my own family won't even talk about."

"That's the way it is."

"So…you notice that my ma never lets me out of her sight?"

Neutral, I waited.

"See, later we found out that Dad had put that rope back around his neck and crawled out on a beam in that old half-timber barn we still have. Dad just crawled out on that beam like a big old coon, tied up the other end of the rope, and rolled off."

Now Moth waited for me to speak. Here was another chance, in Avalanche, for the Dog to say he was sorry for someone else's pain. I did it. I managed. Hell, I was sorry. I shook my head a little, trying to loosen up a sharp new ache above my eyes.

Moth said, "That's when…kinda after that bad thing with my dad…that's when my big brothers…Salt and King, the two of them…starting getting a little off track…a little crazy…you know? I was about ten, so…"

"Yeah," I helped him. "I get the picture."

"So, I mean, they aren't much use to Ma. That's my point. And Ma likes me to be around her."

I nodded. "Right."

"'We're all just as perfect as God could make us,' she likes to say. 'Whatever happens is meant to happen,' she says. But anyway she wants to tear down that barn, history and all."

"And Annie Adams was stopping her?"

He sat quietly, scowling into the candle. Again, I thought he was getting too close. I expected to smell his eyebrows burning. "More or less," he said eventually. "I guess. It's hard to tell with Ma sometimes. She cussed out Annie real good, and as far as I know, Annie dropped the subject because she got the message that the barn was where our dad died and Ma wanted it down. Annie didn't always push too hard. Not always. Just sometimes. I think Ma may have had a little stroke during all that."

"But she's okay now?"

He looked up at me.

"She's healthy?" I clarified.

"Are you kidding?" Moth Kussmaul asked back, incredulous. "Have you seen her? She's got diabetes, high blood pressure, gout, varicose veins, hemorrhoids, about six different kinds of mental illness…That's why I went into medicine. I mean, I'm never going to be a doctor, or a nurse. All I have is a GED. But emergency techs get good training, and they're in high demand." He made a nervous little laugh. "Still, I wouldn't be sewing you up if you had insurance, right? I mean, it's a lot easier to have a doctor do that stuff." He rolled his eyes. "I mean, you should see Ma's hemorrhoids." I took a huge slug of vodka-Tang to wash the vision away. "But anyway," Moth said, "that's why I came down here."

"Yeah…why again?"

"To see how your leg was healing."

"Oh…yeah…right. Well, it seems like you know what you're doing."

He shifted uncomfortably.

"So you've got enough wood?"

"Yup. Thanks."

"So, then…I guess…"

I fought through the heaviness of the moment, through a fresh swirl of my own dizziness, and leaned toward him. I said, "Hey…so Annie Adams often pushed too hard?"

He shrugged his big, soft shoulders. I retreated a step. I said, "Annie pissed off the whole Kussmaul family by painting their barns and refusing to pay them. Am I right so far?"

"Well…sort of…"

"Tell me how I'm wrong."

He kept his gaze on the flame.

"Well…she didn't piss me off, for one thing. I let her have all the access she wanted. I didn't ask for money. I let her paint from the property. I showed her inside the barn. I even let her sleep in there." He glanced up. "Ma didn't know."

"When was that?"

"Last summer."

That surprised me. Or reminded me. "So they've been here how many summers before? Howard and Annie Adams?"

He thought back. "The last three years, at least. With Annie's son, Robin. Who played with Deuce." But he was waiting to say something else. "And the second way you're a little off is that with me, I'm a Kussmaul just like the rest of them, God help me, but I got along with Annie just fine. I liked Annie. We talked a lot. I let her do whatever she wanted on my half-timber. I believed her that my barn is pretty special. I told her I would try to stop Ma from tearing it down. Last summer I said, whatever, cool, get whatever you need…"

Now he looked at me—big, soft, suddenly unfocused blue eyes, as if he had melted them in the candle's heat.

"Last summer," he said.

I nodded.

"Oh yeah," he said. "Last summer was a wild one. Freeman Yoder made a big stink last summer because Robin picked Dorrie a huge bunch of wildflowers and tied them up to Yoder's mailbox on Dorrie's birthday, which happened to be a Sunday, when all the Amish around here were coming in for church service. After that,

Robin got in a fist fight with one of Dorrie's brothers. So Annie wouldn't let Robin come this summer."

"I heard Deuce wasn't happy."

"Deuce...Well, Annie made Robin stay with his real father, and I guess his father sent him to camp. Dorrie gets letters from Robin at my place sometimes."

I dropped another spoonful of Tang dust in his mug. I moved the mug under the water jug and filled it. As I stirred, I said, "Let me guess something."

He looked suddenly uncomfortable. "About my Ma?"

"No. No, no. Annie. Annie Adams was a romantic. Right?"

Still uncomfortable—but more puzzled—he bent back toward the flame, listening to me.

"I mean, she wasn't going to disrespect the traditional ways of the Amish. I saw enough of her to know that. But on the other hand, I'll bet she thought those flowers her son gave Dorrie were pretty damn sweet. Tied up to the mailbox for everyone to see."

Moth was blushing suddenly—that big Kussmaul brow afire— and I wondered suddenly if he was sweet...sweet on Dorrie. After all, who wouldn't be?

"I'll bet Dorrie liked those flowers too."

He nodded. "Yeah. She did. She really did. Only now, because of that, she's not really getting along with her family anymore. Over those flowers, from the starting point."

"So then Annie and Dorrie," I said, still guessing, "they got together and painted a picture for Robin."

He stared into his mug.

"And it turns into several pictures. Because Dorrie's just so dang lovely. And the kapp, maybe some other stuff, comes off. And the pictures turn out to be pretty damn powerful pieces of art. You know anything about that?"

He mumbled, "I don't think I should say..."

I gave him a chance before I came back. "Someone's dead, Half-Tim. I think you should say."

He jerked his head up, eyes narrowed. "I hate that name." The softness had abruptly left him. "Don't call me that."

"I'm sorry—"

"My ma would slap you for calling me that."

"I'm sorry, I didn't realize—"

"She named me Timothy, after her dead brother, the one that ate chalk. She wasn't thinking about barns. But that's how this whole name thing got started. My dad getting drunk and calling me Half-Timber, like that old barn. He thought it was funny. Then my brothers called me that after dad died. The idea for all of us caught on after Salt got his barn, then King. Now all of us Kussmauls are called by our barns. Ma hates it."

I nodded. I said the name he wanted this time. Moth. I told Moth again that someone was dead. I told him the reason for that death might be that Annie Adams painted Dorcas Yoder. He ought to tell me, I said—or tell someone—what he knew.

"But Dorrie's this close to the ban," he protested.

"And Annie's dead."

Now the youngest Kussmaul hesitated. He met my eyes, and I saw something new—a darkness that was almost threatening, like I had better be good to the people he cared about. "Dorrie..." he said, and waited for my total focus. "Dorrie only took her cap and shoes off. But still she could get excommunicated, like Eve and Rachel. The Amish aren't allowed to have any pictures of themselves. Graven images, they call them. Graven images put them above God, and it's very bad. It's devil-work. And Dorrie's father found out about the paintings."

"And how did that happen?"

He stared over my left shoulder, as if he could look through the Cruise Master wall and see up the coulee. "Abe Borntrager," he spat. "Salt's milker—"

"We've met."

Moth Kussmaul leaned in, awkwardly angry. He wanted to make sure I got it. "Dorrie sinned," he said. "Big time. Against their Ordnung. Freeman's a bishop. Dorrie is his only daughter. If those pictures got out, the whole Yoder family would have imploded—just like Eve and Rachel's family."

"And so what happened?"

"Freeman Yoder bought the pictures."

"The *pictures*." I had to stop him right there, like Dorrie, and get the same thing straight. "Polaroids, right?"

He nodded.

"But there are paintings, too. That's what Abe took pictures of."

He nodded again.

"Yoder didn't get the paintings."

"No."

"So where are the paintings?"

With a clumsy, hair-flipping jerk, Moth swung his big head up-coulee again. A small engine whined distantly through the stream-brushed quiet. I didn't stop to listen for its signature.

"In that trailer out there? In Annie's trailer?"

He nodded. "That trailer got locked after Freeman Yoder came down here like a house afire and demanded to have the paintings."

The engine strained closer. I heard it gag and whine over the County Y bridge. It sounded like someone had stuffed a potato in the tail pipe of King's ill-tuned John Deere.

"Moth..." I said, leaning forward, putting my hands down flat on the galley table. "Do you think Deuce killed Annie Adams?"

He shrugged, but this time not so softly. "Why would the little shit lie?" he asked me. "I mean, more than normal?"

"I don't know. Why would he?"

He shook his head and slumped down in the galley seat as the engine noise found its way around the Avalanche Oak and ripped toward us across the campground.

"Could Freeman Yoder make him lie?"

"Maybe..."

"Could Howard Adams make him lie?"

"I don't know..."

"How about one of your brothers? What are their real names, anyway?"

"Boone...that's Salt Box...and King is Conrad."

"How about Boone and Conrad? Would Deuce lie for them?"

But Moth wasn't listening anymore. Now the engine revved right outside, and he sighed mightily and hauled himself up. He put his hand on the door and stared almost wistfully for a moment at my postcard. *Ceci n'est pas une pipe* he read quietly. *This is not a pipe.*

Then a horn beeped shrilly, and Moth pushed the door open.

She was out there, the big, old Kussmaul dam, her housedress up, her shapeless white legs wedged around the seat of a rust-and-gray four-wheeler—this one an old Polaris youth model, listing under the old lady's bulk. She revved the engine again, blared the horn. She backed up expertly so that the headlights blasted through the Cruise Master door. Squinting into the glare, I saw a screwdriver in her right fist.

"I gotta go now," sighed Moth. "It's Ma."

I'm going to Hell because
I chased this moment

And now, I thought, I would finally talk to Eve.

I poured a big second drink, spooned the Tang straight in, and downed it. Then I changed my shirt—replacing a gray sweatshirt with a slightly cleaner black one. I even brushed my teeth.

I pushed outside just as a frozen rain began to fall. But I got no farther than one step across the grass when I stumbled on something soft and heavy, something that burped up a faint warm stink from the pressure of my toe. Another beaver, I hoped. Bigger. One with broken teeth. From someone who actually wanted to help me.

But then I hit it with a lighter flare. It wasn't a beaver. It was a pig. A piglet. Dead. Not much larger than a loaf of good bread. I went back into the Cruise Master for my flashlight. Not much battery left—but enough to make out, as I squatted in the rain, that the little pig had been shaved and partly castrated—it's little white-pink testicles hanging out across a bloody gash. Its throat was slit too. I turned the piglet over, and over again—but that was all.

I sat back on the Cruise Master's wet bottom step, the sleety rain spraying the piglet's blood from my hands. Out of nowhere, I felt too weak to move. I don't know why—over a little pig that would anyway be castrated, that would anyway be brutally fattened and then anonymously eaten—I don't know why I felt such sudden despair.

Or yes…maybe I do know. Maybe what I felt was the despair of something—I still cannot say exactly what—draining through my hands, leaving a deep and lonely bewilderment. Around me were ugly, dark things. Terrible secrets. And a child knew those secrets, a child lived within them, protected them, was going down to keep them in the darkness. His mother was trying to make light. I was trying to make light. But the light had gone off, I was realizing, at the Avalanche Mercantile. My night was over.

I sat down heavily, alone at my galley table. Now pellet rain slashed the Cruise Master roof and sides. I took a long swallow of a new vodka-Tang.

I told myself this: there was something I was missing. Some hole in the way I understood things.

There always was.

That hole was always there. I had danced around it, all my life, always knowing beyond consciousness that I was missing it—you know, *it*—something central, something I had been offered but was too dense to receive. Annie Adams had seemed to get that about me. She had seen that instantly. In the short time we knew each other, all of four cups of coffee, while her husband snored in the teepee, that was how Annie teased me. "Dog!" she would blurt excitedly. Caught staring off at the Avalanche bluffs, I would snap my head around. "What?" Annie would give me her dotty, barn-lover's grin. "Why, whatever you want, my dear. Just let go of what you don't want and do it." At first I thought she was flirting, and then I thought she was daft, and when neither proved true I nervously tried to stick to an instructional mode, where ostensibly I was showing her how to help her feeble husband catch a trout on a fly. Then we got into her learning-style thing. I swear she loved mistakes—something inside the process of them. She botched that blood knot every which way, though she never admitted to doing it on purpose.

"Here, Dog!" and I would swing around from my creek view, my eyes going straight to the latest flaw in the knot she had attempted, while her eyes went straight to mine.

"Will you forgive me, Dog? Can you forgive me? Can I start over?"

"The tag ends go through opposite."

"You never told me about your family."

"I'm not going to."

"What are you going to do?"

"Tag ends go through opposite."

"Okay, Dog. If you'll let me try again."

It was a weird game. Shit, I thought suddenly—I missed her. I missed the Barn Lady.

I reached up to the bunk behind me and hooked down the plastic sack that held Annie Adams' little hard-backed sketchbook. It was a strange bolt of lovesickness—for both of them, I realized—that made me remember two nights ago in the Avalanche Mercantile, the moment when Eve had offered Annie the plastic sack, and Annie had refused it—and then Annie had changed her mind and accepted the sack, saying she needed it, she could always use a sack, as if to make Eve just a tiny bit less unhappy than she already was.

I folded the thin sack carefully, like a treasure, and set it aside. I opened the sketchbook to the pages that Howard Adams had showed me. The mis-tied blood knot. The trico. The dog.

It was time to face that, wasn't it? Time to face the fact that the Barn Lady had a thousand ways to say things, to reach people?

I forced out the questions. Wasn't I supposed to look at that sketchbook the very next morning? And had Annie really not understood that the blood knot, tied incorrectly as she drew it, would snap? And hadn't she said that she would make up her own meaning for the name trico? And for God's sake…was Howard Adams really a dog person?

I knew the answers. Come on, Dog. But I drank a while. While I drank, I noticed that the page before the mysterious sketches had been ripped out. I stared at the little half-moon tear-outs. The pages on either side were smudgy down the center. I wondered about that, distracting myself, trying to stop the voices. But I finally gave up. I let them speak.

And then, as wind rocked the Cruise Master, we—and by we, I mean the Dog, Magritte, my tax guy, Digman, their associate, Annie Adams—we laid that sketchbook out before us and tried saying it aloud.

This is not a blood knot.

This is not a trico.

Look at this…understand this…Dog…

And then hail rattled the Cruise Master roof…and thunder boomed…and I struggled to wake up, struggled to lift my head off the galley table, because she was calling me. She was pounding on the door.

"Dog! Dog? It's Deuce and me. Can you let us in?"

I didn't know how many hours had passed, but it was still dark. My back was stiff with cold, almost locked. I bent my neck upright. My fingers uncurled out of frozen fists. My watch said five-ten a.m. I had been dreaming of bloody creatures, reeling through the night. I limped to the door.

"Dog—Sorry to wake you."

Eve was soaked. She had Deuce in her arms, the kid snoring up through the hole of a cheap yellow rain poncho. Wally splattered at her feet on a leash. She thrust Deuce at me through the door. I got the boy's top half, found his armpits and hung on, while Eve heaved his legs up the steps. The kid was heavy, and somehow Wally was dragged in, choking, behind. I swept my maps and the sketchbook aside and we slung him onto the galley table. I felt like hell myself, so the question was easy.

"Is he sick?"

"No." Eve's kapp was wet, and her hair showed darkly through. The kapp strings dripped. She had wrapped a dirty jacket around her shoulders and kept them dry, but her dress was soaked from the knees down and her red Chuckies were thick and gritty with sand and mud.

"No" she panted. "No. He's sleeping. He's just like King. Once he finally goes down, he could sleep through a tornado. It's just that King started acting very strange and we needed to get out. I'm sorry."

"You walked through the creek."

"It's quicker. King was acting stranger than usual, I mean. He was standing over Deuce's bed with his shotgun, talking to someone."

"Talking to who?"

"No one was there."

"What was he saying?"

She shrugged. She pried her sodden Chuckies off and dropped them in the stairwell. She fiddled unsuccessfully with my door lock. "He was speaking Kussmaul. I couldn't follow. I just grabbed Deuce when King went out to the barn for something."

"Won't he look for you?"

"For me?"

"Yes."

"Me—no. Deuce, maybe. If he remembers what he was doing before he went out to the barn. I turned the TV on. There was a cowboy movie. When he gets back, he'll probably watch that."

Wally continued to strain and gasp. I followed the leash up beneath the poncho to find it triple-knotted to Deuce's wrist. The puppy and the boy were connected.

"It's the only way he would go to sleep," Eve told me. "I had to let him take Wally into his bed. He gets stranger and stranger about Wally."

"Let's get them up on the bunk."

I lit a lantern and set it in the sink. We stripped off the poncho. I used my discarded gray sweatshirt to dry off Deuce's feet and then Wally's thick brown fur. I told Eve to take the puppy, and I got my arms beneath Deuce like under a big load of Moth's free firewood. Carefully, I swung him around—Eve following to keep the leash untangled—and then with a grunt I slopped him up on the bunk. Eve tossed Wally in on top, and I pulled my sleeping bag over the both of them. It was the sudden comfort, I guess, that made Deuce sit bolt upright and look around with startled, unseeing eyes.

"You're in your friend Dog's camper car, Honey. With Mama and Wally."

The boy smiled vaguely. He touched Wally. He touched the ceiling above the bunk. He lay back down. In ten seconds, he was snoring.

Eve slid in behind the galley table.

"It's cold in here."

"Yeah…I forgot to turn on the central heat."

"How's the leg?"

I told her. The madstone had dropped off. The milk had turned green. I showed her the milk.

"Then you're fine."

"I don't feel fine."

"What's the matter?"

I sat down across from her. I closed my eyes to feel it. "I think I have a fever." She reached across and put her palm on my forehead.

"No you don't."

"I'm dizzy, somehow. I'm sick."

She tipped my chin up. She looked in my eyes. "Baby," she said. "You're fine. No rabies."

I sat back woozily, my heart beating too fast. "I'd like to see your credentials, please, Doctor Kussmaul."

"What are credentials?"

"Evidence of your skills, something to make me confident."

She gave me a strange look. "I'm going to Hell anyway," she said. "So if you keep pushing me, maybe you will see credentials." Then she packed and lit her pipe. She gave me a little squint and tilt of her chin as she blew out smoke. Then she changed the subject. "So there's this Amish network," she said. "All over the country. Newspapers, newsletter, people traveling back and forth for visits and funerals. Everybody talks about everybody else. My family in Kentucky found out about the murder yesterday."

I stood up. Something in my vision had caused the Cruise Master's interior to warp strangely. I ran water in my coffee pan.

"My father called me from a pay phone in Paducah to say 'See, see, you're going to Hell, just like I said.' And now he says Deuce is going to Hell, too."

"How does he know?" I said. "Is he in charge of Hell?"

I lit the burner and sat back down. I regretted what I said. Eve was shivering hard. I got up again. I pulled my last dry sweatshirt and pair of pants out of the cupboard above the sink. "Get that dress off," I said as I tugged my raincoat from the back pocket of my fishing vest. "I'll be outside."

So she changed into my clothes. I stood under the whipping cottonwood, smoked a Swisher until the hail knocked it out. Then I felt sick again. I was sweating. A weird kind of panic was rising up inside me—a sense of doom, or disaster, or of somehow being too close to something too big for me to handle or control. I couldn't be fine. I couldn't be.

"My family called six times since supper," she went on as I returned. I shook off the raincoat and hung it. "My mother was weeping, my papa cursing at me in German. They're sending my oldest brother up to talk to me. They want me to renounce."

"Renounce what?"

"Him. Deuce. Say Deuce was a mistake. Say he's the devil's child. Leave him with King and come home. My mother says she's dying."

"Is she?"

"She's been dying for ten years. Ever since I showed pregnant with Deuce. Or no—I guess Rachel showed first, with Kelly. Whatever. We're killing her—me and Rachel. But she's not really dying. Not any more than the rest of us."

My water was boiling. I turned to look at her in my threadbare Levis and my bulky Celtics sweatshirt. She had left her wet kapp on. Her pipe had just gone out and she tapped it in my ashtray.

"Don't let me forget and stand up," she said. "There's nothing holding on these pants."

I turned back to find the instant coffee. I rinsed two cups in jug water. My hands were clumsy. My leg throbbed. My head throbbed.

"Oh my gosh," she said suddenly. "I used to swing on that rope."

I set down an embarrassing cup of coffee, foamy and light brown. "Thank you," Eve said. "What is this?"

"Coffee."

"No...this."

She pointed into Annie Adams' sketchbook, and I told her what it was. I told her I had borrowed it from Howard Adams—who in his shape-shifting grief, I said, wouldn't miss it. My own phrase caught me: shape-shifting grief. Suddenly my gut hurt. I dissolved my coffee and sat down.

Eve turned a page. Looking at a sketch labeled *Yoder's barn*, she said excitedly, "This is the rope that hangs down from the hayloft to the threshing floor. My papa used it to train up a winch line there when he had things to pull up to the loft. Us kids swung on it and dropped off when the threshing floor was packed."

"It's packed now," I said. "I was up at Yoder's tonight." I took a sip. "It's full of grain."

"Oh, my gosh," she said again. "My papa used to hang his jacket on that nail. And this is the latch on the bull pen. Papa had this one crazy bull..."

She looked up at me, still excited but suddenly teary-eyed.

"Oh," she sighed. "Never mind."

But she turned a page and went on.

"My milk stool...it's still there. And this one was Rachel's. See her name carved on the leg? Our biggest brother Amos did that for her. And this is what an Amish milk room looks like. No machinery. Papa ran the cooler with a gas generator because that was allowed. But somehow not cars. Oh, my, stuff like that, how my papa and I used to argue..."

She turned the next page.

"But Rachel never argued," she said. "She always said there was no use arguing. She always knew what she wanted and that was that. Look here—look how clean Freeman Yoder keeps the feed alley. Ever since Dorrie got in trouble with Robin Adams, that mean old man makes her sweep it out twice a day. She hates it. And she's like I was. Dorrie fights."

"Kids do that," I mumbled unsteadily. "They find ways to make their points."

She turned several more pages, uttering murmurs of recognition. For no good reason, my belly turned with her. I was staring at her chewed-up fingers, at her plain silver wedding band, at a burn on the first knuckle of her right thumb. I nearly touched her.

"Do you mind," she said suddenly, looking up at me again.

I looked at her quizzically. Was I caught wanting her? Did I mind what?

"Do you mind if I cry? I think I'm going to cry."

I shook my head: of course not. But I looked away as Eve crumpled forward, wet kapp in hands, and sobbed on my galley table. I stood up—still dizzy—my heart racing. I pulled my sleeping bag neatly over Deuce and his puppy. I moved the lantern down from the sink to the floor so it wouldn't shine on them. I kept an old wool blanket tied up at the foot of the bunk, and I laid that over Eve's heaving shoulders. I tucked it up where the dark hair grew from her long neck and furled up beneath her kapp.

Then I picked up my coffee cup and squeezed forward into the driver's cab. I snapped the curtain shut behind me. I stared out the rain-splattered windshield at Howard Adams' campsite, at the ruined teepee, the dark humps of his wife's soggy belongings, at the silver mini van and the dark shape of the trailer. I listened to Eve sob. I drank my coffee.

Then, after many minutes had passed, the curtain buttons unsnapped and there she stood, holding up my rumpled old Levis with one hand, holding the blanket around her throat with the other.

"King hates it if I cry," she sniffed. "You too, huh?"

"No." I dragged a sleeve across my face, just checking.

I was dry. I was clear.

"No. Not really."

"Can I come up here with you? I like the view."

She squeezed through and took the other bucket seat beside me.

"The sun," she predicted after a long moment of quiet, "is going to come up right over that end of the campground."

"Won't be much sun today."

"Oh, the sun always rises," she said. "but some days it's just harder to notice."

She stared out through the dark, wet window. "She was wonderful," Eve sighed eventually. "Annie was. She was the one who said that to me, about the sun, in the store one morning, and I really liked it. I always wanted a chance to say it."

"I liked her too," I said. "Though I wasn't really sure until she was gone."

Eve sighed. "Yeah. Because she wasn't easy. I never met anyone like her. Piss and vinegar, my papa used to say, though he wouldn't have cared for Annie. But she was full of it. Piss and vinegar and joy. And love for these old barns. It's so sad, because she was just what these Kussmauls needed."

I looked across at her.

She told me, "She saw everything. Annie has a sketch in that little book that shows King's barn, where a woodpecker went after something right in the middle of the i on King Midas. You can barely see it. I know King never did. But Annie noticed." She gathered in Levi fabric and tucked her toes beneath her thighs, cross-legged.

"And Annie drew a spider web framed beautifully in the stovewood nogging on Half-Tim's barn. Ma Kussmaul won't even spit at that old barn—she wants to tear it down and put up aluminum. And Annie sketched the new lock bolts Half-Tim put on the tractor doors this spring. I think she was looking at how the new gets patched onto the old and they don't always go so well together. Annie was truly wonderful. I know Dorrie loved her."

I looked at Eve's profile against the rain-streaked window.

"Your kapp's wet. You ought to take it off."

She made a small snort and kept her gaze stiffly forward.

"Well…now there's a change of subject."

"Take wet shit off. It's a fisherman's mantra."

"You don't know what you're saying."

I didn't. She was right. And she was dead serious, stony quiet for a long moment.

"An Amish woman takes her kapp off for one man only," she said finally, glancing across at me. "Now do you know?"

"I guess I do. I'm sorry."

"Yeah…me too."

We didn't speak then for a long, cold stretch. Rain and cottonwood leaves pelted the Cruise Master. I trembled in my seat.

"Dog…?" she whispered finally. "Will you tell me what's wrong with you?"

"I told you. I'm sick."

"You are not sick."

"How can you say that? How can you be so sure?"

"You want credentials…"

"I was kidding about credentials."

"You weren't kidding. You don't trust me."

"Okay—I wasn't kidding. Suddenly I'm scared. I'm very scared."

"Of rabies?"

"Of rabies."

"Just that?"

"Just that."

She let that hang in the air so long I began to shake hard. "Dog," she whispered finally.

"Yeah?"

"Sit very still. Close your eyes."

I did. I heard her move. I froze. I felt the wool blanket chafe across my forearms. I felt her weight arrive on my lap. "No…Eve…" But I felt her tongue part my lips and shove gently, timidly inside. After a long hesitation, her tongue touched my tongue, and lingered with the touch, both unsure and determined. I felt my shoulders drop. Then I felt my belly clear. I felt my body flood with warmth. I felt a pop of light against the back of my eyelids. Then she pulled back to the other seat, taking the blanket with her.

"There's my credentials," she said.

I opened my eyes.

"I'm that sure," she said. "Spit sure. Okay?"

I nodded. I took a deep, shaky breath. Overhead, Deuce shifted on the bunk. Eve stuck her hand out. I took it. We held hands silently until the sky grew vaguely light.

"You live in this thing," she challenged me eventually. "You're not camping."

"No."

"How long?"

I told her. Three years was the plan. Three years was how long my money would last. For three years I had been trying to figure out what came next.

"And…?"

"I don't know. There's a river up north I've got my sights on, a deep and cold one, and I—"

She pinched my fingers hard.

"Don't talk like that." She turned to look at me. Her voice trembled. "You fool. God damns you if you talk like that, Dog. God damns you."

I looked away out the windshield. The faintest tint of silver had leaked into the churning eastern sky. A pack of leaves fled across the black grass, pursued by a swirl of rain and wind. I gave up. I turned to Eve. I told her.

"I lost someone. That's what's wrong. That's what this is all about. I lost my son. He'd be Deuce's age right now."

I saw that picture suddenly, just as the words left my mouth. My little Eamon would be about Deuce's age. Ten years old.

I said, "I thought I could get over it. I thought I could fish my way out of it. I could tell you what happened, but the story never stands still, never makes sense, never comes out right."

Eve came back beside me. She knelt in the pit between buckets and put her head on my chest, the blanket around both of us.

"He was four," I managed. Now my face was wet. "He was taking a bath. His mother and I had been fighting all day."

"Oh, gosh..." she whispered. "King and I...we fight so much, we...no, go on, this is your story..."

"Yelling and sulking and yelling at each other again. And then Eamon decides on his own that he's going to take a bath. He disappears upstairs and runs the bath himself. He calls down that he's okay..."

Eve waited for me, gripping tight around my chest. But the rest had no concrete reality. There was no way to explain it.

"He drowned," I said.

Eve held on. I felt her fingers grip my ribs. I felt one hard sob before she pressed her face into my collarbone, her kapp into my neck. And in my mind, little Eamon just kept on drowning, I told her. Even right now, as she held me. It just kept happening, over and over, and that if I sat still, ever, for just one day, I missed my son so badly that death looked like paradise.

"Oh...Dog..."

But I was okay when I fished, I told her, when I moved upstream, when I saw new water and found, inside that new water, new life.

"Deuce!" she cried, and she bolted up, out of my arms. She dumped the blanket and tore back through the curtain into the Cruise Master's cabin. She spun around to the bunk and gazed at her child, long and hard. I followed and held her. I felt the ribs along her lean back. I felt the ragged, desperate pulsing of her lungs.

"No..." I murmured. "No...Eve...don't worry. It won't happen to you."

I held her a long time. She reached up and laid a hand to rise and fall on Deuce's chest. Wally stirred.

"He's a good kid," I told her.

"You changed your mind."

"All kids are good," I said, "now that I think about it."

Eve sighed, "Yeah."

My old Levis had fallen around her knees. I could feel her bare legs against me inside the blanket. I picked up her free hand and rubbed her bumpy, shredded nails.

"You're hurting yourself."

"That's meth," she murmured. "Sometimes I can't slow down. But I'm off it right now."

"I can't believe you take that stuff."

"I can't believe I do either. And then there are days when I can't believe I don't."

"King…" I began.

"King is way into it," she said. "But I'm almost all the way out, finally. We're going in separate directions, King and I. He resents every minute I spend sober."

"I think I know why Annie—" I blurted, thinking of habits, money, needs, resentment—the whole avalanche coming down suddenly. "Eve—I think I know why Annie died."

Eve turned inside my arms and looked up. I told her Dorrie had posed for Annie, as a present for Robin in exile. I told her that Salt Box's milker, Abe Borntrager, had found out about it. Freeman Yoder had paid for Polaroids of the paintings in progress, and Annie had wanted to destroy the actual paintings when she learned about the Amish law against graven images. But Howard Adams still had the paintings, and the paintings had value. The milker seemed to have something on everyone involved, and he was setting up some kind of deal. Howard Adams, the milker, her husband, Salt Box and Rachel—something was brewing between them. Maybe with the help of an art dealer in St. Paul. The death of Annie Adams had opened the door. One of them had killed her.

Eve was quiet, still, lost in something.

I raised the Levis gently to her slender hips and sat her down at the galley table. I began to whip through Annie Adams' sketchbook—hand-hewn beams, cracked-leather bridles hung on nails, ten or so pages of barn siding—until I found the trico and the blood knot.

"Look at these."

She stared without comprehension, tucking the blanket around her hips. But my brain was moving—suddenly unstuck. The coffee mug I had filled for her—*I (heart) Iowa*—it was a what? A rebus? Heart was *love*. And to make it work, you said "love" out loud.

So...blood knot, trico...for God's sake...*what?*

"What do they mean to you, Eve. As words."

Bottle caps. I thought of bottle caps.

Little Eamon and I, reading the underside of the Wacker's Root Beer caps. Four years old, and he was better at it. *Waist knot, w(ant) knot. Dad*, my boy was laughing in my ears. *Dad, don't you get it?*

And his mother says, *Wait a minute...what's going on here...you let him have root beer?*

Then I remembered another: *Bee y(oar) s(elf)*.

"Damn," I cursed. "Eve," I said, putting a finger on the trico. "What is this to you?"

"A fishing fly."

"Do you know the name?"

"I wouldn't."

"Trico," I said. "It's a tiny mayfly. But what about the word? Trico," I repeated. "Trico." Giving her a chance. She stared at me blankly.

"Okay. What's this? This sequence of drawings?"

"How to tie a knot."

"Do you know the knot?"

She pushed at her eyes and peered in. "That looks like the knot King taught me when he bought my clothesline too short."

I put my finger on the final, faulty blood knot.

"Just like this?"

She shrugged. "I guess I forgot."

I sat back with a heavy exhalation. I listened to rain and wind whip the Cruise Master. The dead woman was speaking to me.

This I was sure of. But saying what? I fingered the rough paper half-moons where the page had been torn from the sketchbook. I traced the smudges, thinking the page had been torn out in a dirty-fingered haste

Did that have meaning too? Then what?

What?

I sat still and silent, trying to get traction for my thoughts. Eve moved closer to me and shared the blanket. Deuce shifted and sighed in the bunk. Wally stretched open his tiny pink mouth, turned in a leash-addled circle, and re-settled. The lantern bathed us all in a warm, sharp-shadowed light. Outside, the sky was slow to lighten. Eve moved against me. I closed my eyes, brain spinning, and leaned my head back against the wall behind the galley bench.

"Dog…" Eve whispered after a while.

"Hmm."

"Don't sleep."

I was far from it. But I didn't want to talk either.

"I've always dreamed," she whispered, "of a moment like this."

Nervous, I kept my eyes closed. "Yeah…it's nice."

"Dog…"

"Yeah?"

"I don't know much. I told you that. I believe strange things, for reasons I don't understand. But I've always dreamed of a moment like this. I believed it would come to me. A man, a woman, in a storm, safe. A child. A dog. A lantern. Things about to happen, maybe bad things—but at this one little moment…nothing…stillness…hope…"

She paused.

"Open your eyes, Dog."

I did. Her kapp was off. Lush, wet, acorn-brown hair fell in a fat, unwinding braid around her neck and across her chest. Bangs swept her forehead, filled out her face. Her eyes, with the hair to reflect, had changed utterly. They shone richly brown. And her skin held the hair color too, and she moved her fingers, as if to heal them, through the loose, wet turns of the braid.

"I've dreamed of this. I've made mistakes for this. I thought King had this. I'm going to Hell because I chased this moment, Dog."

She moved the blanket aside and let me see her. The jeans had slipped below her hips, revealing a pair of pink-fringed white panties, stylishly boxy, with two tiny diamond gem stones where buttons might be.

"Oh, God, Eve...I don't..."

She pulled me to her.

"It's just happening this way, Dog. It's just happening this way. And I'm not going to miss it...I'm not going to miss this moment."

I eased shut the long curtain that closed in the bunk where kid and puppy slumbered. We were clumsy, and careful, and silent. Pace. Care. Stillness. Eve sat up on the end of my galley table. I undressed her from the waist down. "No," she whispered, as I tried to lift off the sweatshirt. She glanced toward the bunk curtain. "Just touch me."

As I moved my hands upon her small, cool breasts, she whirled the blanket overhead and closed us in. I braced my legs. "Yes," she whispered faintly. I pushed inside and touched her deeply, begging with my lips for her lips. And we kissed through our lovemaking, muffling each other's moans. If we moved too fast, the galley table would rattle, and the puppy would stir. So we went slowly, slowly... slowly...for what seemed an hour...a million secret breaths...and then when Eve finally came, I felt her body shrink and harden, and I felt a wind gust punch the Cruise Master, and then I felt Eve grab hold, inside, and twist the top off me...*Ahh!*

"Sh!"

She stuffed her battered fingers into my mouth...and I returned to earth gasping around them.

"Come here," she whispered, and she pulled me back in. She

grabbed me with all four limbs and squeezed hard and buried us beneath the blanket and held on until there was no more breath.

When we gasped back up into cold air, sometime later, Wally was watching from the bunk, his nose through the curtain, and it was morning. The same dull, silvery light had spilled fully into the coulee. Howard Adams had awakened inside his mini-van. I heard the door slide shut.

Gently, I set Eve back on the bench seat. I leaned over her, her legs still tenaciously attached, like a madstone, and I curled up the black-out curtain. Howard Adams was pawing about in the wet mess of the ruined teepee. He was looking for something. I had Annie's phone, I remembered. I had Annie's sketchbook. Was he looking for them? I reached back and flipped the book closed. I hadn't noticed the back cover before. Annie had written a number there: *10-27-12.*

I watched Howard Adams give up his search. He lifted a camp-fire stone and tottered toward the little lavender trailer. He smashed the stone down on the padlock.

Lock combination, I told myself. He was looking for the trailer's lock combination. To get at the Dorrie paintings. *10-27-12…*

Howard Adams raised the stone again. The stone split on im-pact. He hurled it away and collected another. I felt Eve let go and turn around beneath me.

"He's up to something," I murmured.

Then a horn sounded up on the road. But the Cruise Master window was too low. I pulled pants on. I pushed out the door and battled a wet gust around the corner of my vehicle.

"Dark green Ford Ranger," I told Eve through the open door.

"That's Rachel's."

"Howard's got Annie's trailer open now," I said.

The lavender doors swung wide, flapping in the wind. Howard Adams staggered back to his van. The engine coughed smoke from the exhaust pipe. He backed the van up to the rear of the trailer. He disappeared, but I could hear the clatter of frames as he loaded the van. I shoved the sketchbook in my pocket. I closed the Cruise Master. I plunged across the campground through the rain.

"Hey—" I yelled.

Adams was startled. He peered up at me beneath the dripping brow of his rain hood.

"Hey—what are you doing?"

"None of yours," he sniffed, pushing rain off the end of his nose.

"Shouldn't you be doing something else?" I said, "I mean, beside selling paintings. Don't you have relatives to contact? A funeral to arrange? If you can't get your son on the phone, why don't you drive up wherever he is and tell him?"

"He's not my son."

I glared at him. "His mother is dead."

"He hated his mother. He wouldn't care."

"You're an ass," I sputtered.

Adams stumbled past me. He waved an arm up at the dark green vehicle on the road. Then, "Shit," he muttered, looking at his watch. I watched five Dorcas paintings bump past me—glimpses, fragments, parting shots of beautiful, doomed Dorrie.

"That boy's got his own father," Adams grumbled. "I left a message. It's his problem."

Clumsily, he shoved in the last painting. I stood back as he slopped into the van and roared away. When he reached the Avalanche Oak at the top of the campground drive, he swung the van around, and Salt Box's milker climbed out of Rachel's vehicle to meet him on the other side of the tree.

"Come on," I yelled through the Cruise Master door to Eve. "Let's go! He's selling Dorrie's paintings!"

A house with white carpets

Deuce sat up.

"Stay here," Eve ordered her sleepy son as she tugged her wet Amish clothes back on. "Stay here and lock yourself in."

"It doesn't lock any more—" I said.

"Just stay inside then," Eve barked at Deuce. "Go to sleep until I get back."

He flopped back down. I heard Wally's whine as I slammed the Cruise Master door.

We crashed through the creek and came up behind the Avalanche Mercantile. "King's gone," she panted, heading toward the door. "But here's Abe's pickup with his key in it. Rachel must have met him here. Hang on."

In a moment she was back with her Wal-Mart shotgun. I watched her shove four shells into the stock compartment

"Eve—"

"Go!"

I lurched the milker's rickety half-ton left and swung onto County Y. I heard beer cans clatter across the truck bed. A fly fisherman leaned on the bridge rail, smoking a cigar, deciding whether to go nymph or dry. I wrenched the truck around him. I glanced back to see his middle finger in the air.

As the milker turned Rachel Kussmaul's Ranger up Avalanche Coulee Road, I said, "Eve—I don't think I can follow him in this thing. Even if I can catch up, he'll see us. He'll know his own truck."

"Just go," she muttered at me. "I don't want to follow him. I want to catch him."

"Yeah?" I carved the truck into a tight corner. "And then what?"

I caught the gravel shoulder and made a scary racket. The green truck disappeared over a rise. "Huh?" I persisted. "And then what?"

At the top of the rise, I glimpsed the Ranger on a right-hand turn, flashing through brown stalks of uncut corn. I made the turn. The road was long and flat, tracing the coulee ridge north.

"Eve—?"

She turned on me, her long braid whipping, tense as a weasel. "Can't you go faster?"

"We need to have a strategy. I suggest we just follow them, see where they're going, then back off and figure out how to deal with it. Maybe they're not doing what we think. Maybe they're taking the paintings to the dump. Honoring Annie's wishes."

She ignored that, and I didn't argue. I didn't believe it either. The milker turned west and out of sight. I had to speed up and spot him again before his next turn. Looking ahead, I failed to notice a choice Wisconsin chuck hole, the kind made by relentless frost heaves beneath the pavement. I swerved, but the right front wheel went in—the truck bucked hard—and the little shotgun went off in Eve's lap. The blast tore through the glove box, and the box spilled open, tattered Polaroids flying everywhere.

"Jesus, Eve…"

"Watch where you're going."

"I think you're holding it a little too tight. Let's put the gun down."

She answered stiffly and quietly by packing in a new shell, moving on as if the mistake had never happened.

"Dorrie doesn't know…" she said, "…what the ban will be like. She loves her mom. She loves her animals. She even loves her brothers and her dad, though she won't know it until she can't ever see them again."

Ahead about a quarter mile, Abe Borntrager had stopped the Ranger inside a nascent suburban development—if Westby, population 2,004, could have a suburb. He was backing up. Damn. I clunked the pickup in reverse and drew a steady bead on the most recent intersection. Then the milker reversed his wheels and burst up into the driveway of a nearly finished house.

I stopped my backward getaway. I eased forward again, around the corner, concealing the pickup partially behind a front-end loader with a length of sewer pipe dangling by cable from its bucket. Eve, squinting ahead, sat up ramrod straight and said, "Oh my word."

She lifted the shotgun. She opened her door.

"Eve."

"Hm?"

"No. Don't do it. Stay here. Give me the gun."

She didn't answer. She didn't even hear me. But she stayed in the truck, and I followed her gaze to the big, imitation-barn mail box in front of the house. I checked twice, because it couldn't be. But it was. The box said boldly: *Kussmaul, Boone and Rachel, Kelly, Kirby, and Kirsten.*

After a long, tense silence, as Borntrager, Howard Adams, and Rachel stepped out of the Ranger and moved toward the house, I said, "Eve…take a deep breath."

"I…I guess it's her new place," she stammered. "I haven't seen it before. I didn't realize they were almost done."

She stared through Borntrager's dirty windshield at the raw new structure, half-sided with putty-colored aluminum, the rest in yellow foam insulation with red-taped seams. The windows still wore their manufacturer's stickers. The yard was soupy, rutted clay. The driveway concrete was so fresh it was white.

"Rachel wants to live in town," Eve said. "She always wanted to live in town, since she was little. She always wanted an English house. She and Salt Box have been making extra money for years, but I didn't realize…"

"I guess you two don't talk much."

Eve hung her head. I gently tugged the plastic stock of the shotgun. She held on tight.

"She won't stop criticizing Deuce. Everything with Deuce is my fault, according to Salt Box and Rachel."

We watched Rachel slip off her shoes and enter the house. A moment later, the electric garage door hummed open on Rachel, inside a vast, two-car space, and Eve, beside me, said, "Oh my. Look at that."

Borntrager and Howard Adams each handed her a painting to take inside. Howard Adams stepped in after her, and the milker went back for the next load. Rachel, after a moment inside, returned to help him.

Eve moaned beside me. "Oh, Rachel. Oh, Sweetie."

"Is she an art dealer or something?"

"No. Well, maybe. I don't know. She knows the value of things. She knows lots of people just like herself."

I glanced at Eve. Her face had turned red. Her hands clenched the shotgun.

"No luck, Dog," she said. "I'm still angry. I'm more angry."

We watched the rest of the paintings go in. For the last load, Rachel came out herding a yawning boy a little older than Deuce, a chubby, soft kid in NBA gear—Lakers—and he dragged the final frame inside, sloppily, his mother harping at him not to bump the corners on the concrete.

I tried to clear my head with a sharp shake. The kid went in through the garage, and Abe Borntrager loosey-goosied in behind. Then down the street the other way came Salt Box in his gleaming black four-by-four. Since the milker had taken the driveway, Salt

Box jumped the curb and parked on the muddy clay yard. Round-shouldered, hulking, he clodhopped in through the front door. In a moment, he reappeared, scowling mightily, and set his cowboy boots outside the door.

"She's got white carpets," Eve said. I had a hand on her shoulder, squeezing, trying to calm her down. "I'm sure. She always talked about white carpets. We'd be partying with King and Salt Box down at King's barn and suddenly Rachel would be talking about a house with white carpets and Salt Box would start grabbing her, touching her in private places right in front of us, and she would shriek and laugh and then King would start touching me. King always said I was too cold. I was too Amish. He would always start talking about me liking outhouses too much, and asking me wouldn't I like to aim my pretty little you-know-what down a real toilet."

The electric garage door hummed down. Now the new house was tight as a drum. It was silent, lifeless.

"So your sister knows the value of things. What about Dorcas Yoder? What about the value of an Amish girl's life?"

"Rachel hates the Amish."

"But that's her life."

"She only cares about herself," Eve seethed quietly. "She only cares about having a good life for herself. She thinks she was cheated, growing up Amish."

"But that's her life," I said again. "What about Dorrie?"

"I know," Eve said. I moved my attention to her clenched left hand—small, cold, and sweaty, gripping at the fabric of her plain black dress. I touched it and wrapped my fingers around it. Then she pulled her hand free.

"I'm so angry," she said. "I am so…" She gasped, as if she couldn't stop the words. "I am so…stinky-mouthed angry…at my sister. At my…damn…witch sister…"

She sat up straight—sat up so quickly and erectly it startled me. Then she finally took that deep breath and stepped out of the pickup.

"Stop, Eve."

I leaned over to grab her. But she threw me off fiercely. She shoved the door back at me—it clanged against the shotgun barrel—and she set off up the street toward her sister's house. "Eve! Stop!"

Her wet skirt in one hand, she crossed the clay past Salt Box's pickup.

"Eve—"

"Leave me alone."

"Eve. Think about your family. Think about Deuce."

She had the handle of the screen door. She tore the door open. *Clang!* against the barrel again.

"I'm always thinking about Deuce. That's all I think about. I am nothing but my thoughts about Deuce."

She looked back wildly at me. Her braid had come loose. Her hair was drying stringy and clumped. The brand new door was vacuum-tight. The shotgun barrel was in her armpit when she slammed a shoulder into the crisp vinyl above the door knob.

"But for one day—" she slammed the door a second time "—I'd like to be something more."

Step back to the curb...please

The door gave way on startled looks inside—Salt Box and Rachel, the milker, Howard Adams, three Kussmaul children.

I could do nothing to stop Eve. She raised the shotgun in both hands. Rachel shrieked, stumbled on her thick white carpet, and backed into a blank wall. The children cowered stupidly toward the only furniture in the room, a hulking, oak entertainment center where a television babbled some cheap animation. Howard Adams did the sensible thing—he stepped quickly into the next empty room and shut the door. I heard the keys on a cell phone peeping. Salt Box was nearest the paintings, where they had been arranged beneath the picture window, side-by-side, as if for viewing.

Everybody was in sock feet—even the milker—but Eve and me, and Eve's red Chuckies tracked mud across her sister's white carpet.

"You little bitch," Rachel gasped.

And then I felt my pulse jump. I looked at the paintings. I mean, I *saw* them. And for a long moment, I could see nothing else. I had been a father—granted, of a little boy—but I didn't have to be an Amish papa to imagine what Freeman Yoder must have felt when Abe Borntrager had skulked up bearing photos of the events taking place around the easel at the creek. Freeman Yoder's gorgeous daughter had taken her kapp off. She had taken her shoes off. She had unbuttoned her collar. She had tossed her hair out—full, kinky, chestnut tresses—and she had smiled a smile for Barn Lady, for her boyfriend Robin Adams, that was at once eager, reckless, and shy.

And that was it.

That was the whole story. There was no more to the Dorcas Yoder paintings—and no less—than the graven image of the Amish girl herself, modestly unbound, sitting on a log in a streamside copse of Virginia creeper.

I know we all stared. Even Eve. Especially Eve. The paintings were sensual, surreally beautiful, a fulsome praise of God—unless, I guess, you were Amish.

"Put that damn shotgun down, you silly, mixed-up whore," growled Salt Box.

Eve, her shoulders bunched, darted a glance at him. "Where's King? He's in this too, isn't he?"

"King is on his way. You better put that down before he gets here."

He got himself a cold and silent Amish no. Then Eve backed herself up against the entertainment center, scattering the kids. She aimed the little Snake Charmer out in the general direction of the rest of us and looked down at it. As she did, Salt Box made an heroic move toward her—but I caught him by the belt.

"Hnh…?"

I felt his bulk jerk me forward, but the Dog had waded big streams. The Dog had forded the Green, the Rogue, the Clark Fork. The Dog had done little else for three years, and Salt Box felt my feral strength. He turned, big-browed, and glared at me. I said back, just over a whisper, "Try me."

"Eve," stammered Rachel finally, "get off my carpet. You get off my carpet."

Then she remembered the children and stepped clumsily in front of them. "I always knew you would do something like this. Get out of my house. Now."

"You can't sell those paintings, Rachel. You can't do that."

"He sold them." She pointed to the room where Howard Adams had disappeared. "He sold them, and I bought them," her sister said. "That's my right. And it's my right to sell them again if I want to."

"Be a good boy," I whispered to Salt Box, "and take your children into the bedroom. Bring Howard out."

I let go of his belt. "Go on."

He didn't budge.

"Shoot something, Eve."

That startled her. She looked at me. "Go ahead. Take a practice shot. Show him you can use it."

"That's right," Salt Box snorted. "She don't have the littlest idea how to—"

The shotgun's roar staggered him back. The blast filled the empty house with aftershock. Salt Box looked at himself in a panic. But he was unharmed. Between him and Eve was a gaping, smoking hole in the carpet. Rachel wailed, "Oh no!"

"Go get Howard," I said. "Bring him—"

"No," Eve interrupted. She was trembling. She wiped first one palm and then the other on her skirt.

"All of you," she said, "go in the bedroom with Howard."

They moved, and I stepped up to her, said quietly, "What are you going to do, Eve?"

"Go outside."

"What—"

She swung the gun. "Go outside!"

I backed away. I watched her exhale, shake wild hair our of her face. She reloaded the empty chamber. "Go outside," she whispered. "Please."

I did, and Deputy Austin Vossteig met me on the front walk. His words were clipped, efficient. He looked past me.

"Missus Kussmaul is armed?"

"Yes."

"She knows how to use it?"

"Yes."

"Step aside." He pressed the radio on his shoulder and called for backup.

I said, "It's just about the paintings."

"What paintings?"

I told him.

"Step back to the curb, please. Over by my vehicle."

"These people," I said, "needed Annie Adams dead. All of them. These paintings are worth a lot of money, and Annie Adams wanted to destroy them."

"Step back to the curb, please."

I flared. I had gone through twenty years of *step back to the curb* only to watch some thick-headed cop go in and make things worse. "Look. Give me thirty seconds to explain. The girl in the paintings is Eve's friend—her only friend. Those paintings get out, the girl loses everything. That's all Eve is worried about."

Vossteig was sweating. His right hand went to the taser at his hip. "Curb," he said. "Now."

"They're working together. Kussmauls and that milker. One of them killed her somewhere and brought her to the bridge. That painting scene was a set up. They made the kid take the blame. They think he'll get off."

Vossteig was breathing hard, looking down the street for his backup, trying to calm himself. But the vehicle roaring into the far end of the street belonged to King Kussmaul. A pale blue Lincoln Town Car followed him.

"You're obstructing an officer," Vossteig said. "Move away. Now."

I fumbled the sketchbook from my jacket pocket. "Look at this…"

Vossteig released the taser and put it to my chest. In a swift, smooth motion, he grabbed the arm with the sketchbook and wrenched it up between my shoulder blades. The sketchbook dropped to the ground and he walked over it as he drove me hard toward his vehicle.

"She drew a blood knot and a trico. And a dog. On the last pages of her sketchbook, after she tore one page out. You tell me why a woman who only painted barns and Amish girls would suddenly do that. You think she might have been desperate, captive somewhere, hiding somewhere, knowing she would die?"

"Desperate people about to die generally don't draw pictures," he grunted.

"Right. So when they do, it means something…"

King Kussmaul pulled alongside us. The Town Car stopped at his rear bumper. A siren wailed distantly behind them. King Midas squawked, "What in the hell…"

"Park it, King, and stay in it."

"Eve's in here with a gun!" shrieked Rachel through the bedroom screen.

Vossteig muttered a panicky, "Shit," and let me go.

"Get back in your truck, King."

But King Midas kept coming. Vossteig glanced down the street. His backup was on the way. But I was around him already. Vossteig lunged and pulled me back. He tried to crank my arm again but I twisted out of it. King Kussmaul paused at the door. His eyes were pinpricks. "That's right. You two faggots dance while I take care of business."

"*Take your boots off!*" shrieked Eve's sister through the bedroom screen.

I fought Vossteig. He was thickly muscled and well trained. He worked to control rather than hurt me. He drove me back toward the car once more. But I had taken the humane restraint classes too, way back. I struggled in a phony direction, then ducked suddenly under him, got him up on my back. I had the deputy flipped over in the dirt, had his breath put out with my body weight, and I was rolling off, about to be free, when the backup officer put a foot on my neck.

I lay there, choking, looking up at clear blue sky. Eve's little

Wal-Mart shotgun had two shells left in the stock. I listened for them. The screen door slammed behind King, and Eve cut loose. *Ka-boom!*...and then...*Ka-boom!* Both barrels, I was thinking—in a manner of speaking.

But less than King Midas deserved, I was thinking...just before the taser shut me down.

Never try that again

Or maybe it wasn't a taser. Maybe it was something new they had come up with in the time I had been away from the business.

But when the Dog saw daylight again, it was from the back seat of a Vernon County squad car, on a different street, behind a vast aluminum building. Vossteig was driving. He caught my eye in the mirror.

"Never do that again."

I knew what he meant, but I didn't care to respond. Eve had finished off her family, I thought. King Midas was dead. Eve would go to prison. Deuce would go to Salt Box and Rachel, and they would raise him. I pictured Deuce, on a massive dose of Ritalin, mucking out stalls the rest of this life. My head hurt.

"Never attack me again," said Vossteig. "Or I'll kill you. Never attack another officer. Anybody else would have killed you already. Officer Jorgenson nearly…"

The deputy trailed off.

"Where is Eve?" I asked him.

He took a right. The vast aluminum building turned out to be the backside of Wal-Mart.

"She's okay."

I let a breath out and gathered strength for my next question.

"She shot King?"

"No."

I slumped back in confusion and relief. Vossteig made another right onto the highway in front of Wal-Mart, where the road was torn up to make wider turn-out lanes for the store. I had blacked out in Westby. Now we were five miles south in Viroqua, heading back toward Westby. I didn't get it.

"I heard the shotgun…"

"She shot the paintings."

I tried to process this. She shot the paintings? We stopped for a construction flag, and the bucket of a loader swung past my window, spilling dirt. She shot the paintings. I felt a weird relief that made me suddenly nauseous, as if some terrible worry had dropped from my brain to my stomach.

"What do you mean?"

"Before King got to the door, she collected them up, leaned them one on top of the other. That way two shots ruined them all, totally, twice over. The paintings don't exist anymore. When I got you off me and caught up with King, he had hit Eve in the face, and he had her by the neck."

That was all too easy to picture. We drove a minute in silence. We took a right down toward Avalanche, then a quick left. After a half mile, the road looked familiar: Eve and I had followed Howard Adams and Abe Borntrager down that same road.

Vossteig said, "So, listen…I have to admit. All along, you've been right about some things…"

I didn't jump in. I waited.

"Eve did just care about the paintings. She wasn't a danger to anyone. She's going to get a discharging a firearm within town limits. And her uncle dropped the trespassing charges, so she's clean, legally. She's going home later today on signature. She'll have court in a month or so."

I slid further down in the seat, watched the same turns go by—we were in the same neighborhood again.

"Then I questioned the fellow from St. Paul. The guy in the

Lincoln. He's an art dealer, has a gallery. He was set to pay a hundred grand for those paintings. He thought he was getting a helluva deal, too. He kept talking about some guy, some painter, the Helga paintings, some New England painter who painted his neighbor lady in the nude. He said these paintings had that kind of power. And I do mean *had*. Eve left nothing behind to look at."

There it was—the milker's pickup. I still had the keys. My headache cleared a little. We pulled up alongside it.

"I'm free?" I said.

"In a minute."

He punched something into his on-deck computer. He flipped through a tiny notebook.

"Abe Borntrager is on parole," he said. "Two years ago he swindled an old woman in LaCrosse. Said she needed a thousand bucks' worth of radon abatement. Got caught because instead of radon abatement, he installed a video camera inside her bathroom light fixture—and got caught on a B&E when he came back for the tape." He looked at me in the mirror. "So anyhow, we searched that truck you drove up here. We found these, back in the bed, in with the beer cans."

He showed me a pair of tall, white candles, unlit, crushed and sticky with dried beer.

"Annie Adams bought those at the Avalanche Mercantile," I said, "the night she died. She put them in her pocket."

"Borntrager..." muttered Vossteig, shaking his head. "Most criminals are real dumb shits."

"Yeah," I said. "Thank God."

"We don't know where he is right now. He scooted out Rachel's back door. But we're waiting on a warrant to search his room, along with the houses and barns of Boone and Conrad Kussmaul."

"Right," I said. "Good."

"The medical examiner gave us a little wider window where Ms. Adams could have been killed earlier that night. And after all, there was only one bullet in the victim's body. So we're backing the investigation way up now, looking harder at the stories of Borntrager and these Kussmaul characters, and chances are the kid will come out a lot better."

Vossteig seemed uneasy then. I had my hand on the door handle, but he hadn't released the locks. He didn't speak for a long time. "Look," he said finally. He twisted to look at me straight. "You're lucky to be here. Never, ever try that again."

Half of everything

It was late afternoon by the time I slumped into my lawn chair outside the Cruise Master in the West Fork Campground. The day had flip-flopped to clear and chilly. It would freeze after midnight. So Abe Borntrager had killed Annie Adams, I was thinking. That made it easy enough to fit the pieces together. The milker, leveraged by his picture-taking hobby, brokers a deal with Howard Adams and various Kussmauls, who think they've got money coming. Then Borntrager kills Annie Adams to release the paintings. Thinking he can construct an accident, he hauls her to the bridge and tosses her off. He sets up a painting scene—making a mistake with the wrong painting—and then when Deuce walks into it, he improvises, convinces the kid to shoot the dead woman—and keep on shooting her until someone shows up.

But convinces the kid how? That question wouldn't go away. And how did the little yellow brush end up in the creek on Salt Box's place?

But let it go, Dog, I told myself. *Loose ends are normal. Borrow a chainsaw for the Avalanche Oak. Cut yourself out. Hit the road. Big Two-Hearted by the weekend.*

I looked around the campground. Howard Adams was gone—for good, I was guessing. A pair of SUV's, one gold, one red, turned smartly toward the campground drive and stopped short, headlights blazing into the ancient fallen oak. Three men piled out of each vehicle—big hats, cigars glowing—and cursed the inconvenience as they parked on the roadside and hauled luggage and coolers down toward the dilapidated cabins at the campground's south end.

It was the weekend, I realized. I had been in Avalanche long enough.

I went inside the Cruise Master and fixed a v-and-T. I left the sink curtain open, watching for lights at the Avalanche Mercantile—thinking I would pay a goodbye to Eve and Deuce. As I sat back at the galley table, I heard another engine buzz on the road. I listened—I felt I had heard it before—heard its lack of signifying noise, its low, sulking tone. But I couldn't concentrate. I wasn't sure.

Who was the milker, I kept thinking, to make Deuce Kussmaul do anything? What did he have on Deuce? Photos? Of a ten-year-old? Doing what?

Let it go, Dog.

In only a moment more, the engine buzz was still cautious, underplayed, but louder. Then the machine was in the campground, and I raised the rear curtain. A bulky shape on a mud-flocked four-wheeler, one I hadn't seen before, the driver's head tucked under a round-brimmed black hat, carved a careful, low-rpm circle around the camp of Howard Adams. The machine was a Honda, I saw, and red under the mud. Then the engine roared, grass flew, and the machine was gone.

I lit a candle. Everybody had a four-wheeler. So who was this one? Not King. Not Salt Box. So…Uncle Roundy? Lightning Rod? Where did all the mud come from?

Forget it, Dog. I bent to glance through the sink window. A light had come on at the Avalanche Mercantile.

A minute later I was at the counter, ringing Eve's little bell for service. After a long, nervous wait—what was I going to say to Eve?—I got King Midas instead. The middle Kussmaul brother dragged himself out in a stained white bathrobe, a cigarette dangling from his lips. A pair of black binoculars hung bizarrely about his neck.

"Wuzzit?"

"How's Eve? And Deuce?"

He squinted through smoke.

"The hell do you care?"

"It's just a simple question. I came to say goodbye. Stop being such a dumb shit."

King Midas eyed me woozily. Then he turned away and got himself a beer from the cooler. He eyed me again over the can rim. "You'll see how dumb I am."

He shuffled to the store window. He laddered up on a couple twelve packs of Bud Lite and put the binoculars to his face. "Sonofabitch is coming tonight, I know it." He said, "Here's my theory. Whatever sonofabitch is stealing my showers is that same one that's stealing all them animals."

I let him talk.

"Uncle Tater lost a pig yesterday, and I found it in my shower with its nuts cut off."

"Yeah. Thanks for that, by the way. You dropped it off at my vehicle. But then you decided it wasn't me?"

"Naw. And it ain't Abe Borntrager, either, 'cause that dirty bastard ain't been near a shower in ten years."

He adjusted his binoculars and stared across the West Fork toward the campground. Then he yelled, "Eve—someone here!"

I heard a thump upstairs.

"That dirty bastard Borntrager wouldn't go near a shower," King Midas went on. "They're gonna have to flea-dip that sucker before they can let him into prison."

While he babbled on, I played the whole thing through. It was so sad, so small, and in the end it had amounted to nothing but a pointless death. "Borntrager killed Annie," I said to King, "so all you Kussmauls could finally make some money off her artwork." I shook my head. "But now you're back to worrying about quarters in the shower machine."

"God damn…" he muttered, shifting his position on the beer boxes. "My shower problem ain't Abe. I know it ain't…" He went up on his hammertoes. "I got it figured out now. And there…" he said, " there…the sonofabitch is…"

He lowered the binoculars.

"I knew it."

King Midas shucked his bathrobe. Underneath he had on tight little cut off jeans and no shirt. He had a popped white belly with a scar on it. He ventilated mightily as he reached under the counter, and I expected serious ordnance for the job of shower defense, but what he raised up with was a can of Raid and a golf club—a two-iron.

"You laugh, man," he said, snaking past me, slipping into a flannel jacket and barn boots, "but I done some thinking since I found you washing your damn leg in my sink. I ain't gonna discharge a weapon in there. I ain't messing up my shower stall."

He paused at the door. He glared at me, like I had doubted him, and for an instant I saw him as a seven-year-old kid with scarlet fever, sitting naked in the West Fork. Now the middle-aged King Midas held up the Raid can. He jabbed at me with the two-iron.

"You're trapped in my shower stall, man, this shit will fuck you up."

"Okay," I admitted as the door slammed.

I moved quickly to watch him. From atop the twelve packs, I could see his shape lurch out across the soybean field. Then a voice behind me said, "Dog…"

"Hey, Eve…"

She had put her Amish kapp back on. She looked oddly pale and small. She moved haltingly toward me. I heard more thumps from upstairs.

"Dog…do you pray to God?"

"No," I said. "I fish."

"Maybe that's the same," she said with a little smile.

"Maybe. Kind of. I don't know."

She looked down. She rolled her wrists open and closed, as if they felt new to her. "Where'd King go?"

"To defend his shower."

She nodded silently, dropping her head. She let me wait a long time. Thump-thump! The pressed-tin ceiling shook above us.

"Deuce is going crazy right now," she said at last. "Wally is gone. After you and I left to follow Abe, Deuce untied Wally and let him out to pee by your camper, and Wally never came back. Deucey was out looking all day. But I locked him in his room now, and he's mad."

She reached out. I took her hands. She moved her head against my chest and rested her forehead against the zipper of my jacket.

"Mmmm," I said. "So why'd you lock him in his room?"

She sighed. "Just a feeling."

"What kind of feeling?"

"That he's not safe. That it's not safe around here."

We didn't speak for a while. We swayed a little. I wondered how to tell her I was leaving.

"Good about nailing Abe Borntrager, though," I managed eventually. "Huh?"

"Yeah…"

"I wonder how he convinced Deuce to lie about shooting Annie. You think Deuce has a secret?"

"I don't know," she sighed. She turned her neck, laid her cheek against me. "I wonder too…I don't really see how he could…" We swayed a while longer. Then, "Dog…?"

"Yes…"

"I wanted to tell you that I'm sorry."

"About what?"

"About this morning. About being with you. That way."

My heart sank. "Really?"

She didn't answer. Her breathing picked up to a kind of crescendo and then she moaned quietly and sagged against me.

"Well…just half," was her answer. "I guess I'm just half-sorry."

She gripped my hands.

"I'm half of everything," she told me.

She looked up, and her voice went on unsteadily. "And I'm all of nothing. I'm good. I'm bad. I want. I fear. I have. I miss. I desire. I deny. That's my Hell, Dog."

"Isn't that everybody—" I started.

"No. That's the world outside of the Amish. It's so blurry out here. So messy and confusing. That's my Hell. And I went there the moment I met King Kussmaul."

She held me, and my words popped out.

"I was about to go. I mean, leave Avalanche."

Silence. But no change in the tightness of her grip.

"See?" she said at last. "See what I mean?"

"What—?"

"Leaving is the right thing to do," she said. "And it's also totally the wrong thing. It's both." Tears rushed her soft, acorn eyes. "Dog…I can't stand it…"

She came up on the tiptoes of her red Chuckies. She put her wet face close to mine. She had put something berry-smelling on her lips. Her kiss was soft and sweet and long. Then she laid her kapp on my shoulder. "So just half-go," she whispered into my neck, "and half never, ever leave me alone in this world."

"I—I don't necessarily have to—not right this minute—"

"You mean you could—?—you'd be willing?—but then—"

And that's where Eve and I were, at arm's length suddenly, staring at one another, both a little stunned and teary and breathless, when a sharp *Bang!* sounded through the night outside.

We looked toward the window, then back at one another. And again: *Bang!*

I let my breath out. I loosened my grip on Eve. I grabbed a flashlight off the store counter. "That wasn't a golf club…"

She had closed her eyes. "No..."

Another two shots—*Bang! Bang!*—coming closer. Then from upstairs of the Mercantile, wood splintered and Deuce cried out, "Dad!" Eve followed me out the front door, screaming, "Deuce, stay in the house!"

"King didn't take a weapon," I yelled back. "He wasn't going to shoot the guy."

"No. King wouldn't—" Eve gasped beside me. She was a faster runner, and just as she passed me, King began to howl from across the soybean field, from across the creek.

"Shit!" he bawled. "Oh, my God! Ow! Shit!"

Oh, my God!

Ow! Shit!

I saw his flapping shape on the run. Behind him charged the milker, Abe Borntrager, his loopy stride unwinding to full speed. Then another gunshot—*Bang!*—and King's feet left the ground. His coat blew open as he cartwheeled into the creek. The gunshots ceased.

Eve stopped at the creek edge. I limped up beside her. Her voice came as if out of a small, hollow place. "King wouldn't actually hurt anyone," she finished, "over quarters..."

Opposite us, the milker put hands on knees beside the creek, his lungs spuming steam. I tried to see what he had shot King Midas with. Nothing. I could not see a weapon. Then, from behind Abe Borntrager, the gun fired again—*Bang!*—and the milker went down.

I plunged across the creek. I shined the flashlight on the milker as he lay moaning on the bank. I panned the flashlight beam. King Midas had gone down in deep, fast water. I saw the white liner of his coat, and I pitched downstream after.

I don't have to tell you that the West Fork was icy. But I didn't feel it. I don't recall the cold. I don't recall pain in my injured leg. What I remember is the stones coming up to meet my feet, pushing me off just right, propelling me downstream through waist-deep water. I moved fast. I held the flashlight high, tracking King Midas. But somewhere ahead he sank. I slowed down, kicking back and forth, feeling for the softness of a body. Fifty yards. A hundred. Then I felt him.

I dragged King Kussmaul halfway up onto a mud spit and shined the light on his face. His eyes were open. His lips leaked bloody water. The last shot had come out through his gut, just below the sternum. I raced light into his left pupil. It stayed wide. He was dead.

I sat back on my heels. I fought the bile at my throat. Behind me, Eve thrashed out through the streamside brush.

"King!"

She wailed it from the gut. She hiked her dress and crashed into the stream. But her husband was dead. His feet wobbled in the current. Deuce splashed up beside us.

"Dad!"

Across the campground, the bathroom door slammed. A bulky figure moved through the yard light. A four-wheeler turned over, revved high and rough, spat gravel up the campground drive, and skirted the Avalanche Oak. The machine fled hard, engine banging, north.

"You bastard!" Deuce screeched, his voice so pained and raw that it was then that my adrenaline peaked and I felt the despair, the confusion, sweep in. The killer wasn't Abe Borntrager. It wasn't King Midas. The violence in Avalanche had nothing to do, I thought, with the Dorcas Yoder paintings.

And then—closer—something staggered, wheezing, toward me across the campground grass. I shined the light. Two dull red dots shined back. Then my light caught a small pink mouth with tiny sharp teeth. The thing fell down, struggled back up, wanly wagged a tail.

Wally...

Eve wretched behind me.

"Oh...King..." she wailed, and she bent and struck her husband's body, struck it and struck it with her fists, kicked it, as if to kill him once again. I looked for Deuce, to shield him. But the Avalanche Kid was crashing back across the creek, racing toward the Mercantile.

Deuce—!

Eve Kussmaul stopped flailing and went to her knees in the icy current. Her dark skirts held air, her apron spread out and rode the ripples, and for a long and precious moment she looked like a lotus, her pale arms outspread, the white bulb of her kapp nodding like the tip of the flower. Then, keening in deep, vestigial German, she fell forward onto the corpse of her husband.

I scooped up Wally. The little puppy sagged like rubber in my arms, but still he strained and wriggled, in slow motion, trying to lick my face.

I limped across the campground to the bathroom. I knew the smell before I saw the blood. If you have ever cleaned a large fish, or gutted a deer, you know the odd, metallic scent of blood in volume. It sticks in the nose and throat. It makes you weak. You can't mistake it.

I hit the light switch. Footprints. Dog and human. Curves and smears and pads of bare feet tracking watery blood out of the shower stall. Across the floor before the urinals were strewn King's two-iron and his Raid. In the stall, blood pooled on the white plastic chair. The stinging scent of rubbing alcohol rose about a spilled brown bottle. A blood-smudged towel hung on the clothes hook.

I backed out. I laid Wally in the sink. His little brown body sunk and molded into the oval depression, and he sighed, his eyes rolling up at me. I looked for wounds, and he was bloody enough to have lost a pint, but he seemed to be in one piece. I rolled him, ran water on him. As the blood washed away, I saw that he was uncut. Yet he was drugged, or injured, somehow. I rolled him back. I took my jacket off and covered him. He sighed again and closed his eyes.

I turned the lights out. I closed the bathroom door. Eve's moans sounded above the slow, smooth gurgle of the West Fork. The milker rolled and twitched and crawled, going nowhere. I limped back to the Avalanche Mercantile and dialed 911.

When I emerged into the cold night, I had one strange and dreadful moment of calm—looking up at a gibbous moon hung up in the Milky Way—before an engine roared to life and lurched past me: Deuce Kussmaul, aboard his father's gagging John Deere Trail Buck, toting his mother's Wal-Mart shotgun.

"Deuce—!" I hollered.

But he was gone.

What was Annie Adams saying to me?

And to where Deuce had gone, no one knew—except to know that that place would be the place to find his father's killer…and Annie Adams' killer…and maybe, I worried, the bodies of the Avalanche Kid and his mother, who had lurched away blindly after her little boy in her husband's truck. Eve hadn't known which way to go, she hadn't even known exactly how to start and shift the truck, or where the headlights were, but she had torn away in low gear, west, into the dark.

Again the West Fork campground became a crime scene, and this time I was inside the tape. The Cruise Master pulsed with red-and-blue lights. It bobbed in a sea of motion and voices. Radios squawked like strange, scavenging birds in the night. I answered questions, answered them again, answered them a third time, and then I paced, and lifted curtains, and drank vodka without the Tang. I felt heat on my forehead. I felt scratchings in my spine.

Rabies…after all, I thought. The madstone hadn't worked. Nothing, I told myself, nothing about this scene could be trusted or understood. Nothing, for sure, except the deviance of Borntrager.

The verminous peeper had been holed up inside my Cruise Master when the shooting broke out at the bathrooms. Crudely, with his trademark clever stupidity, he had been trying to squeeze me. Faintly and sloppily, using my red map-marking pen, he had scrawled a note right onto the Cruise Master's faux-paneling wall. He had unpinned my *This is not a pipe* postcard, let it fall to the floor, and in its place he had tacked up a dark and grainy shot of Eve in my lap behind the Cruise Master steering wheel, kissing me. So that was the pop of light I saw through my closed lids. On the wall, Borntrager had been telling me, *Mister in my bisnis Im in a pikkel now but so are you—see this picher. I will show it to King. Now you leave the kees to this vehikkel or else I show it to King and he will kill you for sure.*

I guessed Borntrager had just finished up the con and walked outside when the shooting started. There was something, always, about the timing of guys like him. I lurched back across the width of my tiny living space. I swept aside the black-out curtain. A bulldozer had shoved the Avalanche Oak down into the campground. The earth was gouged, frenzied with spinning lights. A sheriff's cruiser rocked up the grade, spun its rear wheels, then burst away on the road above.

I smelled Eve in the space around me. I crawled up into my bunk. I smelled the Avalanche Kid. I smelled the puppy. A moment like this, I remembered Eve saying. Safe inside, a storm outside… and then my mind skipped.

Annie Adams had been captive. I felt sure of that suddenly. She had been caught by the killer, and she had known that she would die, but she had had time and space—inside somewhere—before it happened. To defend herself, she had possessed nothing more than her sketch book, her candles, her Snickers bar, the small, clear plastic bag Eve had given her at the Mercantile, and her little yellow brush. Hell—I changed my mind—she wasn't defending herself. She couldn't. She was defending the rest of us.

I sat up, hunched beneath the bunk's low ceiling, and I remembered the single page torn out of the sketch book. Where was that page? What was on it? Was it nothing? Had the killer torn it out? Or had Annie Adams hidden it? I had a sudden memory of her mangled right arm, trailing downstream of her head in the current below the bridge, her profusion of leather bracelets nowhere in sight. Where were these things? The bracelets—the torn page. Did they matter? How did they fit with blood knot, trico, dog?

I slugged vodka, thrashed over in the bunk, tried for one foolish moment to make it all go away, to relieve myself in sleep.

But a minute later I was rolling off the bunk. I ripped line off my reel. As lights spun outside I hunched over my galley table, under my Eve-scented wool blanket, and I tied blood knots. Over and over. Male and female ends. Twining into each other, looping back, penetrating those self-made loops, twisting, tightening, knotting up. I pulled. They held.

Then I tied blood knots wrongly—as Annie Adams had first tried to tie them, and as she had later sketched one in her book. I made just one wrong turn. I made one small but significant error inside the helix of the knot. I made the mistake again, again…then in different ways, then random mistakes…tying blood knots until it was dawn and the crime scene outside had evaporated with the pale light of a cloudy autumn morning.

Then I pulled. I pulled. I had done the same in front of Annie, to prove she couldn't tie the blood knot any old way. She knew that knot was bad. She knew the sight of a bad knot would jar me. I pulled, and the miscreant knots held…they held…they showed strength…they showed rigid, tenacious, impressive strength…and then they snapped.

Every last one.

And someone knocked at my door.

Make it hurt

"How's the leg?" asked Moth Kussmaul. "You doing okay?"

I was hoarse. "Fine."

"How about wood? Okay on wood?"

I shook my cluttered head. Wood? Wood was the stuff you burned in a campfire. "Uh…I was okay yesterday…and I didn't make a fire last night…so…"

"Because I see they bulldozed that oak down the hill and I can get the truck in here, drop you off a whole load."

He didn't look any better than I did. He looked pale, a little shaky. I glanced past him out the door. There was his ancient red Chevy—filled to the sideboards with split and seasoned oak. An Amish kapp showed through the rear window, just above the heap of firewood. I stepped out on the frosted grass.

"It's Eve," he said, "She ended up at my place last night. We found King's four-wheeler hidden off the road up by the tri-county corner. But no Deuce. And now my Ma's gone."

Eve got out. "Thank you," she told him numbly.

Moth Kussmaul hobbled awkwardly after his sister-in-law. "Hey, Evey—sit down. This is the campground. You're not home yet."

"This is fine," Eve managed. "I'll walk from here."

"Just let me unload some wood for Dog here, and then I'll—"

Eve walked numbly past him. She stumbled past the Dog. She went inside the Cruise Master and shut the door. Moth Kussmaul blinked after her, a pained look on his haggard face.

"I'm fine on wood," I told him again.

He seemed beaten and heavy, stuck in the frozen grass. "Yeah," he sighed. "Yeah. Okay."

Eve was spooning the last of my instant coffee into two cups when I climbed back aboard the Cruise Master. She had just set the pot on the flame when I caught her nipping a small white pill between her lips ahead of a slug of jug water. She swallowed. I had a wad of smelly old coats under the sink. I put one on each of us before I said, "Meth again? Now?"

"When else?"

I looked at her.

"Why not?" she challenged me. "I won't rest until I find him."

"Last night..." I began.

"Ma Kussmaul is gone too."

"I heard. But how? Is someone missing a vehicle?"

She shrugged forlornly. "No."

"How about a horse? A buggy?"

"Some investigator told me Freeman Yoder had been questioned but wouldn't talk to them. So they have a warrant. They're searching Yoder's place today."

She shivered. I could almost see the meth rushing to her brain. She held her chewed fingers around the gas flame beneath my hot water pan, catching stray heat.

"I'm sorry about King."

I watched her fingers lower closer and closer to the blue flame. I swear I saw her skin glowing. "Eve..." I pulled her hands back and held them. They were nearly too hot to touch. "Eve...don't. Please."

She yanked her hands out of mine. "Deputy Vossteig called all the farms in this coulee and Norwegian Coulee. He asked them to look in their barns and call back if they found anything. Two called back."

I took her by the shoulders. I sat her down on the galley bench and put the wool blanket around her trembling shoulders.

"Yes?"

"Lightning Rod's girlfriend was all hissy," she said through chattering teeth. "I guess they're missing another twelve-pack of Mountain Dew and another side of bacon."

"I feel their pain…" I muttered. I sat down beside Eve and massaged her steel-taut neck. I touched the dirty-green tattoo, the choker of thorns.

"And Uncle Roundy," she jittered out, "is missing a deer rifle. And you know Uncle Tater—the one with the high voice? He's missing altogether. His wife said he never came home last night. I guess there's one vehicle unaccounted for."

"I forgot which one he was—Uncle Tater."

"He's nobody," she said darkly. "Just a brain-dead dirt farmer. Ma Kussmaul's other little brother, the one they didn't kill off in childhood."

We sat silently for a while. Eve flinched and kinked under my touch. The water boiled. I poured it and made two cups. I asked her, "You're sure you need caffeine…?"

"I'm sure. It levels me out."

"What about funeral stuff for King? Do you have to worry about that too?"

She shook her head. "Salt and Rachel will handle that…"

"That's nice."

No answer—except from outside, that quintessential Avalanche sound: the distant buzzing of a four-wheeler.

"No. It's not nice. The idea is that since I can't keep King alive," she said, "I can't be trusted with his funeral." She cricked her neck sideways. "Something like that."

I let out a ragged, mournful breath. The engine buzzed closer.

"You want to hear my vision of Hell," I said, "at this point? After a week in Avalanche?"

She tipped her head the other way, wanting more of my touch. "Make it hurt," she said. "Push harder…"

"Four-wheelers," I told her. "In my version of Hell, everybody rides a four-wheeler. You want to move six feet to the right, you fire up your four-wheeler. When your cell phone rings, you start up your four-wheeler and drive around for good reception."

The latest horseless buggy rumbled a slow circle around us. I thought I knew it. Not by name or sight. But, in the same way that I absorbed the call of a new bird around a new creek in a new place, I knew suddenly that I'd been hearing that engine. It's sound profile had worn a slight groove. I knew it. The clean engine—or the slow one, the one that stayed in low gear, tried not to excite itself, tried to stay in the background. The one I heard after Dorcas Yoder's friend escaped the hay loft.

"Last night too," I told Eve, "and I think several times in the days before that, that guy, or whoever, comes through the campground. Muddy red Honda. He likes to circle the teepee—just mosey around it—even after Howard Adams knocked it down. But this is the first time in daylight."

As I spoke, the engine slowed. The sound dropped to idle and drifted away from us, then back, then away, then back again—then suddenly, for the first time, the four-wheeler muttered right up beneath the Cruise Master window.

"So I guess now we'll see who it is," I said. Eve was closer. "Go ahead," I told her. "Quickly."

Eve leaned away from me and yanked up my black-out curtain. "Oh!" she gasped, and the engine shrieked back in a panic.

She turned to me as the four-wheeler raced away.

"That's it!" she cried. "That's who did it!"

"What?"

"That's who killed Annie and King!"

"Who?"

"I don't believe it…how can he be…"

"Who?"

"That," she said, "on that machine, that was Deuce's buddy. Annie's son. That was Robin Adams."

That Adams kid

"I should have known," she panted at me as we hurried down the long gravel drive to Yoder's farm. "Deuce has been taking food from the store for about two weeks now. I wasn't telling King. But I should have known he was giving it to someone."

"And Dorrie," I said, "was seeing someone in Yoder's hayloft. She had these strange pictures—"

Eve looked at me.

"Body parts?"

"Private parts."

"Weird? Black-and-white? Not really porno?"

"Yes."

"Deuce has them too. Printed out from a computer."

"But what would Robin Adams be doing with pictures like that? Where would he get them? Why would he be passing them out?"

The ground around the Amish barn and house was crowded with buggies and horses for Sunday worship.

"Maybe Dorrie can tell us. You talk," I told Eve.

"No. It has to be you. I'm in the ban. The Amish can't even look at me."

"Then—"

"You distract Freeman," she told me. "That shouldn't be hard.

He won't want you to say a word to him where people can hear. I'll try to get Dorrie alone."

Amish kids played around the buggies—and then stopped cold, staring wide-eyed and silent as we made our way to the house. It was hard to say, as I scanned their faces, what worried them more: the gimping English, or the Hell-bound woman they were supposed to shun.

The door to Yoder's house was open. Amish boys worked to line the large central living room with benches, and beyond that, girls and women worked in the kitchen. Word of our presence had spread in Amish German, and a teenage boy ran screeching past us: "Papa!"

"You a detective then, after all?" the old man said coldly to me when he appeared from around the house, "playing yourself off as a fisherman?"

No, I told him. I was the opposite. Which gave him a chance, I said, to set things on the right course before the real detectives got here. They had a warrant to search his farm, I told Yoder. Yes, I answered him: during church if they decided to.

Freeman Yoder hitched ahead, favoring his left leg, while the Dog, in tow, limped on his right. The Amish bishop led me to his barn. He took me down one of his feed alleys, and when we reached midpoint he turned on me with a furious, glittering stare.

"My daughter is still a child. She doesn't know her mind."

"I don't want your—"

"I'm not finished, English. These Zook girls, Eve and Rachel Zook, look at their lives. Hellish, ruined lives. A crying mother. A father insane with rage. Brothers angry enough to kill a man. Now people are dead. That's what comes of the likes of you chasing Amish girls."

I stared at him, bewildered.

"Dorcas tell me you been meeting her in my hay loft. I wouldn't believe it if I hadn't caught you there myself."

"She's lying," I stammered. "She's protecting someone."

Still his eyes gleamed with rage.

"I don't want your daughter. That's not why I came in your barn the other night. Someone else was in there with her."

His face went red inside the rim of his round, white beard.

"The two of you were alone," he argued. "Dorcas told me so."

"No. She's lying. As I came up the loft ladder, her friend went out the hayfork doors and down the side of the barn."

"That's impossible. That's thirty feet down. I would have found a dead man."

I challenged him. "Let's look."

He stumped out the far end of the feed alley and left the barn through a broad door between two calf pens. Freeman Yoder looked up. A rope dangled from the hay fork pulley. There was a jump at the end of it, onto a hard-packed wagon ramp, but a healthy kid could survive it.

Now Freeman Yoder hung his head, his rage against me slipping away. I watched his gnarled hands clench. "Must be that Adams kid," he figured at last to the dirt. "The dead woman's son."

I said, "So we agree."

I waited. After five long minutes, Freeman Yoder brought his beautiful daughter to the barn by the scruff of her neck. Eve followed silently, and Amish eyes watched from every window and corner. When Freeman Yoder had driven Dorcas deep into the same feed alley, he turned to me. "Tell the English wife she doesn't need to be here."

"I'm not leaving," Eve said back, straight to him, her eyes sharp and tight with meth energy.

Freeman Yoder looked at me.

"Tell her to go."

"I won't go."

Dorcas Yoder, her head bowed, said, "Eve's my friend, Papa. I won't say a word if you make her go."

The old man bounced his icy glare between the three of us.

He pushed his black hat back and scratched his balding head. He muttered something in German and Dorrie said back, "Yes, he will, Papa. God will forgive you. He'll forgive us all."

For a long moment, Freeman Yoder stared fearfully through a dusty window along the edge of the feed alley. He knew—we all knew—that the eyes of his people stared back in, but the dust was thick, and Dorrie began to speak.

"Robin ran away from his summer camp," she told us all. "To see me."

Freeman Yoder dropped a work-scarred hand on the dusty sill.

"He stole a four-wheeler and drove all the way down here on back roads, at night. He stole gas from people's garages and barns. He did it because he hates his parents. And he did it because I said I wanted to see him."

Her father's hand worked its way along the sill, sweeping nails and dust and bird dung toward the corner.

I said, "Robin's in trouble, Dorrie…"

She hung her head. She kneaded the pleats of her skirt. She began to shake and sniff.

"Dorrie," I said, "at this point, you want to want to help him do the right thing."

"He—" she started. "They—"

She had begun to cry quietly. "I asked Robin to come. I mailed him letters from up at Half-Tim's." She sniffed. "Half-Tim gave me stamps."

"Robin was angry at his mother?"

"Yes."

"Because—"

"Because she stopped him from being with me. Robin was very angry."

"He's in trouble now," I told her. "Very big trouble. You're part of it, Dorrie."

"I knew he was breaking into people's barns, taking things. He found those pictures, those pictures of people's private bodies, and he stole them to show me. I told him taking things was wrong. But Robin said adults were always doing wrong things and then pretending they didn't…and so he didn't care."

Freeman Yoder swept the sill. Eve put her arm around the girl. I felt like crying myself. Adults doing wrong. A kid destroying himself in protest. The Dog had been there, in that Hell. The Dog would always be there.

I asked Dorrie, "Did Deuce know Robin was here?"

She nodded. "Deuce gave him food from the store. I gave him an Amish hat and jacket and a lantern and matches."

"So where is Robin?"

"I don't know."

Her father wheeled on her in a storm of rage and dust.

"Wo is der Junge?"

"Where is he, Dorrie?"

Eve squeezed her shoulder. "It has to go this way now, Dorrie. We have to find Robin now. You have to tell."

It was a while before she spoke. One brave Amish youngster jumped his head up to the dusty window—just a hat, a blur of flesh, then a clatter below the outside wall of the barn. Dorrie whispered, "Up on the tri-county farm."

That stopped me. "You mean…"

"Half-Tim's place. That's what Papa calls it. The trico farm."

I looked at Freeman Yoder. His head was lowered now. His boots scraped at the dusty concrete floor.

"That's what it's called on the Amish farm map. Papa wants to buy it for Amos. I mean, after…" She looked around for help. Her father stared at the floor. Eve and I looked back at her, puzzled. "The farm where the three counties meet on the map. Someday Ma Kussmaul is going to…you know…she won't live long, Papa says…and when she's gone Half-Tim will get a job in a city somewhere…so the trico farm…"

I turned to Freeman Yoder.

"They're coming for you today," I told him. "Maybe with some reason. But they're going to end up with Dorrie, too."

He bent his neck and showed me the top of his hat. He didn't speak.

"Robin Adams," I said, "is hiding up in the half-timber barn, on the tri-county farm. His mom, snooping around, found him there. She went up to confront him, and he killed her. She tried to say, in her sketch, that it was a family thing gone wrong. He tried to make it look like an accident, but Deuce got involved. Deuce worshipped Robin. He agreed to take the blame. Robin is still in the barn. He's waiting for Dorrie to get loose and come with him." I glanced at the girl. "He tried to take a shower and panicked when King Midas caught him. He's had to do something with Deuce and Ma Kussmaul to stay hidden. And Dorrie has been helping him hide."

Eve's head was sunk now too. I looked at Dorrie. "Isn't that right?" I asked the girl. I was sure of it. I needed to be sure of it. I needed the relief of having put things together at last.

Trico was the barn, I thought, the place, the hideout; Annie's own son, her mis-tied blood knot, was the killer.

And so it threw me—when Dorrie whispered, "No."

Bacon...I smelled bacon

No, Dorcas Yoder said.

No, she denied. Robin Adams hadn't killed his mother. No!

She didn't know who did. But it wasn't Robin. And he wasn't hiding in the half-timber barn. He was hiding on the farm property, but not in the half-timber.

Eve held her as she shook. Freeman Yoder put both work-gnarled hands on the sill and hung his head, nudging a strand of straw back and forth with the toe of his boot. The boy she loved had been in every barn and garage in the coulee, Dorcas Yoder told us, stealing gasoline, food, tools, horse blankets—anything he needed to survive. He was in an open cave somewhere up on the coulee wall. Yes—he was waiting for her. But he was innocent of murder, she claimed, and he was up where there were boulders in the forest.

"I'll stay with her," Eve told me, and she stepped wild-eyed and meth-hot between Freeman Yoder and his daughter.

The old man backed up a step.

"You go find Robin," Eve told me.

I walked north along the stream bank, skirting a half-mile of Salt Box's tidy pastures, until the coulee narrowed and clogged with the unkempt fields of the tri-county farm. Then I thrashed and slipped up the steep west wall—nagged, all the way, by how things had fit together so suddenly, and had just as suddenly fallen into chaos in my mind. How had Annie Adams had time to sketch her rebus? Was there a torn page somewhere? Had her son held her, tormented her, before he…what? How had he killed her? How could a son kill a mother? Why hadn't he just shot her, like he had King Midas? And what was he doing with his sad and grimy pictures of male and female anatomy, when he had his own parts, when he had a gorgeous and willing Dorcas Yoder right in front of him? Where had he gotten the pictures?

I wouldn't know until I found Robin Adams, I understood, and I pushed on up the coulee wall. I beat my way up through black cap brambles and rain-slicked leaves. The under-forest was dense, and dim, but the subtle vacancies of deer trails stood out and I followed them, branching up until they began to wind around through car-sized boulders that had been grown over by the forest.

I stopped to catch my breath. I thought I smelled wood smoke.

Through a gap in the trees I could see the coulee floor below. I was looking down, I realized, on the tail end of a long, snaking, weather-grayed wood pile.

I moved on through heavy underbrush. The wood pile, glimpsed in flashes a quarter mile down through the trees, seemed to worm north with me. I kept my nose to the smoke. I kept my feet on the soft, black center of the trail, avoiding leaf noise. Ahead, generations of white-tailed deer had squeezed through damp, moss-padded chunks of the coulee wall, and I stopped at a point too narrow for my shoulders. A shape some distance in front of me, boulder-like, was nonetheless something else. Something muddy, not mossy, with pipes, and a wide, cracked seat: four-wheeler. Red Honda.

I listened. I saw no light ahead, but the smoke was the sweet, wet fume of a doused fire. And bacon. I smelled bacon. Far downhill, the wood pile had expanded. It had become ten feet high, double wide, the wood carefully regimented, pewter and frost-rimed—but then suddenly it was broken open, at one point, on raw and steaming tree flesh. As I wondered at that, I heard movement ahead under the next big boulder. I heard paper crunch, something clink, a soft mutter.

My Glock. I should have brought it. I hesitated a long time, wondering if I should go back. But Robin Adams had heard me coming. I felt sure of that. He had doused his fire, mid-bacon. He was waiting for me. He was caught. He was panicked. If I turned my back, I thought, the kid would shoot me too, like he'd shot King and the milker.

I approached the muddy Honda. The boy had left the key in. I took it out. I know he heard the *snick* of the key hole as it closed. In the back of the vehicle, in its little fenced bed, Robin Adams kept a two-gallon jug of gasoline. It sloshed as I lifted it. He heard me, of course, as I climbed atop the boulder that sheltered him.

Moss peeled away as I edged toward the boulder's front, into a strong bacon smell. Robin Adams was beneath me. He heard me. In the forest dimness I couldn't see well enough to move smoothly and so I scraped and skidded toward the overhang that sheltered his hole. I shoved the gas jug ahead. Moss and leaves and pine needles cascaded off into his still-steaming fire pit.

"Who is it?" came a small voice from beneath me.

"We'll see about that in a minute."

I dumped gas over the edge. I slopped the whole two gallons over the front of his hole, over the Amish hat and bulky coat that I could see dimly atop over a pile of firewood, over the dry bed of needles where his feet stuck out. I soaked his doorway until there was no gas left. Then I pushed the jug off the edge. It thumped and bounced and disappeared into the downhill brush.

"Now come out of there," I said, "with your hands empty."

He didn't move. The Dog snarled.

"Come out. Hands empty. Or I drop this match."

Dog on pup

It nagged me, the way Robin Adams came out.

He stumbled out like a…well, like a kid, with a precious piece of Lightning Rod's bacon in one hand, a Mountain Dew in the other.

I nearly dropped the match.

"Jesus Christ, kid," I said, the tiny flame flaring in my face. "I said hands empty."

He jettisoned the Dew. He stuck the bacon in his mouth.

I blew the match out.

"I nearly dropped this." My heart hammered. "I said hands empty."

He was a tallish, thin kid, shivering hard. He had Annie's bright eyes and curls. "Sorry," he stammered. "Sorry. I didn't realize I was holding stuff."

"Step out and away from the hole."

"Okay."

I jumped down into the gas fumes.

"You have a rifle in here?"

"Yes."

I found it quickly. I swung the barrel at him and he froze.

"You stole it from a farm with a round barn?"

He nodded. His clothes were misfit Amish pants, suspenders, and bulky black jacket.

"Dorrie gave you the clothes?"

"Yes," he croaked.

"You have a flashlight in here?"

"It's by the entrance. Left side."

He had a big mag light, a foot long, but its batteries were weak.

"Which barn is this from?"

He let a breath out. I put the pale light in his face, saw freckles and dirt and badly chapped lips.

"King Midas," he said.

He cautiously raised one hand. He threaded fingers through his heavy curls and scratched his scalp hard.

"Was Dorrie planning to give you a haircut the other night?"

He nodded.

I followed with, "Where's Deuce?"

He shrugged. I looked him over carefully. He was a kid—maybe even a pretty tough kid, when he had to be—but I could overpower him, Dog on pup, if I had to. So I lowered the rifle. I turned my back and aimed the flashlight into the cave. He had a few hairy blankets. He had most of a twelve-pack of Mountain Dew. He had a tube of beef jerky and a case of Otis Spunkmeyer muffins. He had a little pile of tools: screwdrivers, channel locks, a hammer.

"You know what's been going on in this coulee the last few days?"

"I don't know," he stammered. "I've seen a lot of cops."

"And you figured..."

"I figured they were looking for me."

"Dorrie didn't tell you?"

His voice rose. "She won't. She won't tell me what happened. She acts like I already know and I just won't tell her. She just cries and begs me to run away with her. But we don't have any money. We won't get anywhere."

I turned and once more raised the weak light between us. Robin

Adams closed his eyes against it. He agonized over his words a long moment. "My mom's dead," he scratched out finally. "Isn't she?"

I nodded.

The boy turned in a clumsy circle. Then he flopped down on the pine needles between us. He began to weep. And things began to shift and slide in my mind. The blood knot. The knot of blood, kin, family—flawed to the snapping point—a nice idea—perfect for a state-paid shrink—but the kid hadn't killed his mother. That wasn't what Annie Adams meant.

"Where did you get the pictures, Robin?" He hesitated. "The ones you and Dorrie were looking at in Yoder's hayloft."

"I busted into a barn a couple of days ago, right down below. The half-timber barn where Dorrie works. I took some tools from the tool room. I mean, nobody used that barn. Everything was caked with dust. I went down into this cellar thing, this dirt room dug out below the stalls and I found this lamb in there...he was...he was crying..."

I urged him to go on.

"Somebody...had cut his stuff off...his balls and stuff...and sewed him up...and he looked real sick. He wanted out. I let him go. And in that same room, I found those pictures...and some other stuff...And I...and I..."

I waited for him.

"I got caught," he said. "I got caught in there. I got chased out."

He looked like he would run again. I raised Uncle Roundy's deer rifle. I tried to slow my pulse. Tri-county farm. Blood knot. Pipes that were not pipes that were not not-pipes. I braced myself.

"Who chased you out?" I asked him.

"The old lady," Robin Adams said. "Ma Kussmaul. She said anybody who came in that barn was asking to die."

Tell me, Deuce. Damn it. Tell me.

From the edge of the western woods, at cold and early sunset, the original Kussmaul farm looked awash in gray waves of stove wood. I was surprised to see that the famous half-timber barn was a wee, slumped thing, riding precariously inside ringed breakers of split oak and hickory—waves and rows and alleys of cord wood that swept and swelled and marched north to surround a small and sagging once-white house. Smoke rose wanly from the crumbled chimney, as if to make the point that the effort was useless, trying to burn all this wood. It would never happen. There was another direction, another reason, for all of this stored-up Kussmaul energy.

I rolled under a disused fence and stood up in the abandoned eastern high pasture. I spooked a pheasant out of chest-high wild parsnip, watched it rocket noisily over the wood piles around the antique barn. In the other direction, toward the crumbling farm house, a screen door squeaked and slammed. I walked wide around a reef of dry oak, getting an angle on the house in time to see Moth Kussmaul lumber out on the porch. He lit a cigarette and smoked it slowly, watching the smoke curl away through the shadowy canyons of fire wood. From my distance, his posture made him look sad, injured, exhausted. I imagined he had done a lot—far too much, I guessed—to tolerate and protect his mother. But where was she?

Where was Deuce? What had happened? What was the old lady's secret in the barn?

Moth lifted a gym bag off the porch floor, limped heavily to his pickup.

"Moth!" I called, crashing downhill through the weedy field. "Moth, wait!"

But I was too far off. He didn't hear me. He levered gingerly, like an old man, into the pickup, and he eased the vehicle quietly away up the long gravel drive to Avalanche Coulee Road. He turned south, toward the Avalanche Mercantile, County Y, and the highways beyond.

Leading with Uncle Roundy's deer rifle, I entered the house. The foyer was cold and rank, clogged with boots and coats and bags of garbage. The first room, the kitchen, smelled like cabbage, mold, and fried chicken. Someone had just cooked. The oil was still warm in the fryer. The iron sink, amidst dirty dishes, held the feet of a chicken. The window above the sink was taped around the edges, where it met the sash. Beyond it, framed in cord wood, was the weathered outhouse that I had seen in the milker's Polaroids. I looked back down at the sink. No faucets. I looked up. Low-watt light bulbs. Electricity...a phone on the wall...but no plumbing.

I moved on. There were three other rooms in the house, all cluttered with junk but unoccupied. I could see that Moth and his mother shared one bedroom, Moth on the top bunk. Fist-sized holes in the paneled wall connected that room with a living room, where an ancient television murmured the weather report to no one. It was going to be a peach of a late-September day...cloudless until noon, a soft breeze, high in the seventies. Probably tricos in the morning, blue-winged-olives in the afternoon...those thoughts drifting through my head as effortlessly and pointlessly as the flies that buzzed when I cracked the third door.

A fetid whiff hit me and I staggered back, slamming the door. I pinched my eyes shut for a long moment, trying to make my heart slow down. I knew the smell. The smell wasn't flesh. It wasn't blood. It was ammonia. Guano.

I cracked the door again. Chickens lived in the third room. The old sash window on the north side was blocked open, and the birds came and went, roosting in the closet, on the old roll-top desk, in the book shelf, pecking along the dung-littered plank floor. There were twenty of the creatures…maybe thirty. Two appeared dead on the filthy floor. The others blinked at me, uncertain, and then, one-by-one, cautiously, they began their funky tiptoe toward me, clucking softly, heads bobbing and cocking, looking to be fed.

I closed the door. I hurried outside and gulped the brisk coulee air. I had to check the barn next, the cellar where Robin Adams had been asking to die, and I felt fear ripple through me. But before I could step off the porch, I felt the presence of another ripple—some vague but real energy ticking south-to-north through the vast shoal of cordwood in front of me.

I raised the rifle and listened. With my eyes, I followed the wave south. Something stirred there, inside the woodpile, where it had toppled into disarray between the house and the barn. Coons, most likely. Or rodents, and something hunting them. But I had to walk that way anyway.

It was as I drew alongside the tumbled mess of split oak that I understood that the disturbance was very new—today new—the same patch of raw wood I had seen from up in the avalanche. The weathered surfaces of the surrounding wood pile were silvery for a hundred yards up and down, and in all the subsidiary joints and annexes and side-piles. But right here, where the pile had collapsed, the inside wood-flesh was freshly exposed, was tawny and moist, releasing heat and crawling with earwigs. And that anomalous, dark brown, polished piece—hard plastic—that was the stock of Eve's Wal-Mart shotgun. The stray boot wedged between two slabs of oak…that was Deuce's boot. The pile had collapsed on him. Or been pushed in.

"Deuce!"

He moaned.

I tossed wood aside. I flung aside a whole cord of wood, but it seemed to get me nowhere.

"Deuce?...Deuce!"

I hurled and clawed, but the massive wood pile thwarted me, sucked down and collapsed in on itself, as if the Avalanche Kid were the drain through which all the hoarded, stockpiled, misspent Kussmaul energy would go.

I had to back out. I was crushing the kid. I had to break seams into the pile, so that the ten-pound hammers of oak and hickory would fall the other way. Then, getting space finally, I waded in— sinking in, shoving out. "Ouch!" wailed Deuce. I was stepping on his leg.

I tossed all the wood off his body—and he sat up, as if to show me his spine was okay. Then he whimpered..."Dog?"...and fell back, shivering. I opened the shotgun chamber and then the stock compartment. He had fired the last shell.

"Deuce? Can you hear me?"

I tapped his arms and legs. He didn't cry out. He didn't flinch. But he was hypothermic. I wrapped him in my coat. I stuck his hands down the front of his pants. I took my flannel shirt off and capped his head with it. I looked over my shoulder: the sun had ig- nited the tree tops above Robin Adams' cave, but solar warmth was thirty minutes away from the coulee bottom.

I figured I would get five seconds of focus out of Deuce before hypothermia shut his body down. I wiggled his shoulder.

"Where is she?"

His voice came out stiffly, slowly. "Who?"

"Your grandmother."

Faintly: "Hmm...?"

"Tell me, Deuce. Damn it. Tell me."

"In the barn," he shivered. His eyes fluttered shut. "I guess..."

I remembered a sight before me from Annie Adams' sketch book. Half-Tim's new lock, Eve had observed—the new imposed on the old, the two not matching—but the barn lock was broken, its bolt dropped and stuck in the frozen mud below. The doors were made to swing out, but the mud ruts stopped them, and I saw from frozen tracks that a knobby-tired four-wheeler had been parked there recently, blocking the door.

I limped around the barn, keeping an eye on Deuce as long as possible. He didn't move. But now and then a breath steamed up from the heap of wood.

At the south end of the half-timber barn, I found a rusty green tractor with its left back axle propped on a hickory chunk, the wheel off. The empty tire had rolled away toward the creek, and a barn cat sat on it, watching me. I peeled a blue plastic tarp off a hump beside the tractor, uncovering a gas-fired air compressor. An air nozzle lay in frost-scorched clover at the end of the hose. A drill head sat on top of the engine housing. The threads on the tractor's wheel base were oily, bright silver studs on a plate of rust. Like the wood pile, this was a new disturbance. Someone had taken the wheel off.

The tractor tire's inner tube, I thought. Annie Adams could have been floated down the creek on the tractor's inner tube—the one I found shredded the morning of the murder. She could have lost her little yellow brush along the way.

Then I saw an entry to the barn. On the creek-side wall, the ancient stove-wood nogging had been smashed out, leaving a narrow hole into the barn. I squeezed in, wondering how Ma Kussmaul could manage it—how she could manage any of it, from getting in and out of the barn, to cutting up animals, to killing Annie and floating the body down the creek, to setting up the painting scene and then setting up her grandson. How...and why? I wondered.

I pushed through the broken stovewood-and-mortar wall. Robin Adams had been generous in describing as simple dust the filth inside. The floor was strewn with old, moldering straw that was caked together with the dung of the birds that lived in the rafters. Spider webs—decades of spider webs—hung in every direction, thick as hanks of hair, flocked so heavily with dust that they sagged and tore. The walls were leaned with tools that hadn't seen use in twenty years, and the shadows behind those tools rustled as the barn's vermin hunkered down to wait me out. The roof was no more than twenty-five feet up, and from its central beam hung a rope from which the useful end had been long ago cut off, trailing only a single long strand down to head height. The Kussmaul father, I knew suddenly, had hung himself from that rope. Where was she, I wondered? Where was the mother?

But I had only five steps through the deep straw to wonder.

"Who's there?" she rasped at me.

The voice came from below. I kicked through straw to find the plank floor. I pulled a rope handle. There was the dirt room Robin Adams had described, not quite as dark and filthy as I had expected, but instead more lived-in than the barn. The hole was lit somehow—I raised up, looked around—by a box of outside light that had been channeled in, perhaps by mirrors, from the upper wall of the barn. And there were things down there: boxes, papers, a chair.

"Who's there?" the old woman rasped again, looking up, her neck wobbly and losing strength, like a baby's.

I told her who I was. As I did, I understood that this cellar was maybe the only place in Moth's life his mother couldn't get into. Or out of.

She shivered. Her neck gave up and her head dropped.

"Oh, holy God," she mumbled as I stared down at her. "Please stop him."

I looked up and around in the murky first-floor light. It wasn't only frozen mud, I realized, that stopped the barn door. The doors were tied shut from the inside—with leather thongs, with Annie's leather thongs—as if to stop someone from coming in. Ma Kussmaul wheezed desperately up at me as I stepped over the cellar hole. Those leather thongs—I touched Annie's great redundancy of hippie bracelets—had been perfectly blood knotted together to form one long rope capable of wrapping around the door pulls a dozen times—strong as steel. Annie had stayed in here, then, protected for a few precious minutes by perfect blood knots, while her killer removed the tractor tire and smashed through the nogging.

Then my eye found it. My eye was yanked to it. The old rope that hung Herman Kussmaul...the strand on the end of that was not of the rope but rather a last leather thong—and the blood knot connecting them was tied wrong. But it was Annie's wrong. Annie's and mine. Our wrong. The one she teased me with. Both loops through the same hole. The flaw she and I had gone around and around on. She had sketched it that way on purpose. She had sketched just as she tied it—to catch my eye.

I kicked away the straw beneath Annie's sign to me. It was easy to find the piece of folded paper. It was thick. Like sketch paper, looped and tattered on its torn-out edge, smudged down the middle by her desperate fingers. *My Dear Dog...*Annie had begun. *Should you ever find this...*

"Oh, holy God," Ma Kussmaul moaned as I tucked the note away and climbed down to her. "Please stop him. He's my baby. He's just as perfect as God could make him. Please stop him."

Asking to die

Moth Kussmaul's faded-red Chevy pickup was parked beside the campground bathroom. I could see it from a rise on Avalanche Coulee Road as I limped hard south toward the store. I had cut the thongs and pushed the barn doors open. I had carried Deuce inside the house and smothered him in blankets. I had hauled out Ma Kussmaul and asked her to phone the sheriff and try Eve, in that order. I glanced over Annie Adams' desperate note as I ran. Eve was outside by the time I reached the Avalanche Mercantile.

"Half-Tim's cutting on himself." My heart hammered. My leg pounded. "That's what it's all about. He's using the campground shower to try to stay clean. Deuce and his grandmother are all right, but anybody else who gets in his way right now is asking to die."

"I'm going with you."

"No," I said.

"He'll bleed to death," Eve said.

"Eve—"

"I'm going with you."

Her methed-out eyes startled me. "I'm going with you," she repeated. "To make sure he stays alive long enough to suffer in prison."

The bathroom light and fan were on. The iron-scented water was running. Steam filled the small, smelly room. "Moth…" I called from the doorway.

I heard back, faintly, "Oh, no…"

I raised Uncle Roundy's deer rifle.

"Moth, it's Dog. And Eve. We're out here. We're armed. Just step out slowly."

The water stopped. I smelled blood. "Oh no…" he muttered. Then he screamed it: "No!"

There was a clatter. A bare leg shot out beneath the plywood half-door. A scalpel skittered across the rust-stained concrete. Eve drew a sharp breath behind me.

"Why?" he wailed. "Why won't you leave me alone?"

"Just step out, Moth."

"Why won't people leave me alone?"

The plastic chair scraped inside the shower cell. Moth Kussmaul's voice, thin and rage-filled, echoed around us.

"Or help me? Why wouldn't anybody help me? My old man just makes fun of me. *Half-Tim.* Then he checks out. My mother, she doesn't do a damn thing but try to control me. *You're just as God made you, Timothy…*My big brothers, hell, they know about it but they don't do nothing. Salt doesn't speak to me. King looks at me like he wants to shoot me, like I'm some two-headed goat. No doctor will talk to me, 'cause I got no insurance…Fuckers."

"Timothy…" Eve began.

"I got nothing against you, Eve. I got nothing against anybody that leaves me alone. You and Dorrie have been my friends, all along. I like the Amish. They don't start shit. They leave other people alone. I'm sorry for your sake that I shot King—but he started talking about his fucking hot water, his quarters…when I got this to deal with. And I'm sorry if I hurt Deuce. I'm sorry about the way I tried to make it all look because I was desperate. Okay? But don't start fucking hassling me now. Please. I've been working on this too long."

He was quiet a long time. "Oh, no," he whimpered finally,

and a rivulet of blood appeared beneath the door. "Oh...no!" he screamed.

Then it was quiet again. Just the faint sounds of a packet torn open. A slurp. Then, "Okay...okay...okay..." he murmured. "Wally times three," he muttered, and he slurped twice more.

I glanced at Eve. Her eyes were hard and dry, black pupils bloated. Her jaw quivered. "Why did you have to kill—"

"Animals? *Practice!*" screamed Half-Tim. "You think I'd do this to myself without practice? What's a few dead animals—compared to my life? And King? Worried about a few quarters? Are you kidding me? Wouldn't you snap too?"

Eve hung her head. We waited. We heard him moving slightly, slowly, inside the stall.

"That kid of yours, Evey," he mumbled. "He got into my shit more times than I can count. I had to do something to keep him off me. And I never really hurt Wally like I said I would. I never meant to hurt Wally. I just dosed him with a little of this oxy to see how much I needed for myself. And then anyway Deuce got a piece of me with that shotgun. That's not helping."

The water stopped and we heard a screwdriver grind in the coin slot. We listened to water restart and pound the aluminum walls of the shower stall. Little rivers of blood swirled toward the drain. "So Annie Adams got into your barn," I said eventually. "She found the animals."

"And she let them go," he seethed, "before I could see how they heal. Which killed them, of course, the dumb bitch. And then she comes back. She wants to talk. To help me. She gets in my business again. She starts telling me she's going to stop me. She starts saying Ma should know about my plan. Ma had a right to know. Mothers had a right. Then she starts telling me I should stop my plan and get some counseling. 'Forgive some people and then see how things look,' she says. When she doesn't know shit about me. When I've been working on this forever. When I'm *this* close..."

He muttered to himself again. More blood appeared on the floor.

"I didn't plan to hurt anybody. But people just wouldn't leave me alone. You don't know what it's like. Nothing is going to stop me. I have to do this. Or die. At this point, either one is fine."

I glanced at Eve. What did he mean? Do what? She shook her head.

A rivulet of blood ran beneath the shower door and split in two, then three. I clenched my teeth. I walked a fine line suddenly. The good Dog wanted the truth out, the good Dog wanted justice for the dead, the good Dog even wanted help for such a damaged young man—but the bad Dog wanted to unload the hunting rifle through the shower wall. I felt Eve's hand on my shoulder.

She said, "We can take you to a hospital, Timothy. Or I can get bandages."

A chair scraped back. Feet slapped through the blood and water. Moth Kussmaul's agonized face appeared above the plywood half-door, his feet below it. Blood twisted down through the hairs on his calves and ankles, ran through his toes. He croaked, "Bandages? You think I need *bandages?*"

He fumbled at the hook-and-eye latch. Slowly, clumsily, like a man so stoned and so aggrieved that the world was moving out from beneath him, he stumbled forward and he nudged the door open.

I don't know what Eve did—except see it finally, the Kussmaul family secret, and scream.

I know what I did. The rifle. I went numb, and I dropped the damn deer rifle.

Go, Dog, go

Moth Kussmaul stood naked and two-fisted before us. His right hand aimed Uncle Roundy's deer rifle—the rifle I'd just dropped—straight at my vital organs. His other hand loosely pointed the rifle he had used on King and Abe Borntrager. One of Deuce's shotgun volleys had grazed him with a few lead pellets around the right foot, through a boot probably, and those wounds bled slowly and steadily.

But the shock to me and Eve was that Moth Kussmaul had cut himself, a dozen times on each leg, from the knee to the groin. Most were old cuts, crudely sewed up, knobby and half-healed. A few at the top looked newer, like the oozing, red-rimmed, neatly stitched beaver slash on my right calf.

And at the top…

And at the top…where his battered legs joined…Moth Kussmaul was just as God had made him.

Like his ma had said.

He was just as perfect as God could make him. But God had messed up.

I understood something now. *Half-Timber*, his own father had dubbed him, moronic with drink, and then later, as the kid hit adolescence, his father had fought Ma Kussmaul, on the kid's behalf I imagined, and then hung himself in despair.

Half-Timber, his big brothers had called him, knowing about it, not knowing what to do about it, and so doing nothing. *Half-Timber,* the whole tiny world of Avalanche—his neighbors, his sisters-in-law, the Amish—had called the young man, unaware of Half-Tim's tiny upright penis, no larger than the top joint of a man's little finger...unaware that below that he had labia, detouring around the faint pink eye of a childish vagina, and below there the labia kept on going, falling out of the female form and back into the male, wagging a small pair of testicles on either side as Half-Tim lumbered forward.

Eve gasped again. I heard her feet move. But my eyes were locked at the joint of his mangled legs. That's where Half-Tim was bleeding. From the sprung sack below one testicle. And now he had the rifle at my head.

I moaned, "Jesus."

"There is no Jesus," he said back, in slow motion. "There is no God who makes things just the way he intended. There is no intention, no plan. There's just me. I'm alone. And I'm doing this. I'm going through with it. There is no more time left."

I whipped around. Eve was gone.

"Put the rifles down, Moth. You're going to bleed to death."

"I can do it. I studied. I practiced. I've got the drugs. I can do it."

"If you survive, you're going to prison."

"No shit. And guess who won't be there with me. No Ma. Finally."

"Put the rifles down, Moth. We're going to the hospital."

"No," he said. "No. You're going to die now, Dog. Like the rest of them. For getting in my way."

"Moth...you don't have to kill to do this. Think about it. You didn't kill Deuce. You didn't kill your mother."

"They're blood," he monotoned back. "They're family."

"But you killed your brother King."

He wobbled on his unsteady legs. The barrel of his Uncle Roundy's rifle touched the side of my head. I considered briefly the willpower of the youngest Kussmaul. In my scrambling mind I saw the ocean of cord wood, the years of blowing off a raging energy, storing up more.

"Your brother wasn't armed," I said. "And I'm not either."

"You don't know," he droned on. "You don't know what it's like. Growing up around here. No help. No money. No insurance. No one helped me." He breathed raggedly. "Fucking coupla quarters..." he slurred. He had medicated himself against the pain, I realized—his pupils were glittering, soulless pinpricks—the opposite of meth eyes.

"Now no one is stopping me...not now...no one."

I took a deep breath. I took a last look at Moth Kussmaul—male and female strands, mis-tied, flawed, about to snap completely, the story of his final unraveling told by a dead woman, left in a note beneath the straw.

Go, Dog, go.

Now or never.

I lunged.

And Moth shot me.

Life, breath, everything stands still

The Dog entered the ranks, then, of those who understand that it doesn't hurt that much to be shot. Not really.

The first instant of a gunshot wound, even at point-blank range, is more of a painless blast of force—like getting hit by a bus that you never saw coming. It knocks you straight out of your shoes, straight out of your thoughts, out of your past and your present and out of time altogether. Life, breath, everything stands still.

I was outside in the West Fork campground when I next had senses. I was running across cold black grass, but I couldn't have told you, yet, whether I was running across my childhood backyard in western Massachusetts or across the infield at the Kentucky Derby or across a tundra in Nowhere, Alaska.

But I was alive and I was running. I was tripping. Branches raked my face. I hit a barbed-wire fence, at full speed, and I bounced, and then I knew where I was.

I was at the far south end of the West Fork campground, near the creek's big dogleg west. I was running from Moth Kussmaul—who couldn't run. Whose pale form tracked me slowly, steaming and bleeding, stumbling toward me out of the gloom, sweeping a pair of rifles.

I crawled along the fence line through stinging nettles. I crawled through thistles. I crawled across the tattered, reeking carcass of a deer. I crawled through a cold spring feeder that set me trembling uncontrollably. The initial, global non-pain from the rifle shot had settled at my chest. The impact had attenuated to a sharp-hot spot low in my left ribs. I put a hand there. It didn't feel like much. There was no blood on my hand. But I didn't know how I had managed to run. Suddenly, I couldn't breathe at all.

Moth Kussmaul had limped down to the spot where I had crashed into the fence. He had lost me. He turned a circle. Desperately, I tried to get a breath in. I tried to move. Where was Eve? Where the hell was Eve?

No air went deeper than my collar bones. As the dizziness washed over me, I lunged up, stupidly, airless and utterly uncoordinated, and I charged ten steps across the wide open grass, back toward the Cruise Master, and then my legs collapsed beneath me.

I dreamed, as I lay there, gasping up at the stars.

I saw things.

I saw Deuce Kussmaul, his grubby little hands in Wally's groin, screaming "No!" I saw King's hands around Eve's throat. I saw Salt Box, sexed and vicious, climb a woman, punish her with his weight. I saw bald and beaten old Ma Kussmaul—stalking, weeping, coping, praying, eating, snooping, wounding, trying to get everybody through to God's own finish line, where stood Freeman Yoder with a stick of barn wood, ember-tipped, painting crosses with the smoke.

I saw my own dead, curled, water-grub little boy.

I screamed it aloud: No!

And then all at once, around me, I smelled them. I heard them.

Horses.

Horses. All around me. And buggies. Creaking, clicking, reins slapping. Surrounding me.

A hand in mine. Then shouts and screams. Gunfire. Moth Kussmaul, bawling like a calf.

Then quiet.

Enjoy your dinner date

It took her five days of practice, and Eve only had her learner's permit, but she was a more-or-less legal Wisconsin driver when she pulled up in King's pickup to deliver the Dog—subtract various pieces of rib and skin—home from the Vernon Memorial Hospital in Viroqua.

Along the way, she filled in some of the holes in my head. Howard Adams, she said, had come back, had dealt with Annie's death and his stepson's pain in a passable fashion. He had admitted that, once Annie was dead, he had been talked into selling the Dorcas paintings. Borntrager had put it all together, using his leverage on Rachel and King, demanding a hefty cut. Howard Adams had tried to apologize to Freeman Yoder—who wouldn't speak to him. Wally had sobered up and seemed uninjured, no worse for the wear. But I was distracted. I kept checking to see that my seat belt was fastened.

"What's your problem?" she said. "This is how I drive. I'm a beginner."

I laughed. Laughter hurt.

She said, "King taught me about horsepower. He said this truck has two hundred and fifty horsepower. That's so English. Two hundred and fifty horses, when one horse is enough."

"Maybe you ought to get a horse now. And a buggy."

"Maybe I will."

"And paint both of them," I said, "bright safety-orange."

Then she laughed, and that didn't seem to hurt at all.

"Go to Hell," she told me.

"All by myself?"

She glanced at me. She was taking us downhill with both feet on the brake pedal, nursing out the hill's gravity like spreading cold honey on hard bread.

"Sorry," she said. "I'm busy tonight."

She scooted up on the seat of King's truck to prepare herself for the next corner. I watched her. She didn't wear her kapp. Her acorn-brown hair was cut—in a cute, acorn shape. She wore a blue gingham dress...and still the red Chuckies, though they looked washed...and I couldn't see the pipe anywhere on her. She chewed a finger on her left hand.

"Busy with what?" I asked.

The corner was a tight one, with a guy on a brand-new four-wheeler—a relative no doubt—ripping up the other way. Eve solved her anxiety by pulling onto the shoulder and stopping entirely. A milk truck nearly hit us from behind, blaring its horn as it cut into the oncoming lane. Eve pulled out and continued as if nothing had happened.

"Well," she said, "while you were in la-la land, up there in your hospital bed, I arranged a dinner date."

"La-la land?"

"Deuce taught me that."

I tried to turn the topic. "How is Deuce?"

"Very quiet," she said. "And a little sniffly. Pretty shook up, overall. He misses his dad. But he knows things weren't good, and he seems okay that I've got a date."

I looked away at one of the Amish farms high in the north branch of the coulee. Her date made me jealous, and I didn't like the feeling. For a good half mile, I sat there hurting in a dozen places. I sat there thinking the hell with it. Take the kid out fishing once more, like I promised. Drive all night. Big Two-Hearted River by sunup.

"A date," I said. "That's nice."

Eve smiled silently. We came up behind an Amish buggy.

"You know what I always wondered?" I asked her. "How come Amish will ride in cars, but they won't drive them?"

"They won't *own* them," Eve corrected. "They think owning cars makes it too easy for families to spread out. Cars make people more isolated, the Amish think, and cars make it too easy for people to move too fast and too far, without good reasons. You can't just take off on a horse and be in Disneyworld tomorrow."

I thought about myself and my Cruise Master—my tool of isolation. Had I gone too fast, too far? *Dog—this is not a fishing trip.* So what was it? Disneyworld? Where was I now?

I looked at beautiful Eve. "Speaking of horses," I said, eager to duck my own questions, "didn't I hear them? The other day when Half-Tim was after me? Horses around me? And buggies? In the middle of the campground?"

She nodded. We were hitting the coulee bottom. Those horses and buggies were King's kids, she told me. King's party posse. They had been having a vigil party in the King Midas barn.

"How did they know?"

"That's where I went when I deserted you in the bathroom. I went for help. When those Stoltzfus kids heard gunfire, they rode to the campground. They're brave kids. They've been through a lot. They saved you."

Eve seemed content to crawl along at ten miles per hour. I sat back a while, eyes closed. I could hear them now—the horses, the Amish teenagers, the spuming breath of Moth Kussmaul as he tried to focus on them, shoot them, shoot me, explain himself, deal with all the hassle.

"So what happened to Moth?"

Eve sighed heavily. "I saw him go off down Y, naked and bleeding and all. It was horrible. So sad. He still had Roundy's rifle and his own, too. Then…"

She looked at me.

I said, "Vossteig?"

"Yes. He was all the way on the other side of the county when he got the call. He caught up to Half-Tim by the Yoder farm. He yelled for Half-Tim to put the rifles down."

I waited.

"Tim didn't put them down," she said. She breathed a while to gather strength. "So," she sighed, "Vossteig backed off, let him run himself out. About an hour later they found him unconscious in Uncle Tater's barn over in Norwegian Hollow."

"He's alive...?"

"So far."

She drove another hundred yards. Now, across the West Fork, I could see the Cruise Master. I could see Deuce Kussmaul standing on my picnic table, waving a fly rod, practicing. He had a decent loop going. I felt a strange flood of relief, remorse, and panic.

I was supposed to take her kid fishing? While she had a dinner date?

Easy, Dog, I told myself. *Drive all night. Big Two-Hearted by sunup.*

"Thanks," I said, getting out beside the Cruise Master.

She smiled. "You're welcome."

"Enjoy your dinner date."

"Oh, I think I will."

I stood there like a lummox—like a goddamned wounded yak—steaming, puffing, stinking, one hand on the pickup's side mirror, staring off over the West Fork. I didn't want to let her go.

"What do I do with Deuce, after fishing, since you won't be home?"

"Dorrie's father is allowing her to babysit for me," she said.

"Freeman Yoder—allowing her—?" I switched to flummoxed. Flummoxed felt slightly better than jealous. "But you're in the ban—"

"Freeman is taking it easy on her. He even let her spend time with Robin before Robin went back to his real dad, and he's allowing them to write letters to each other. And the other day, when I was practicing my driving on Avalanche Coulee Road...guess what?"

I couldn't.

She grinned. "Freeman Yoder waved at me. He flagged me down. He said to tell you he located a bent-hickory rocking chair in his workshop, one a customer never came back to pick up, and you can have it—oh, and there it is! He left it in front of your camper. It's so pretty..."

I'd rather have the damn dinner date, I thought, but glanced at the rocker. Wally slouched in it, licking a paw.

"So just drop Deuce off at the store?"

"Right. Dorrie will be there."

The Avalanche Kid had stopped his casting atop the picnic table. Eve leaned over to call her scowling, silent son. "Deucey? You be good. Dorrie will feed you supper at five o'clock. Let Dog tell you the time. Bring me a trout, if you catch any."

I worked my ribs a bit, trying to tip the pain one way or the other. I let go of the mirror, and I turned away from Eve Kussmaul. I turned away and bit my tongue.

"Have a good time tonight," I said.

"Sure," she said happily. "You too."

Just like in the video

She pulled away up the campground drive. I took my waders off my clothesline and tossed them on the grass in front of Harvey Digman's new bent-hickory rocking chair. I bumped the puppy out and sat down in the rocker. I felt like I would never get up.

I called out to the boy, "Your cast looks pretty good today."

Deuce started it up again. I sat down and pulled my civilian boots off. It hurt to bend that far. I began to work my sore leg into the waders.

"But you want to pause a little longer on the backcast, give the line time to straighten out and load the rod like a spring. That's where your power comes from."

"I know."

"You do?"

"Dog, I *know*."

"You know?"

"My mom bought me a video."

"She did?"

I got the sore leg set in the wader boot and pushed the good one down. A god damn video. I straightened up against the back of the rocker, letting the pain leak out of my ribs. Then, grimacing, I bent again and got my boots on. A dinner date. And now a sonofabitch fly fishing...video. When I stood up to hook my suspenders, the Avalanche Kid was pausing in his backcast, loading the rod, shooting out a nice, flat, thirty-foot cast.

I gimped around and stood behind him—suddenly grouchy as a wounded bear. His line whipped the top of my head, tangled around my ears, and he stopped, his cast broken, his line slushing down around his feet.

"What the...?"

"Now what are you going to do?" I said.

"What do you mean?"

"Fly casting is not always such clear sailing," I grumped at him. "There's usually a tree somewhere."

Deuce scowled at me—that big, red, Kussmaul brow aimed down, like he thought he had horns. "Trees don't just jump in behind you."

I taught him something then. I taught us both something right there. "You'd be surprised," I said.

We fished his Uncle Salt's stretch—by permission. It was late in the day, late in the summer, and in parlance of fishing, the store was closed. The show was over. The fish were down. At Deuce's shoulder, I said all those things and more, trying to keep the kid's hopes in check. But the Avalanche Kid and his puppy plunged ahead of me—in the Wal-Mart neoprene waders his mom had bought him—and he slashed that stream to pieces, cussing under his breath. He peppered good water and bad with an oversized yellow humpy. He snagged fescue, bottle grass, New England asters, milkweed, box elder, black willow, angelica—and the Dog stumped and wheezed along behind him, naming his new nemeses.

"Damn it!" he cursed once, looking back to see his humpy gripped in a fist of sticky burrs.

"Burdock," I told him.

"That wasn't there before! That moved!"

"I told you you'd be surprised."

He ripped the line forward and sank the humpy in my thumb.

"Hey," I said, watching the blood bead out, "now you finally caught something."

Near dusk, the chill falling fast around us, Deuce let me change his fly and move him upstream from a riffle that swept beneath a willow snag. I pulled his wader belt to keep him low. "What—?"

"We're stalking now." I grabbed his arm before he could cast.

"What the—?"

"We're going to catch a trout. Are you ready?"

"I've been ready all day," he groused.

"Then listen to me. You won't hear this in a video."

He stared straight ahead, his cheeks flushing hot pink.

"Make your puppy stay. Then get on your knees…"

"I don't pray."

"Kid, you've been praying all day. Just not the right way. Now get down on your knees in the water and crawl about ten feet forward." I grabbed him. "No. You're making mud. Slow down. About a foot a minute."

He tried to move again in ten seconds. I grabbed his belt and pinned him to the stream bottom. He was exasperated.

"I'm just supposed to sit here, doing nothing?"

"Do nothing if you want to," I answered. "Me, I'm going to watch that kingfisher over flat water up there. I'm going to hope he gets something."

Deuce squinted upstream.

"He's just sitting there on a branch, doing nothing."

"About like you are."

The kid sighed. The kingfisher dove, skimmed the stream, missed, streaked chittering to an upstream perch.

"Now move," I said, and the kid kneed one foot forward.

"This," he muttered, teeth chattering, "sucks."

In thirty minutes the sun was behind the west coulee wall. The kingfisher was fed—a nice, fat chub—and I had Deuce ready. I had him shivering on his knees, midstream in the riffle, the West Fork just as quiet and clear-running as the moment we had walked up on it. I had him swing a muddler minnow out into the current ahead of him and then find the fly—speaking in tactile terms—and, once he had found it, tug it up and back, until he felt the muddler as if it were swimming, struggling, just beyond the tip of his left hand.

"Now strip line," I said, "and let the current take your fly down under that snag. There…yes…yes…now twitch it back."

And there was his trout.

"Yes!" Deuce gasped, and he set the hook.

The heavy brown rolled and dug beneath the snag. But Deuce turned the fish, tail-walked it out of the willow, risking a break-off to make the trout fight in open water.

"Right…" I said as the trout went deep. "Perfect. Now let him pull himself out against the rod—"

"I *know*…"

"You saw it in the video."

"Yes," he huffed. "So I know."

I backed away. I sat on the bank and smoked a Swisher. In time, Deuce got the trout close enough to net. I creaked up to standing and waded out.

"I can do it," he told me—and he did.

"Just like in the video?" I asked him.

"No…" he chattered. "No…that guy never got wet."

We sat on the bank in chilly darkness. Deuce gutted his fish and put it in his new creel. I smoked another Swisher and thought about the road. I followed a map in my head. North to LaCrosse, coffee there, then east across the center of Wisconsin to Highway 51, coffee again, then north again to the Michigan border. That's about where the sky would lighten. Then I'd take some lonely, triple-digit, Upper Peninsula highway farther north—

"Dog?"

"Yeah, kid."

"What time is it?"

"About five."

"Dorrie's waiting," he said. "You'd better drop me off."

I dropped him off. We chuffed manly goodbyes at each other. I walked back to the West Fork campground, down the bulldozer ruts where the Avalanche Oak was pushed aside. The entire history of Annie and Howard Adams had disappeared while Deuce and I were fishing. Only the teepee's circle of dead grass was left behind.

Icy dew clung to the spindles of Harvey's slick new Amish rocker, but I didn't care. I wanted to sit outside. I wanted to watch the Avalanche sky deepen one last time. I wanted to see the Milky Way spill and swirl between the coulee walls. I wanted to hear the screech owl's wretched squawk for its mate.

Or some such bullshit.

No. I wanted Eve.

I wanted Eve so badly I could not find the strength to walk the five more steps to the dark and empty Cruise Master. So I sat there—ten minutes, an hour—I don't know. Long enough and numb enough to have a sad string of thoughts: 1) get heavier jacket; 2) get vodka bottle; 3) get drunk; 4) get up early and leave.

I rose stiffly and opened the Cruise Master door...but I smelled something.

I smelled warmth. Heat.

A match hissed and Eve said from the galley bench, as she leaned to light candles, "I thought you'd drowned."

My galley table had been transformed. Eve had draped a white linen table cloth over it. She had set up two tall white candles in silver holders, spaced perfectly around a vase of purple asters. There was a meatloaf and a round of white bread and two giant tomatoes, terraced out and dribbled over with oil and salt and dried mint. There was a six-pack of beer. There was a fresh pillow and blanket on my loft bed. There was a gas heater fanning heat across the tidied floor.

"Almost..." I told her. "I almost did drown..."

She stepped up. She took me under the arms and squared her hip bones against me. She was blushing, suddenly breathless.

"Well you didn't."

"Not yet."

"Shhh—" she hissed.

She took my hat off.

"So now," she said, "do you want to go to Hell with me before...or after supper?"

In violation of the law

Eve and Deuce Kussmaul left Avalanche sometime the next afternoon. They didn't say goodbye, except to post a note on the door of the Avalanche Mercantile.

Closed.
Thank You for Your Business.
For Information Please See Rachel Kussmaul,
S671, Coulee Road

I rattled the store's door knob. I walked around the side and rattled the door knob to the house. It was a crisp, windy day—the last one in September. Eve's sunflowers were taller than my head, and song sparrows fanned the air below their bowed heads, trying to be hummingbirds and peck out the plump black seeds. A squirrel surfed the big wheel of the tallest flower, bending it nearly to the ground before he jumped off.

Eve had her own special chair back there, scalloped steel, sky blue. I put my hands in my pockets and walked over to it. I sat down. It took me an hour before I could do it. But at last, under a ragged vee of honking geese, I wept for her, and for Deuce, and for Annie and King, and for myself.

Deputy Austin Vossteig dropped by as I walked the stream the next morning. He gave me fifty bucks. He gave me the number of an uncle in Eau Claire.

"My dad's big brother, Elmer Vossteig. Good guy. Tell him you need a new headlight and some decent clamps for that tailpipe."

"All for fifty bucks?"

"No," the deputy grinned. "He'll do it free. That's gas money."

Then he held out a folded piece of paper. I knew what it was by the scalloped edges and the thick feel of the page between my fingers. It was the torn sheet from Annie Adams' sketchbook, the one she had led me to with the trico and the mis-tied blood knot, the one I had skimmed as I ran south to find Moth in the campground shower.

"We took it from your pocket when we went through your clothes at the hospital," Vossteig told me.

I accepted the note but left it folded in my hand. "I read a bit of it the other day," I said. "I'm not sure I can take any more."

The deputy shrugged. "It explains some things," he said. "Ms. Adams snooped in that half-timber barn. She found animals that Timothy Kussmaul had cut on for practice. She let them go. Then when she came back on the night you got hurt, Kussmaul caught her, and he blocked her in, and he said he was going to kill her. She heard him outside with some kind of power tool—which was the drill to take off the tractor tire, to get at the inner tube—to float her down the creek, because if you remember there were Kussmauls and Amish all over the roads that night. She tied herself into the barn so he couldn't get at her, and she wrote this note before he smashed in through that stovewood nogging on the south end."

I said, "So...Annie Adams was alive...when he took her downstream?"

Deputy Vossteig shrugged again. "Looks that way. He clobbered her in the head with something from the barn, in order to get her out and onto that tube. But the official cause of death ended up as drowning, not blunt trauma or gunshot. So he didn't kill her in the barn."

I said, "I think she dropped that little yellow brush in the stream on the way down. On purpose." I thought a minute, recalling the bib pocket of Annie Adams' overalls. "Then Moth Kussmaul must have pulled those candles from her pocket and dumped them in Abe's truck on the way back upstream, to point you guys toward Borntrager—in case Deuce didn't do as planned."

Vossteig rubbed his eyes. He looked tired. "Yeah...well, that... he was trying to point us every which way, it turns out. He was panicked, is my guess." He reached down and flicked burrs off his crisp pants cuff. He was hesitating to say something else. "I have a friend," he managed finally, "who had a niece born like that. Hermaphrodite. It happens. Not a problem when you deal with it right away."

He didn't get all the burrs. He picked methodically at them. "But you don't deal with it...my goodness...you get hormone problems, you get gender problems, you get the whole horrible secrecy thing..."

I watched his big, clean fingers remove the burrs and flick them, one by one, into the grass.

"But growing up out here...growing up Kussmaul...I did a little research this morning. There was not a single medical record for that kid...not one. There was going to be some damage somewhere."

He sighed. His pant leg was clean. He straightened up.

"But Deuce finally talked to us, after you got shot. He went out to shoot a beaver, he said, but he met Timothy Kussmaul hauling Annie Adams down the stream on that tractor tube. Deuce said Kussmaul had her tied down on there, gagged, and the kid said he knew she was drowned by that point. Then," Vossteig said, "Kussmaul grabbed the kid's puppy. He made Deuce go over to the campsite and get her painting stuff. He told him to get a painting of the Amish barn. That's how the wrong painting ended up on the bridge. Then Kussmaul threatened to kill the puppy unless Deuce shot the body—or if he told anyone later. I guess that it made a pretty clear choice for the kid. She was already dead anyway, Deuce kept telling us. Her whole head was underwater. He knew she was dead. So he shot into the air a dozen times, waiting for you to look, and then when you got there, he put one bullet into her. Kussmaul let the puppy go later. That's why Yoder found the dog, up on his farm."

Vossteig looked away, up coulee. I almost opened the note. But what didn't I know already?

"Borntrager's still with us," the deputy mentioned. "He'll survive. The DA's working on a plea bargain with felony extortion, and Borntrager is filling us in on some of the stuff going on down here in Kussmaul country."

Again, I nearly opened the note. But why, I wondered. Why bother? Why did the Barn Lady try so hard to speak, when she knew she would die anyway? What was so important? I had felt earlier that she was saving the rest of us. But from what?

"And so," said Vossteig, "we busted a meth kitchen in a barn up on the bluff. Then state Fish and Game had a look inside the round barn, and there will be poaching charges on that one. Sometime this week, the county assessor is going to have a look inside the salt box barn…"

I nodded. But I still didn't unfold Annie Adams' note. I didn't think I could take the rawness, the ramblings of a woman about to die.

I said, "So Annie tore this page out because she figured Half-Tim would go through the sketch book before he dumped it."

Vossteig nodded. "We found his prints all through the book."

I felt shaky. I felt the kind of trembling one feels after a near miss—and after one steps into the new and deeper water of a life to be lived beyond the old way of seeing. Vossteig clapped a sympathetic hand on my shoulder.

"Some fishing trip, huh?" he said.

"Not at all," I murmured. "Not at all."

I went back to ruminating over my Swisher then, after Vossteig left me sitting beside my gear on the banks of the West Fork. I wondered about Eve, where she went, what she would do.

And then I found myself wondering about love. I mean, I really *wondered*. Did I feel it? Had I felt it? Could love go on, I wondered, in the aftermath of tragedy, in the miasma of fault and guilt, in the absence of the loved one? How? How did it work?

I should know that, shouldn't I?

I should know something so important.

I closed my eyes. I had a brief but clear image of a fish getting away—of a big fish breaking off—was love like that? Was it all guile and filaments and stress and struggle and loss and blame? Or was love bigger than that? Was it—after injury—the willingness, the going forth again? The pulsing of the heart back open?

I opened the Barn Lady's note. I skipped over everything, all the sordid detail between *My Dear Dog* and the end, where the thick, charcoal-pencil handwriting nailed the word *everyone* hard and dark and then began to trail away...

...*be kind*, Annie Adams was scrawling, writing fast, urgently, like what she had to say could not wait another second...*and understand*, she scrawled...*and love someone...and, in all of your precious lives...forgive...*

I folded the note and put it away. I wiped my eyes. I blew smoke up past them.

Forgive, huh?

Forgive who? I wondered, trying to stay stupid, stay innocent, for one final second.

And that's when I saw, at last, the perfect trico moment. Staring at the West Fork through my cloud of bad smoke, I saw, in a pocket of sunlight the shifty sky had let through, a vast swarm of tiny mated mayflies. I saw the frenetic dance of insects that had merged their genes and entered their death dance—the females hopping up and down in microcurrents of air above the stream, the males in gymnastic clouds around them—each and every one of them willing, destined, to die within minutes.

My hands moved without me—tied blood knots, tied on a trico

fly. The stream bubbled like champagne, and the trout had been waiting as long as I had. Up and down the West Fork they began to sip and splash and boil the surface. I trembled again, in a fearful excitement, suddenly and wildly desperate to *fish*...to have a day, to make a journey...to scribe with my own two legs a broad and brainless circle, out and back...while I could...while time stood still.

I started just below the bridge. A crisp breeze blew leaves from the trees. The asters and sunflowers nodded. Monarchs flitted from milkweed to milkweed. Massing birds swirled in the treetops. Geese honked. An Amish buggy clip-clopped in the distance. I raised my rod exactly when the trico spinners began to fall, surrendering their lives to the hungry, rising trout.

My line was in the air. It was poised, perfectly—my loop coiled, my rod ready to load the cast, my feeding trout picked out—when a car door slammed on the County Y bridge.

A young guy, a game warden, walked to the bridge rail.

"Sir," he called down, "this is October first."

I nodded. I flicked my trico spinner pattern up beneath the bridge. The tippet rolled tenderly out. The fly touched down, soft as milkweed duff. A nice trout took it.

"Sir," the young man said, speaking more loudly, "the Wisconsin trout fishing season ended yesterday."

I let the line go slack. I let the trout shake off. I reeled up.

"Oh," I said.

He watched me.

"Oh," I said. I climbed out of the West Fork. I sat on the bank.

"You're in violation of the law, sir."

"Oh."

I bit my fly off, reeled up, and laid my rod down. I laid myself down in the tall grass, nose up into the high blue sky.

I guess I had disappeared to the warden. I guess he couldn't see me.

"Sir?"

I knocked my hat back. I tossed my sunglasses inside the hat's grimy straw cup. I let the blue drape over me. I let the breeze toss leaves against me. I let the tall grass snap with hoppers and the short under-grass tickle me over with its tiny, traveling masses. I let the stream flow on its own. I let the fish feed on.

"Sir?"

No. Not a fishing trip at all. Not now.

Maybe I'd get a pipe.

Like Harvey's, like Magritte's...*like Eve's*...

Maybe I would go fishing. I hadn't ever been fishing. Not yet. Not me.

Then "Oh," I sighed, staring at the perfect sky, hearing the creek plunge on, hearing the warden pull away.

"Oh," I sighed, understanding for at least one short moment that as much life as I could stand was still out there, was still inside me too...was still, in flush, wherever I could want and hope and bear to seek the things I loved.

Then, "Oh..." I sighed, slipping back in the tall grass. "Oh... Oh...Oh."